The Dandelion Clock

by

Mary Lesser

Also by Mary Lesser

Books one and two in the Cornish series:

The Lemon Juice Summer
Apple Blossom Honey

The gifts of Mr Karim

Acknowledgements

Thanks to my friends:

Robert Ketchell for sharing his inspiration as a master
Japanese garden designer, who described the garden as "the
space beyond the everyday world".

Steve Beech, sound engineer, for his kind advice
on the world of outside broadcasting.

The Dandelion Clock

Simon Sherwell was born lucky, according to his Gran and her reading of his stars. Not that this down to earth gardener would believe a well aspected Jupiter could possibly have any influence on his life.

It was love at first sight when Simon saw Clare Palfrey through a Tudor mullioned window at Trelerric House in Cornwall. Then a chance discovery by a local historian reveals they may have loved before.

Talent spotted after designing an award winning garden, Simon, who'd never had a job interview in his life, finds that fate throws him chances and opportunities to make a future for them both.

****

This is book three in the Cornish series that includes 'The Lemon Juice Summer' and 'Apple Blossom Honey'

For my father
Carl Stanley Hopkinson
who never knew his own father.

ONE

The day I started work at Trelerric House was the first time I set eyes on Clare Palfrey. I was staring at the old Tudor house trying to make sense of the feelings it aroused in me when I saw a face through a mullioned window. I'd never seen a prettier, sweeter face on any girl. She had the sort of face where a lifetime of looking wouldn't be sufficient. With her pale skin and dark hair she was like moonlight and I thought I was seeing a ghost through the old wavy glass, it wouldn't be the first time. Then she laughed at something someone said behind her and I heard the sound. It made my spine tingle. At first I thought she was Sam Latchley's little sister and therefore right out of my league. He was my boss although he was barely seven years older than me. He was also the heir to the Trelerric estate even though he was the son of a younger brother. I tried to explain it all to mum when I got home that night.

'It's amazing, the old house I mean. It's been there since Tudor times and kind of speaks to you. In a funny kind of way I recognised it. I know that sounds weird but when I saw it I felt like I'd found my way home.'

Images of the house as Sam walked me around the place were playing through my mind. I got back to the bit my mum was interested in.

'Anyway,' I continued. 'The older brother died in a car crash in France about ten or so years ago. The younger brother, Sam's dad, still farms the estate and lives at the farm. It's called Home Farm.' I paused while mum put some more home grown vegetables on my plate. The freezer was full of them. 'The older brother's widow still lives in the big house, she's the one who was an actress. I haven't seen her yet but I've seen her Jag. It's gorgeous, I'd love a car like that. Sam said he also had a sister. I think I saw her today.'

Mum told me to get on with my food and stop gabbling but I could tell she was interested. I was hungry, I'm always hungry and mum's a good cook. She has a way of cooking vegetables in what she calls a medley, all in together with a knob of butter and a sprinkle of celery salt, it's delicious. I smiled at her across the table as I ate. A petite, fiery brunette, quick to assess people or a situation, she'd done everything she could to keep us together after my dad walked out on us when I was baby. She'd taken any job she could to make ends meet; cleaner, dinner lady, waitress. Finally she'd got work as a postwoman, it had been the saving of us and she loved it. Like all Sherwell's she liked to be active and outside as much as possible. Gran and Gramps had helped with babysitting as they lived at the other end of the village. Sometimes I'd thought that they were my real parents and that mum was my older sister because she always had a young fresh look about her.

Mum's work ethic had rubbed off on me. 'Never mind what they say at school Simon. It's what you do with your opportunities my lad. Cornishmen are grafters and honest work never hurt anyone. And you'll never go hungry if you can grow food. It's what your grandad always says.' Most of Gramps garden was turned over to growing fruit and vegetables. His family, the Sherwell's and grandma's family the Minhinnett's, had always had their fingers in the soil and I'd inherited their love of it.

Despite having been married, mum dropped dad's name as soon as he left us and reverted back to her maiden name, so the village knew me as Simon Sherwell. Her view had been that you needed a name you could be proud of and I think there had been plenty of sympathy for her. I never knew my paternal grandparents, all mum told me was that my grandfather had been a widower and had gone off with a woman who wasn't interested in any grandchildren she wasn't related to.

I grew up appreciating the value of money and that you had to earn it. As a little boy I used to earn pocket money by collecting and delivering the weekend newspapers for some old folk down my end of the village. Then I started walking their dogs, feeding pets when people went on holiday, washing their cars, mowing lawns and weeding and finally learning about plants and gardening from anyone who cared to teach me. Something about me made people confide and I was always happy to listen to the people I did odd jobs for, never being bothered by the age difference. When people were patient and kind I could soak up information and never needed telling anything more than once. At school if a teacher was short with me I used to get noise in my ears and just stop listening.

School was something you had to go through. At first I'd loved it, making friends and playing games. Most of my friends adapted to the teachers' expectations quite quickly but I didn't always seem to fit the mould. There were some things I loved, like painting and drawing and I always enjoyed stories. I've got a good imagination, too good sometimes, often finding myself away in a daydream, a personal world prompted by colours and words and then finding myself at a loss to understand what was going on in the classroom. Because I was well behaved and quite shy I avoided trouble, but I didn't always catch instructions and sometimes wondered what I was supposed to be doing. Teachers seemed to think I was a bit slow and I was a very average student. Sport was okay and I really enjoyed doing martial arts as an after school activity. Since I wasn't the fat lad in the class, or the geek or the dumbo, nobody wanted to hit me and I was pretty much left alone.

When school finished I hadn't a clue what I was supposed to do with myself and with no particular vocation I carried on with what I'd always done, working for my old folk in the village and picking up any odd job that was available. With a reputation for being helpful and reliable I got word of mouth recommendations which led to more work.

By the time I was twenty I was taking care of the gardens at three holiday cottages, helping out at several small gardens and working as a casual labourer for a builder. That was the year I met Daniel Pencraddoc. I already knew the woman who became his lady because I looked after her brother's garden. It's quite something to be on first name terms with the local dot com millionaire but Daniel Pencraddoc was just an ordinary bloke who had some good ideas and made his pile. It was his lady, the artist Miss Frazer who reckoned I had some skill with a pen who made the real difference though. She gave me the confidence to go to college to do a short course in technical drawing and computer-aided garden design. Daniel helped me with the technology since computers were his thing. Then I did another short course on basic horticulture and I got really lucky because on a college visit to view the gardens at Trelerric House I hit it off with Sam Latchley. He introduced himself to us all as the 'head gardener, the only gardener, and the heir to the estate'. I said I reckoned he needed a bit of help then and made everyone laugh. We got talking later and he offered me some work. That was the only job interview I ever had.

Coming to Trelerric brought a sense of familiarity which was uncanny. It seemed as though the stones knew my hand, and my hand recognised the shape of the land. I loved the place and from the first day cared for it like it was my own. Sam Latchley was great to work for, he had good ideas and his mind was always active. He'd planted a new orchard, reintroduced bees, helped his parents on the farm when necessary and charmed the socks off everybody. He was funny, quite a role model, the brother I'd never had, and I began to model myself on him while at the same time making myself indispensable. As usual I didn't have a plan, but I'd found something I was more than comfortable with and I just followed my instincts.

My mum never seemed worried about what I might do with my life. All she ever said was find out what you like doing Simon, and go and do it. It didn't stop there though, she was always giving me advice. Mum couldn't tolerate sloppiness, slovenliness or slipperiness in people. Her words, not mine. I was naturally methodical and honest, but it was sometimes like having a sergeant major around, living with her. Once in a moment of frustration I'd asked her if my dad had left us because she was so bossy. That had taken the wind out of her sails but to be fair she'd thought about it and answered my question.

'I should clout you for that because you're cheeky, my lad. But no, he left because he couldn't cope with a baby or with responsibility. We were too young, and he still wanted to be the lad about town. He was a flirt and an entertainer and he'd not had the chance to spread his wings. We never should have got married but there, what's done is done. At least I had you. And you're nothing like him.'

I began to notice that she never said anything horrible about my father even though it must have been one hell of a struggle without him.

'Who am I like then?' With the selfishness of youth I'd been eager for identity.

'In attitude you're very like your grandad, my dad. Laid-back and considerate. But you've got my nose and we've both got my mum's fine skin. And you're a Sherwell with your fair colouring and blue-eyes, whereas I've got your Gran's colouring.' She didn't say anything about what my dad looked like. 'Cut you in half and Sherwell is written right through you like a stick of rock.'

That had made me laugh out loud but later I'd asked Gramps about the Sherwell's. We'd been working together on his sizeable vegetable garden where we often had good conversations. For an ordinary man he was a great reader, he never dismissed a book until he'd had a good look at it. He was also an amateur historian, fascinated by Cornish folklore and legend, and had done a fair bit of research into our family history.

'There's been Sherwell's here as far back as I can go Simon. We've moved through several villages locally, pursuing jobs and pretty women I suppose, and settled down over the decades with the best of both everywhere between Calstock and Caradon. We've worked at the mines, at the local big houses and manors on their estates and market gardens, even done a brief stint as bargemen on the Tamar. But we've never gone far unless we've had to join the army and fight for our country. There's something about being in Cornwall that suits a Sherwell.'

Later I'd thought about mum and whether her heart had been badly broken. I never knew of another man in her life but either she was very discrete or simply not interested. Her focus was me and Gran and Gramps. I'd thought then about settling down with a woman and wondered how to go about it. How on earth would you know when you wanted to, when you'd found the right woman? That was another thing I'd asked Gramps about. He'd smiled and said I'd know when it happened. Daniel Pencraddoc had said much the same thing once, we'd been working together on some hard landscaping he wanted doing, laying endless granite cobbles. He'd come back home to Cornwall when he inherited his grandmother's family home, the one I'd worked at up on the moor. He'd had the whole place gutted and sympathetically modernised and extended. One day he'd found Miss Frazer sketching in the garden and had fallen in love.

'It was instantaneous Simon. All it took was one look and a couple of words exchanged and I knew I wanted her in my life, for the rest of my life.'

Now they'd got two children, Flora Rose Frazer and David Frazer Pencraddoc. My mum tutted a bit because they weren't married but I told her that's modern times. She'd muttered something about how did the children know what name to call themselves, Pencraddoc or Frazer, but I'd stopped her. 'I'm Simon Sherwell, yet my birth certificate has me down as Simon William Buckland. How confusing is that?'

I'd liked girls at school but there'd been one called Chloe Elaine Baxter who was quite special in my eyes. She was my first proper kiss, backstage during the school play. She'd been playing a lead role in a sexy backless strappy dress and I was doing the stage lighting. There was something about standing in the dusky privacy of the wings with the smell of lights and dusty curtains which was absolutely thrilling. In her stage make-up

Chloe had seemed older and sophisticated. She'd initiated the kisses and was bold in her demands. We'd got intimate as we got older, again she'd taken the initiative but I hadn't complained. I'd liked her a lot but she went away to study and the last time I'd seen her she'd told me she had a boyfriend at university. That was how I knew I'd been dumped.

I'd been working at Trelerric House for about four months when Lucy Huccaby moved in to work for old Mrs Latchley, the widowed actress. I'd never seen glamour before, Mrs Latchley kind of shimmered even though she was about Gran's age. One day I'd been working on the front terraces and had just cleared everything into the wheelbarrow and was standing by the camellias observing my work when Lucy came into view walking Coco, Mrs Latchley's long haired chihuahua. For a moment my heart jumped and I thought I was looking at Clare Palfrey, in the half light of a midwinter afternoon there seemed to be a resemblance, but Lucy moved differently and was taller. I'd waited until she was out of sight and then taken myself and the barrow off to the greenhouses where Sam kept everything. I remember asking him what he thought of her. When I wasn't thinking about my work I was thinking about women.

Clare wasn't often at Trelerric. I'd finally learned that she wasn't Sam's sister but that she sometimes came up to the house and helped her mum, Maggie, who was old Mrs Latchley's housekeeper. Her real job was as a veterinary nurse in the village. Sam, who was no fool, noticed my interest in Clare. Well, I had asked quite a few bloody obvious questions about her.

'Bright, attractive, loves animals, great with children.' Sam said when we were sorting stuff out in the potting shed. 'She babysits for my sister's two at The Lodge at least twice a month on Saturday nights. If you're interested I'd suggest you do something about it, a girl like that is going to get herself noticed pretty soon.'

I'd straightened up and looked at Sam carefully when he'd said that, seeing him as a competitor. He had everything to offer and I mean everything. Whereas I lived with my mum and drove an old car that one of my elderly gardening clients had let me have for a tiny sum when he became dependant on his wife. I also owned a tidy old campervan but you couldn't start life with someone in that. The enormity of making my own way in the twenty-first century hit me for the first time and that evening I'd spoken to mum about it.

'I've got savings, but probably not enough for a deposit on a house. I could rent, but then I'd never be able to save. I don't know if I've got a secure job, but I've always got on by taking whatever comes my way. I've never been short of work but I've never made a plan mum. I don't know what my future holds. Am I thick?'

'No, you are not thick. You might not have the silver spoon that your boss has in his mouth, but you've got strength and health and ability. And I think you're nice looking but then I would wouldn't I?' Mum had ruffled my hair, which I hated. 'And one day I suppose Gran and Gramps little house might be yours, if they don't have to sell it to pay for their health care in their old age.'

Blimey, that had never even occurred to me but the very idea was horrible. 'I can't look at making plans for my future which involve Gran and Gramps popping their clogs. I can't even think about it. The thought of either of them being ill makes me feel sick.' I said.

One weekend I read something in a newspaper about pensions and savings for millennials and had to sit down because it was all a shock. Basically I came to the conclusion that I was living at the "have not" end of the social scale and that I had to do something about it. I thought back to a conversation I'd had with Chloe when I'd asked her about the university boyfriend. She'd told me that he had plans and was going places once he'd got his degree. But what she'd said next had stuck with me.

'You're a really lovely bloke Simon but you're basically just an odd-job man. You have to get out there and make something of yourself.' Somehow she'd made me feel like a loser, someone with a ragbag of experiences but nothing that could be put on a posh CV to impress anyone. But what could I do? It was time to get smart. Only I couldn't help wondering how, and why, I'd never been told about these things before.

TWO

I quickly realised that Sam's interests did not include making a move on Clare. Anyone with an eye in their head could see that he was set on Lucy but he told me one day that things were complicated because he'd made a big mistake in seeing a woman called Helena. I'd noticed this posh blonde who kept on turning up at Trelerric in her blue Honda and hanging around, wearing lots of make-up and showing enough cleavage to leave little to the imagination. Exciting when you don't usually see much of that, but not my kind of woman. She turned the charm on and off depending on whether you were useful to her. My mum would have described her as false.

'A piece of advice my son,' Sam said over a mug of tea in the potting shed where we had a couple of comfy old wicker chairs. Once again he'd let his phone ring and not answered it because it was this woman calling. 'Don't think with your dick.'

I laughed at the way he spoke to me, it was like being back on the building site with the guys over at Darleystones, Daniel Pencraddoc's house on the side of the moor. But this was funny. 'What do you mean by that?' I knew perfectly well what he meant but I was curious about the detail.

'I mean that I made the stupid mistake of going to bed with a woman who fancied a shag as much as I did,' he said. 'I thought it was just a one-night stand only her fancy included terms and conditions which hadn't occurred to me. If this was the olden days she'd have me up before the beak for plighting my troth and spoiling her virtue. Then I'd either have to marry her or be declared a cad and a bounder and be hounded out of the parish while people jeered and pelted me with sheep dung and rotten vegetables.'

Sam liked talking like this, he saw the silly side of life but he was quite deep. Fortunately the sort of books my mum read and left lying about had taught me a few things and I understood what he was going on about. Mum was keen on historical romances even though she sometimes doubted their factual accuracy. My guilty secret was that I rather liked the moist heroines depicted on the front covers and quite enjoyed a soppy read. I put it down to having a romantic streak and being in touch with my feminine side.

'So what are you going to do about the busty blonde then?' I asked.

'Find an opportunity to let her down gently I suppose. I've been a fool by backing off. I thought she'd get the message and leave me alone but if anything she's redoubled her efforts and is chasing me even harder. I'm going to have to spell it out, that's she's not part of my future. I just hate upsetting people.'

'Wimp.' I said.

I had a lot of work on. I was at Trelerric House four days a week and gardening for my regular clients on the other three days. On top of that Sam had asked me if I fancied looking over some college notes and photographs of his because old Mrs Latchley had decided she wanted an oriental-style garden putting in the bare courtyard outside her rooms. He wanted to know if I had any ideas since I'd done a garden design course. I did, my imagination just flew, spurred on by pictures and articles I found on the internet. All the training I'd done came back easily and I was happy working with pens, ink and watercolours, which was fortunate since I didn't have access to a computer with a design programme.

Meanwhile the weeks were warming up and we were working hard preparing for opening the house to the public for Mothering Sunday. Gardening in the Cornish climate is a tough business because it rarely gets cold enough to stop things growing. There's a pause of a couple of weeks when you think you've got everything under control and then plants start sprouting all over the place. Sam and I were busy with seedlings and cuttings in the greenhouse as well as all the outdoor jobs. Weeding was a pain because Sam's dad farmed organically and got rather heated if he saw weedkiller, even though we only used it on the paths around the house and the tea room they'd made by converting the old stables and tack rooms. I was a bit in awe of Sam's dad who was the nearest thing to landed gentry that I'd ever met. Despite being a sheep farmer he dressed well, often with a waistcoat and a tweedy jacket with a cap. He was fair and blue eyed like me and I found myself studying what he wore and noticing how he behaved. It was my way of learning things.

Hard work made us hungry and Sam liked to pop into Maggie's kitchen to scrounge something when he could, and took me along a few times as support. That way he sometimes saw Lucy and sometimes I saw Clare, so I was happy to fall in with his plans. Maggie shook her tea towel at Sam one day and told him he was a ruddy nuisance.

'But look at this poor starving boy Maggie,' Sam said, indicating me. 'You can't turn him away, look at his big blue eyes. He's only a puppy.'

Clare was with Maggie that day and had gone into peals of laughter. I'd stood there entranced by the lovely shape of her throat as she threw her head back. Her teeth were white and even and her eyes sparkled. How ever could I have thought I'd seen a ghost when I first saw her through the Tudor window? She was so alive and vibrant. It was Clare who had got some plates out and opened the big fridge. 'Come on mum, they're both famished. There must be something they can have. Mrs Latchley only eats enough for a bird.'

I found myself sitting at the kitchen table eating with Clare and her mum and Sam, all of us chatting like old friends about the estate, the farm animals and the dogs. Maggie asked me if I had any pets.

'We've got a cat. A big old ginger boy called, oddly enough, Ginger. He followed me home one day last year and just moved in. People in the village reckoned he'd been dumped by a couple who took one of the holiday cottages I look after.'

Clare shook her head. 'It happens. We've had a box of kittens left in the porch without food or water, an old dog left tied up outside and last week a box turned up with a couple of unusual lizards in it. People split up and find they can't cope financially, or decide they've become allergic, or just get bored with keeping a pet after the kids have left home. I suppose they think it's better to dump the pets at the vet rather than in the bin.'

'The tales you tell us at home sometimes Clare, I think we're not really a nation of animal lovers.' Maggie said.

'What about microchipping?' Sam asked. 'Wouldn't the dog be traceable?'

'These animals are never traceable. We do our best to home them and the rescue places are fantastic. But there are always losers. It breaks my heart.'

I could have been eating newspaper for all I knew, I just sat and gazed at this pretty and compassionate girl and delighted in every second in her company. In a lightbulb moment I decided I'd take Ginger to the veterinary surgery to let them give him a health check and a worm tablet. As casually as I could I asked her what days she worked with the crafty idea of making sure she'd be there when I made the appointment. She was way ahead of me though.

'Wednesday's good, I usually do a stint on the desk in the afternoons. Three till six. If you make the appointment for then I'd be able to say hello to him.'

I stared at her, all my nerve ends on fire. If I wasn't mistaken that was as good as an invite. 'Nearer six, after I've finished here.' I managed to speak normally. I was already planning to ask her to accompany me to the pub afterwards for a friendly drink together. My local was The Wheal, but her local was The Hogshead. Either way if it was likely to be a date I intended wearing something other than my gardening clothes.

I don't know who was most shocked, mum when I said I was taking Ginger to the vet or Ginger when I picked him up and put him in the cat carrier I'd had to go out and buy.

'Why this all of a sudden Simon? There's nothing wrong with him and the vet's expensive.'

'I just want to be sure he's fit, that's all mum. We don't know his background.' I said as I carried him outside to my car. 'Just being a responsible pet owner.'

Mum had eyed my clean blue jeans and blue and white checked shirt with suspicion. 'Well, I hope he appreciates the effort you're going to,' she'd sniffed the air. 'And the aftershave. And put some newspaper around the basket in case he pees in the car. You'll never get a girl to feel romantic with that sort of stink in the back.'

Ginger moaned his displeasure all the way and I found I had lumps of ginger fur all over my shirt. To make things worse Clare wasn't on the desk after all. My hopes plummeted and I felt like a prat as all my plans and rehearsed conversations collapsed. The duty vet was a tired pouchy-eyed middle-aged man with bad breath and I felt sorry for Ginger when he got a thermometer poked up his backside before being felt all over, weighed and prodded and then given a worm tablet. He slunk back into the basket after giving me a thoroughly disgruntled look. It felt as though I'd lost a friend.

After paying the bill and taking Ginger back to the car I stopped and tried brushing yet more fur off my clothes because I didn't want it all over the upholstery. A sweet voice spoke behind me and I jumped.

'It gets everywhere doesn't it. I think they shed extra fur when they're frightened. I usually get it off with sticky tape. We use loads in the office.'

I turned round and Clare was standing there looking neat and official in her maroon and white veterinary nurse outfit and with her hands thrust into the pockets of a denim jacket. She smiled up at me and all the colour rushed back into my world.

'He's not very happy with me.' I said lamely.

'P'raps he doesn't like your aftershave, they're funny about smells and scents.'

I felt myself blushing but her voice was quite matter of fact.

'I'm not criticising you, I like it. But they teach us this stuff. When you work with animals it's best to be as neutral as possible. They smell us and read our expressions. It all tells them what they need to know, like us looking at a book.'

This wasn't one of the conversations I'd imagined having with her. I'd seen myself fully in control of the situation and asking her if she'd like to go to the pub with me when she got off work. I'd wanted to say something gallant like "I'd like to get to know you better". Somehow it had worked in my mind, but here we were standing facing each other in a potholed carpark and she was starting a lecture. Just like my mum.

'You sound like my mum.' Oh crap, I'd actually said it, not just thought it, but she laughed.

'Is she nice? What's her name?' Clare asked.

'She's called Gwenna. Yeah, she's okay. She was a bit surprised that I'd decided to get the old boy looked over.'

'Well I think you're kind.'

We stood there looking at other. This was the first time I'd got this girl on my own and I couldn't think of anything sensible to say. I was noticing her smooth dark hair, the way it was tucked artlessly behind one ear. I saw that her ears were pierced but she wasn't wearing any earrings. Her eyes were clear, the greenish side of hazel, not the witchy green of her mum's eyes and she was smiling at me. Something spoke in my head and it went along the lines of "mate, she just said you're kind and she liked your aftershave so bloody do something before it's too late." I realised she was moving her shoulder bag to the other arm and looking as though she was about to make her excuses and leave so I finally seized the moment. Better late than never.

'Have you finished for the day then?'

Clare nodded.

'Fancy a drink or something?'

Again she nodded.

'Is The Hogshead any good? Only I've not been in there. My local is The Wheal.'

Clare looked at me considering something. 'Well, it's okay, if you don't mind the sort of place where you wipe your feet on the way out. And I need to get out of my work clothes, I hate these polyester trousers, they're uncool in all sorts of ways. And your poor cat ought to go home.'

'The Wheal then, it's decent. Shall I wait for you while you change?' It was starting to go more like I'd envisaged.

'Yes, okay. I live down there.' She pointed in a direction behind me.

I opened the passenger door. 'Hop in, I'll take you home to change.'

My confidence returned.

I waited in the car with Ginger and spoke to him gently but was rewarded with a cold stare. Clare didn't take very long and appeared in grey skinny jeans with a green top under her jacket and, I noticed, earrings. Little gold mice. I took that bit of dressing up as a good sign.

'Mum started the Spanish Inquisition but when I said I was just going to the pub with you she shut up. It was like magic.' She pulled a funny face.

Ginger started moaning again as soon as I started the car. By the time I pulled up outside my house he'd reached a full throated yodelling wail. Mum appeared at the door as I switched the engine off and immediately composed her expression when she saw I had company.

'Is he all right then?' she asked, glancing quickly at Clare.

'He's fine mum. This is Clare by the way.'

Clare got out of the car and put her hand out to mum who shook it awkwardly. 'I work at the vets. And my mum works at Trelerric House. It's how I met Simon.'

Mum, who liked straight talking, immediately relaxed and said a polite hello. 'We're just going for a drink mum. I'll be back later after I've dropped Clare off.' I nodded to her and smiled and left her to minister to Ginger who was now swearing in the cat basket and shredding the old towel I'd put in to make him comfortable.

Rather than walk the quarter mile to the pub I drove us, it gave me something to do with my hands. It also meant I couldn't drink which was a nuisance. I like pubs, there's something about the atmosphere and the smell of beer and woodsmoke that I find welcoming. The Wheal served decent food as well and I felt my stomach growling. Clare heard it and giggled.

'Mum says you can eat anywhere and anytime.'

'It's true. I'm always hungry. Do you fancy something? My treat.' I asked her. My casual jobs provided me with a fair bit of cash, most of which I usually put into my savings once a month. This was a special occasion though so my wallet was in funds. Clare smiled at me, a bit shy at first, then said she was starving too so we ordered moussaka. Normally I would have ordered the steak and ale pie but I wanted to seem more sophisticated. We took a corner table for two and as I sat down Clare shrugged her jacket off. I immediately got up to help her and got into a scuffle as she wasn't expecting assistance. We ended up grinning at each other in a confused way, both of us holding the jacket.

'I was trying to be polite.' I said.

'Polite is good. What shall I do with it?'

'Let go of it. Sit down and I'll put it over the back of your chair.' I suggested.

It was nice the way she did as I asked and let me retrieve the situation. Dignity restored I sat down again and raised my glass of coke to her. 'Cheers.'

Clare clinked her glass of white wine and smiled at me over the rim as she took a sip. 'Oh, that's nice. What is it?'

I thanked my lucky stars I'd seen the bottle the barman opened. 'Sauvignon Blanc. Crisp and with a green finish.'

Clare looked at me, startled. 'Wow. Are you a wine expert then?'

'No. I made the last bit up.'

To my relief she burst out laughing and then sat back and regarded me, a smile playing over her lips. I complimented her on her mouse earrings and made some chat about liking animals. The food came and I really enjoyed it, I don't think I'd ever eaten moussaka before. There was a slightly sweet taste to the dish which I liked but couldn't identify. Clare said it was nutmeg, but explained that she only knew because Maggie, her mum, being a cook-housekeeper, was a terrific cook. Clare wouldn't have a pudding because she said she didn't want to look like one.

'But it's different for you Simon. You work very hard, you need the calories.'

'You won't be disgusted if I dive into the sticky toffee pudding with extra sauce and ice cream then?' I joked.

Clare shook her head. 'No. But will you let me try a bit? Just a taste?'

I found myself gazing at her mouth, her nicely shaped lips, wondering what she'd be like to kiss. With an effort I focussed on her eyes. 'You can have anything you like if it's in my power to give.' God, I sounded like a creep.

'You sound like the lord of the manor bestowing favours.'

Then she just smiled at me, a secret little cat smile. I wondered whether she had any idea that she'd got right under my skin.

THREE

It was turning out to be a lovely summer. I finally produced a set of garden design drawings for the oriental-style courtyard that I was happy with and showed them to Sam. He pursed his lips and let out a long slow whistle.

'Bloody hell. They're marvellous. How on earth did you do this?'

Well, the answer to that was lots of research, thought, care, planning and effort but all I said was the one word. 'Talent.' I was actually being cheeky because I was nervous but Sam didn't react.

'In spades mate.' Sam said in his deep, posh voice. 'You make it look easy. There's no way I could produce something like this. Not at this level. We need to show Aunt Flick as soon as possible. I think you've got a winner here.'

He was right, she did like my drawings and so did Lucy, but the best bit was that Clare's mum gave us some lunch and she saw them as well.

'Look at these Maggie. See what a clever lad he is.' Sam said, unrolling the drawings.

'You made these Simon?' Maggie sat down at the kitchen table in Trelerric House and smoothed the corner of one of the drawings almost respectfully with the palm of her hand. 'How on earth? Who taught you?' She was looking at me with surprise.

'I dunno. I've always drawn and painted flowers and buildings. Then I did a garden design course, nothing fancy like a degree.' I was hoping I didn't come across like a total wuss. Flowers indeed. Maggie wasn't concerned though.

'Well I think you could go far with a gift like this.' Maggie said.

Well, my talent certainly landed me with a job involving a lot of physical labour. Sam more or less left me to get on with the hard work involved in preparing the ground for the courtyard garden, only helping when there were rocks to find and move into position, which was a heavy old pig of a task. I got fed well in Maggie's kitchen though and as the weeks went by I was included more and more in the working of Trelerric House.

After that first meal at the pub with Clare I cast about for ways to see her. Like a complete plonker I hadn't asked for her phone number, but then she hadn't asked me for mine. I spoke to Gramps and he suggested inviting her to the cinema.

'There must be something on for you young things down Plymouth. Find out what she likes and take her out one night. And you could go down to the Royal William Yard, the old warehouses are all tarted up now as fancy restaurants with swanky lighting. I've always loved the old dockside. I took your gran down the other day as a surprise.'

I was surprised, I'd never realised that they had a life and went out together. You kind of think of old people just mouldering away together in front of the telly with a plate of jammy dodgers and a mug of tea.

In fact it was Clare who got in touch first. I was in the potting shed cleaning up at the end of the day when she appeared at the door. 'Hello. Sam said I'd find you in here.'

'Clare!' I was bowled over with pleasure and felt my face light up. 'I was just thinking about you.' My mouth had operated without engaging my brain. What a lame statement. I'd spoken the truth though and I think I'd sounded genuine.

'Nice thoughts I hope?'

Now we were both talking bollocks. Taking refuge in safe, trite conversation. We both gave a nervous laugh but I spoke first. 'I was thinking about what was on at the cinema in Plymouth and whether you fancied going down there with me at the weekend.'

'That would be nice.' Clare looked pleased. 'But I'm babysitting at The Lodge this Saturday and I wondered whether you'd like to keep me company. It's only about four hours, and Mrs Marquand said it would be okay to ask you.'

Mrs Marquand was Sam's married sister. I knew her name was Alice, but I'd not had any reason to get to know her. My brain was grappling with the message that Clare had asked if she could invite me into their home as company. It felt significant and important. The thought that she wanted to spend some time alone with me made me go hot all over. I gripped the handle of the hoe I was holding and told myself to calm down.

'That's er, that's kind. Of them I mean.' Oh crap, I wasn't handling this at all well. Clare was looking uncertain at my bumbling response and I suspected that it had cost her something to plan this and to come and find me. Just like my mentally rehearsed conversations when I'd decided to ask her out that first time, when I'd thought it had all gone to pants. This dating thing wasn't easy.

'I mean yes, I'd love to. If you're sure they don't mind.' Shut up, shut up, I was thinking. Stop blundering about and accept the invitation that this lovely girl has just given you. Be cool. Ask what time you should pick her up. Clare spoke before I could.

'If you could pick me up from home at five thirty, they always go out at six. They're usually back by about ten cos it's only dinner with the family over at Home Farm. Mr Marquand will be grateful because he'll be able to have a drink if he doesn't have to drive me home.'

That was sorted then.

I started on my clients' gardens very early on Saturday and because it was good dry weather I steamed through the work. By mid afternoon I was back home in time to shower and change. Mum audibly sniffed at the odour of male grooming products emanating from the bathroom but she wasn't being sarky. 'She's special then, this girl?' Mum asked.

'She's lovely.' I couldn't explain what it was about Clare, there was something about her which made me feel good about things which is a curious thing to say because I'm an optimistic kind of bloke. It wasn't just that she was pretty and kind and smart. I couldn't find the words to describe how it felt when I looked at her.

'Well I hope you're getting something to eat. Do you want a sandwich now in case there's nothing doing?'

'I'm okay thanks mum, I got fed tea and cake today and I grabbed a pasty from the farm shop between jobs.' For the first time in my life I felt too anxious to eat, I just wanted to get off, but first I made sure the inside of the car was clean. It was an old jalopy but I liked to think of it as a classic and I kept it washed and polished. Briefly I wondered if I'd ever have enough money to buy the sort of cars they had at Trelerric House. There was some serious metal up there.

Mum was still speaking. 'Well, I'm going to my tai chi class and then out with some of the girls for the evening's bitching. Have a nice time and behave yourself. If she's special it's worth waiting for.'

I kissed her on the cheek, gave Ginger a stroke, he was friends with me again, and let myself out. Clare was ready when I arrived and apart from waving hello to Maggie there was no-one about. I realised I'd never seen Clare's dad. 'Is your dad around?' I asked as I pulled away.

'He's gone fishing with Ed. It'll be sea bass for dinner tomorrow. He loves his fish. He loves bringing stuff home for mum to cook. He pretends to beat his chest and be a caveman providing for his family.' Clare smiled. I knew that Ed was her older brother and that he lived with his girlfriend down at Mevagissey.

'I quite like fishing.' I said conversationally. 'I like the idea that you can just take off in the boat and go somewhere else. Gramps used to take me out fishing quite a lot when I was a kid. Now I don't seem to have the time, I'm working all hours.'

'You should make time for things you like Simon.' Clare said seriously. 'You don't want to end up wishing you'd spent time differently. Ah, we're here already.'

We were a bit early but the door opened and Mrs Marquand was clearly pleased.

'Hello Clare. And hello Simon, I've heard all about you but we've not met properly.'

'Nothing bad I hope Mrs Marquand.' There I went again, falling back on safe but dull prattle. How not to get noticed. But I spoke to my clients this way and they seemed to find it reassuring.

'Call me Alice, please.' She smiled but didn't respond to my boring comment. 'Tom's already in bed, Grace is just waiting for you Clare. And here's Jon. Jonathan this is Simon, he works with Sam.'

I noticed she didn't describe me as Clare's date, or boyfriend, or whatever.

'Hi.' Jonathan, her husband, a burly slightly florid man with curly sandy hair and blue eyes stuck his hand out and gave me a strong handshake. 'Good of you to help keep the zoo under control tonight. They've been fed and watered so I hope they'll stay caged and calm. Clare knows how to deal with them anyway. Brought your whip Clare?'

I thought he was trying too hard to be jolly and Clare only gave him a brief smile before going inside. A little girl I recognised as Grace was waiting for her. Grace looked at me doubtfully for a moment and then gave me a gap toothed grin. 'You're my uncle's friend. I've seen you before.'

'That's right. And I've seen you playing in the garden. So that's alright isn't it.' I said to her, recalling that she'd been found picking Sam's prized English bluebells one day, much to his dismay.

There was a brief flurry of activity and then I was on my own in the hall. Clare was upstairs with the children. Mrs Marquand, Alice, had indicated the kitchen and the sitting room, she didn't call it the lounge, and had told me to make myself comfortable. I opted for the kitchen which managed to be both smart and homely, noticing Grace's drawings stuck to the wall above a seriously high tech coffee maker. I was standing there looking at them when Clare came in. She looked so pretty with her dark hair clipped back and a few loose strands around her face, I really wanted to kiss her but we hadn't got to that stage yet. And it felt kind of odd, being alone, apart from the children upstairs, in this unknown but rather upmarket house. For a moment I wished quite fiercely that this was all ours. A good life, with children of our own and a future together.

Clare was busy with the kettle and hadn't noticed anything. 'They've left us some quiche and salad if you're hungry,' she said, making tea. 'It's perhaps not your idea of a Saturday night out, but it's a job which gives me a bit of spare cash and it's reliable. And I like the kids.'

I told her I understood all about the value of cash paying jobs and keeping in with reliable clients. Then we had a sensible conversation about work ethics and sat down like adults at opposite sides of the kitchen table while we demolished the quiche. Clare picked up my mood though.

'Is this what it's like, being a grown up? We'll be talking about the mortgage and the children next.' She giggled suddenly and glanced at me, her eyes dancing. Impulsively I stood up, my instincts telling me to go round the table and kiss the living daylights out of her. The strength of my emotions stopped me in my tracks, what if the Marquand's came home unexpectedly and found us in a clinch?

'Where's the loo?' I said, not needing it but thinking I ought to splash cold water on my face and possibly other parts of my anatomy. What was it Sam had said one day? "Having a hard-on isn't actually personal growth".

Clare pointed down the hall and I found it after mistakenly going into the dining room. God, this place was nice. The loo was hung with framed certificates, the sort of clever but understated thing confident people like to do. Jonathan had some qualification in estate management and Alice had a degree in biology. There were some swimming certificates belonging to

Grace and a couple of odd blurry black and white photos which I eventually realised were the things hospitals give to pregnant women. Back in the kitchen Clare had tidied up and was putting our plates into the already loaded dishwasher. It was such a homely scene that once again I found myself making wishes. This time I walked over to her and took hold of her hands.

'You're being busy. Do you feel comfortable doing these little jobs or are you as nervous as I am?'

'I'm nervous.' She was looking up at me seriously, her eyes wide. Time was spinning round in my head. We'd done a lot of talking this evening, at the pub on our first night out, even in the kitchen at Trelerric House with her mum and Sam there. It was time to make some sort of statement about why we were meeting. Gazing down at her I opened my mouth to speak. I could feel my heart thumping.

'Are you going to kiss each other?' A little voice spoke from the doorway. Grace was eyeing us with a detached kind of interest. 'Daddy kisses mummy sometimes. I woke up and couldn't find my cugga.'

'What's a cugga?' I asked no-one in particular.

'It's Grace's cuddle blanket. It helps her sleep.'

Grace was clearly wide awake now and enjoying our full attention. 'Can I have a story please?' She was looking at me with her cornflower blue eyes, her fair hair flat on one side where she'd been sleeping. As a newcomer to her domain she'd sized me up as someone who had absolutely no authority and was clearly open to blandishments.

'I'm not sure I have any stories.' I felt helpless, but then remembered her drawings. 'I could draw you a picture if you promise to go back to bed afterwards.'

This was clearly an acceptable deal and she climbed up to the table expectantly.

'There's paper and crayons in that basket.' Clare said.

'I prefer a pen, or a pencil.' I saw a pencil by the telephone and took that. 'Here we go then Grace. What's your favourite flower? No, don't tell me, I shall guess.' I pretended to make some sort of mystic mesmerising gesture with my fingers in front of Grace's eyes. 'Ah, I've got it. You're a little girl who likes bluebells.' I quickly sketched some bluebells down one side of the paper. Grace was delighted. 'What next?' I asked her.

'Mushrooms. I like mushrooms.' She responded.

'Okay, how about like this.' I drew a cluster of mushrooms at the bottom of the paper, smaller than the bluebells and leaning at different angles so that I could show their gills.

'Very realistic.' Clare was peering down at what I was drawing and she casually placed a hand on my shoulder. I felt her touch go through me like an electric shock.

'Dandelions!' Grace was really getting into this.

'Shush, not so noisy. Don't wake Tom.' Clare said.

I drew a large dandelion with its jagged leaves and then had an idea. Busily sketching I did a small figure wearing a nightie kneeling on one of the mushrooms. 'Who's that?' I asked.

'It's me.' Grace's voice hissed.

That was what I wanted her to think. I did a rapid bit of hatching and shading and smudged it with my thumb.

'Clever girl.' I said. 'And what's this?' I drew a small dandelion with a seed head as though the little figure was holding it. Then I drew little winged seeds floating away. Grace was leaning over my arm and making small noises of appreciation. 'That's a dandelion clock', I told her. 'If you blow on them gently the seeds float into the air and if you count you might be able to tell the time.'

'Which means it's back to bedtime my lady.' Clare said, gratefully. 'So I can tell mummy and daddy what a very good girl you've been.'

Grace knew she was beaten and out-manoeuvred. I smiled at her and carefully wrote on the top of the picture, "Grace in the Garden" and signed and dated the bottom. 'There, put that on your wall Grace. It's all about you.'

Clare was looking at me in a funny way, her lips slightly apart. I had the distinct feeling I'd done something good, something that had impressed her. She took Grace back upstairs while I mooched about on my own, prowling round the sitting room feeling like a burglar casing the joint. After the Marquand's got home I drove her back down to the village and got out of the car to help her out. Clare seemed surprised but pleased by the old fashioned courtesy.

'Thanks Simon. And thanks for coming over. It was nice to have company for a change.'

I stood back as she got out of the car and then closed the door behind her, thinking her words sounded formal and leaving me momentarily unsure how to react. 'The quiche was nice as well.' I responded like an idiot. Nice, what a dull word it was. Why the hell couldn't I think of something funny or sexy or interesting to say?

Clare gave a little laugh which seemed a bit fake. 'Yes, well er, goodnight then Simon. Thanks for driving me home.' And she turned to go.

'Clare.' I spoke her name urgently and she turned back to me. 'Clare, I'd like to see you again.'

We stood there in a moment of indecision and then she stepped forwards and put her arms up round my neck. 'That would be nice.' And she kissed me.

A few days later Sam spoke to me. 'Alice showed me that picture you did for Grace when you and Clare were babysitting. Alice is going to get it professionally framed.'

'You're joking.' I was surprised.

'Not joking. It's brilliant.'

'But it's just a pencil sketch.'

'It's good Simon.' Sam was looking at me thoughtfully. 'You need to believe in yourself.'

But I was thinking about Clare, about the way she'd looked at me that night. And remembering her kisses.

FOUR

'Simon, what would you ask for if you were granted three wishes?' Clare put down a book she was reading, something about a genie and a housewife, and looked over at me. We were sitting in the back garden at my house on a warm Sunday afternoon.

I considered her for a moment, loving the way her nose wrinkled when she was concentrating.

'No idea, haven't really thought about that sort of thing.' I responded lamely.

'What, you've never had wishes?' Clare asked.

'Well, yes of course I have. But they were to do with wishing mum could find a decent bloke, or wishing that grandad wouldn't leave teabags and a dirty spoon in the sink. It sends Gran nuts.' With one hand I caught the cushion she threw at me. 'So what are yours then?'

'The ability to fly,' Clare started counting on her fingers. 'Perfect health of course. Oh, and the ability to see into the past.'

'Why not the future?'

'Because the past has happened and the future hasn't. I'd like to see what life was really like in places like Trelerric and Plymouth in olden days. And if I could fly I could just sit up in a tree or something and watch, without them knowing I was there.'

I liked the idea. 'That could lead to a whole lot of new legends, undiscovered folklore. I know,' I said, the idea grasping my imagination. 'The legend of the watching lady, or the flying lady. Portents of doom and all that. I could draw that.'

Mum came outside with a tray of cold drinks and some homemade shortbread which she'd topped with caramel and chocolate. It wasn't even tea time but mum always looked after the inner man. Being a postwoman kept her lithe and fit and she had no qualms about calorie intake. 'What are you two nattering about?' She handed me a drink, I was sitting cross legged on the lawn cleaning and sharpening my secateurs. 'Damn, I forgot the plates.'

'I'll get them Mrs. Sherwell.'

Clare got out of her seat and I watched her pretty figure retreating as she went off to the kitchen. She and mum had struck up a friendship since we'd been dating. Mum liked the fact that Clare had inherited her own mother's practical abilities and Clare admired the way that my mum coped with what life had thrown at her. There was that curious mutual respect that two women who recognise each other's capabilities have. Mum said that Clare had a sensible head on her shoulders. I told mum about the three wishes idea.

'If wishes were horses, beggars would ride,' she said dismissively. 'Isn't that what the proverb says?'

'Yeah I know, but it's not very optimistic thinking like that mum. Clare has ideas, she thinks about what's possible.'

Clare, returning with three plates, heard what I said and planted a kiss on the top of my head. It was one of those little things that make your day complete. Living in Cornwall, with the sun shining, your mum and your girlfriend getting along in the garden and a plate with something wicked on it to tide you over between lunch and dinner. The cat keeping us company. Could it get any better? And I've always enjoyed the company of women.

'How high would you fly if your first wish was granted?' I wanted to know.

Again there was that nose wrinkling while Clare thought. 'Not very high, just like in dreams when you find you can leave the ground and float over it while no-one else can. Enough to lift yourself over bushes and small buildings.'

I was nodding, I'd had those dreams myself. Dreams where I could just fall forward with the knowledge that I wouldn't hit the ground but simply rise above it and swim like a dolphin through the air. Dreams of letting go and then seeing landscape from a new angle. Landscape which might include sights and views of times past. It was a seductive image.

Clare was smiling at me. 'You're miles away Simon.'

'I was thinking about the past, and about flying through time. Sam sometimes talks about Trelerric as though the past was just yesterday. He says he's smelled women's perfume and men's sweat in the Tudor house, and thinks he's heard voices sometimes.' I paused, remembering. 'On my first day there I saw you though a mullioned window. I thought I was seeing a ghost but then you laughed.'

'Have you seen a ghost then?' Clare asked the question seriously.

I glanced at mum. 'Sort of.' Mum already knew the story and remained non-committal. Clare raised her eyebrows and looked interested so I decided to tell her the story.

'It was when I was little, about ten years old. One of my very old guys, one I fetched the papers for and washed his car — his name was Walter, was really kind to me. He was the first person, apart from Gramps, to teach me about gardening. But he was also interested in wildlife and taught me about bullhorns and the small people that live in Cornish landscape.'

'Bullhorns are snails aren't they?' Clare asked.

'Yes. Walter never killed them, he never killed anything. He said he'd seen more than enough death on the battlefield. He'd been an artilleryman. Anyway, Walter taught me about slow worms, lizards, hedgehogs, and also about the things that live in ponds. He called them the small people, he had a theory that the natural world was behind what the Cornish think of as knockers, piskies, fairies and spriggans.'

'Knockers lived down the mines didn't they?' Clare was keeping up with me. 'The miners respected them and used to leave food. But spriggans? I've not heard that name.'

'Spriggans are spirits. Walter said spriggans were everywhere, even in the stones up on the moor. He said you had to respect everything you worked with because it was all subtly connected by energy. He opened up a whole world that was right there before my eyes but which I hadn't really seen before.'

'That's lovely,' Clare said. 'But what about the ghost?'

'Well, Walter had been hurt when he was in the artillery. He walked with a really noticeable limp. It used to trouble him but it never got him down, and he said that one day he'd walk again without a limp and without any pain. And on that day he'd be truly happy.' I sat and thought for a moment. 'One morning I woke up and ran downstairs to mum.' I saw Clare glance at mum. 'I told her that I'd just dreamed I'd seen Walter, I'd been standing in the lane outside his house and he was walking down the path towards the gate to see me. He was smiling at me, looking really well and happy and walking without a limp. The garden looked fantastic, everything was perfect, the colours were brilliant. Then I found myself in bed.'

Mum was nodding now and looking at me, ready to take the story over.

'Simon told me about Walter, as innocent and as pleased as anything about seeing his old friend looking so well. I had to tell him that Walter's wife had just phoned and told me that he'd passed in his sleep during the night. She didn't want Simon going round while all the funeral arrangements were being sorted out and the family was grieving.'

Clare looked astounded. 'So you saw Walter at about the time he died, looking well and happy and in a nice place. But in a dream?'

'It seems that way. I haven't got any explanation.' I said. 'I was just happy for him. I was only a little kid.'

'Mad.' Clare breathed.

'Possibly, but not spooky. Not floating about wailing and wearing a sheet.'

We were all silent for what seemed like ages. I started tidying my tools up and Clare sat staring into space. Mum started the conversation going again.

'I hear that boss of yours has been seen out with a dark haired young lady up at The Wheal recently.'

'If she's got dark hair then it's Lucy.' I said. 'They've got feelings for each other, it's plain to see.'

'As the nose on your own face.' Mum said meaningfully. And she took the empty plates and glasses back to the kitchen.

'They go to our pub?' Clare said. 'What if we bump into them there?'

'So what if we do?' I said, liking the way she called it "our pub". 'I'm not bothered. He's with his girlfriend, I'm with mine. It's a free country.'

'I'm your girlfriend then?'

'I bloody hope so. If I'm not too weird for you.'

'I'm okay with weird. Boyfriend.'

Since babysitting for the Marquand's Clare and I had started seeing quite a lot of each other. We just clicked, we were on the same wavelength. We'd been to the cinema, for walks by the sea, had a picnic on the moor and found we could talk about anything. The only thing we couldn't do was spend serious personal time together, simply because there was nowhere for us to go. Any private time we got was on a dark night in the car up on the moor. It wasn't very satisfactory. I began to think about booking a weekend away in a nice hotel somewhere, but before I had the chance to pursue the idea the Latchley's asked if I'd be able to help them with some big event they were holding over the summer. It meant reorganising my other jobs because it involved some weekend work, but I came up with the idea of moving my old campervan up to Trelerric so that I could stay over some nights. Sam's mum let me put the van up behind an old granite barn across from, but out of sight of the farmhouse. I found myself a secluded corner alongside a handsome old granite trough and some attractive but rusting old farm machinery which had bindweed and foxgloves growing through it. The corner was a sun trap and the huge trumpet shaped flowers were already in bud. In Cornwall things arrive early. Sam's mum gave me permission to cook on my camping stove and told me I should use their downstairs shower room. She'd originally had it put in for Sam and his dad to use so that they didn't bring the farm into the house and occasionally she washed the dogs in there but the facilities were clean and decent. The main thing was that Clare started coming up to see me after work so we often ate together as we began to explore our feelings.

One evening I had the bright idea of having a barbecue. I rigged up a contraption using a couple of old breeze blocks, a discarded metal tray and an old oven shelf. Sam's dad was very particular about the look of the farm but boy was there some junk in the old granite barn next to where I was camping. I'd gathered kindling and found some dry wood, and had a bag of barbecue briquets ready. Clare turned up with a tub of Maggie's own coleslaw, another tub holding marinating cubes of meat, some cherry tomatoes and a couple of ready-baked potatoes wrapped in foil. I poured her a glass of wine and attended to the fire. It was a warm evening and the heat made me sweat. Then some of the old wood sparked and spat tiny embers onto my bare arm which made me swear and Clare laugh. This was all macho-male cooking stuff though so I decanted the briquets once I'd judged the wood to be burning properly, and then had to stand back when a great belch of smoke issued. By now Clare was in hysterics.

'You've got soot on your face and smuts in your hair!' She was gasping with laughter.

An hour later I felt as though my face had melted. I was hot, hungry, covered in smuts and stinking of smoke and, I feared, sweat. Clare stepped forward having carefully skewered alternate pieces of chicken, pork and jumbo prawns and placed them over the heat. I went to turn them and forgot that metal gets hot, very hot. More swearing ensued as I sucked my burnt fingers while Clare folded a cloth she'd brought and calmly dealt with the situation, with a huge grin on her face. I noticed she'd also put the foil wrapped potatoes on to heat.

Finally she pronounced everything ready and we balanced paper plates on our knees and ate with fingers and plastic forks.

'The potatoes will be a bit dry by now won't they?'

'No, I cut them and put some butter and grated cheddar inside before wrapping them up.'

They were delicious. She'd even remembered to put black pepper on them.

Clare told me she'd had a few boyfriends, including one from school and one when she was at The Duchy College first studying veterinary nursing, but no-one she was serious about. I asked her why the last one hadn't turned into anything special.

'He was okay at first, but then he got all needy and kept sending me soppy cards of teddybears wearing sticking plasters and pretending to be cute and brave. I thought they were pathetic, I mean, I'm a veterinary nurse and deal with animals who've had injuries and operations. When I told him I didn't want to see him any more he got terribly upset and said he'd do something awful to himself. He nearly freaked me out, it was like emotional blackmail. Mum reckoned he'd got issues as soon as she met him.'

I didn't pursue that but told her about Chloe, my girlfriend from school, although I didn't say anything about the way she'd made me feel like a loser.

Clare seemed to be a good judge of character, she was lovely to be with and anyway it was early days yet. And here I was, at last cool and composed enough to enjoy the moment, watching the late evening sunlight dappling her face as she chattered unselfconsciously about her job and ideas while I listened and quietly exuded smoke.

'Penny for them Mrs Latchley?' I'd been heading for the downstairs shower room because I needed to use the facilities. Sam's mum, Jane Latchley, was standing at the back door to

Home Farm, staring out at her rockery. With the farm and all the work that entailed, her own garden consisted of a simple spacious paved and gravelled seating area surrounded by a large curved rockery. I'd discovered that alpines were her passion and found myself hoping that she wasn't wanting to redesign the place, I'd got enough work to do. Then I noticed she was holding a letter in one hand. 'Not bad news is it?' Hoping I sounded both neutral and friendly.

'Oh, hi Simon. I was just thinking about the Latchley Book and Chronicle. It's been on my mind for ages to get something done about them, I mean translating into modern English and written up so that we can understand and refer to them easily. I've had another letter from overseas, someone tracing their family history and finding the Trelerric lands mentioned in their old family papers. It fascinates me what people find in their great-grandparents old trunk, long forgotten in the homestead attic. The things people wrote down before they died, about where they came from and so on, often long after they'd made the one-way trip to a new life.'

I was interested and said so. 'My grandad has done some family research, he's got back to 1841 but says it gets complicated before that.'

'Yes, before that you have to rely on parish and any other local records. It's a bit hit and miss. That's why Trelerric is so special, we have the estate records to refer to and they're comprehensive. The last couple of centuries are readable with patience, but the Tudor period is difficult and whenever anyone with a peculiar handwriting style has written an indecipherable script.'

I just stood there nodding and looking at her. I'd heard Sam talk about these records and what a source of information they were about the development of the estate. There were some old maps he particularly liked and had promised to show them to me one day. I was comfortable with the thought of all that information listing all those lives springing from the Trelerric lands. I had a visual picture of the old house with tendrils flowing from it like vines all over the globe, producing buds, flowers, fruits and seeds. 'It's living history isn't it.' I said.

Jane Latchley looked at me, a bit amused. 'Yes, I guess it is. And these days people seem to want to get in touch with their past. Perhaps it's because modern times are so uncertain at the moment, with so much global trouble. Do people think they'll find something safer and more secure in previous times?'

I just shrugged my shoulders and Mrs Latchley turned to go back inside. 'Ah well, if you know anyone who wants a job deciphering the books let me know.' It was a throwaway comment, she didn't mean anything by it.

'Oh,' I said to the back of her head. 'I think I do know someone.'

She turned back to me. 'Really?'

'Well, in the pub the other night I was talking to a lady called Sally Evans. I met her because she came over to Darleystones a couple of times when I was working there. That's Mr Pencraddoc's house. He'd found some old stuff there which she was interested in.' I realised Mrs Latchley was looking at me patiently, but clearly wanting to get on. 'Well, Sally works at the museum in Liskeard.' I continued hastily. 'She's got contacts in Plymouth and Truro who know about antiquities and conservation and stuff like that. Sally said she was starting a course doing research for a qualification.' I stopped for a moment, trying to remember what it was that Sally had said she was interested in.

'Go on Simon.'

'Something to do with trade and commerce in Tudor times, the movement of goods, um, tin and copper and lead going from Cornwall and what got brought back — you didn't want an empty ship. She said there was no profit in it.'

'Well, that's interesting, but what does that have to do with Trelerric?'

'I told Sally where I was working now and she said that Trelerric had its own quayside, like lots of the old properties on the River Tamar. And that she'd already seen some early documents connected with Trelerric House.'

I'd got Jane Latchley's full attention now. 'Oh, so she might be able to find references to what the original de Lachele was trading in. We know he was an entrepreneur, there's a mention of commodities like wool and hides in our own records. I think fruit was referred to in one of the documents we have. Cherries to Plymouth or something,' she said. 'But that was much later, I'm a bit vague on the details.'

'Maybe Sally ought to take a look at what you've got.' I said.

'You could be right Simon. What an extraordinary fount of knowledge you are. You never cease to surprise me.'

'It's not what you know, it's who you know.' I said. 'Apparently.'

She laughed and went indoors.

FIVE

Summer at Trelerric House was manic. They'd got the big Trelerric Vintage event on for about six weeks and the whole family, plus some relations and helpers were working flat out. Because it was such a popular attraction the local television people turned up, which caused more work as they wanted to film old Mrs Latchley being interviewed in the gardens. Sam wanted nothing short of perfection but it was fascinating watching the little film crew working, all the kit was lightweight, miniaturised and portable.

When I wasn't weeding, hoeing, dead-heading and sweeping I was helping Sam's dad with customer tickets and parking duties and when I wasn't doing that I was working with Sam doing greenhouse work. Clare was busy as well, doing something for her diploma which involved a written assignment so I saw a little bit less of her. Texting was sometimes all we managed, it was frustrating in more ways than one. Finally we got to the closing night at August Bank Holiday and Jane Latchley put on a feast at Home Farm for everyone who'd been involved. Since Clare had helped her mum in the tea rooms on her days off she was invited. I think people were noticing that we were together. That evening I was reluctant to let her go.

'I've got to move the old van out now the event is over.' I said. 'And I think I've got to find some way of getting my own place so that we can be together.' I noticed the thoughtful look on her face. 'With winter coming, I mean.' We'd done a lot of kissing and some serious cuddling, but so far we hadn't gone all the way. Clare was passionate but curiously reluctant to let go completely. All she said was that she wanted to be in the right place when she did it. I wasn't sure whether she meant the right place in her head or the right place like somewhere of our own. Probably both. And I really fancied the idea of us being together. The thought of waking up and finding her next to me was intoxicating.

A few weeks later old Mrs Latchley, the ex-actress who'd commissioned the Japanese courtyard garden, dropped a bombshell. She asked Sam to let me know she wanted to see me so after a quick splash at the cold tap in the greenhouse I went round to the big house. Maggie was there and she bossed me about, insisting I drag her comb through my hair before she took me into Mrs Latchley's rooms. I'd been in once before, the day Sam took me in to show the lady my courtyard design drawings, so I knew I'd have to take my boots off. I just hoped my feet didn't pong. I needn't have worried, there was so much perfume in the room from the lilies she favoured that nothing would have been detectable.

'Simon, thank you so much for coming and at such short notice. Do sit down, I've a favour to ask you.'

I thought about the way Sam's dad moved and sat myself squarely on the little chair she indicated, with my back straight and my gaze level. It was hard looking at her, like looking straight into the sun. She was curiously dazzling with her actressy ways and for an old lady, she was very good looking.

'What can I do for you Mrs Latchley?' I asked.

'Well, I have some news. I'm to be married shortly to Sir Hugh Flinton and I will be spending time away from Trelerric House. Hugh lives at Flinton Hall near the Malvern Hills.' She looked at me expectantly but I didn't know where that was or where this was leading so I just sat still and looked amiable. 'Hugh has been admiring the work you did on transforming the courtyard outside,' she waved an elegant white hand to the French windows. 'He'd like you to come up to Flinton Hall after we're married and take a look at an area of ground he wants developed. It's a sort of wedding present to me.'

I was gobsmacked but managed to make a congratulatory noise about her marriage. Just how old was she, I was wondering. Much older than my mum, so possibly there was still hope for her. I came out of my thoughts and realised that Mrs Latchley was staring at me, waiting for an answer.

'Oh, wow. Well that's a surprise. I don't know what I was expecting but, well, what about my job here? I'd have to get permission from Sam and his dad I expect.'

'I've already been presumptuous and spoken to them both at supper last weekend. I've told them what Sir Hugh would like and why, and the family wouldn't dream of disappointing me.' She spoke in a silky smooth voice and smiled at me in the way of a woman who always gets what she wants. 'And with Trelerric house and gardens closed now until next year it's the perfect opportunity for them to lend you to me.'

Oh bugger, I was thinking, It would mean being away from Clare. How could I stand it?

Mrs Latchley took my silence for acquiescence. 'So I'll be in touch regarding a suitable date and you can discuss your fees with Sir Hugh after you've seen the project. Is that suitable?'

I was feeling dizzy and right out of my depth. There was nothing for it, I couldn't bluster my way through this. 'Mrs Latchley, I'm honoured, truly I am. I've done hard landscaping and made changes in a small way for some of my clients, but never anything on this scale before. The courtyard out here was my first proper attempt and it was a sort of a favour to Sam. It was a way of proving to him that I'm good enough to work here. I'm pleased with it and I'm really glad you are, but I wouldn't know how to go about starting a project for someone like a "Sir".'

Mrs Latchley was looking at me closely and I felt my colour heightening. Suddenly she smiled warmly and the illumination in the room went up several watts.

'Simon, I hope you don't mind me calling you Simon, but I realise I don't know your surname.'

'Sherwell.' I managed to blurt.

'Simon Sherwell, I like your honesty but even more than that I appreciate your talents and ability. I believe that if you have a particular talent you should use it to your advantage. I recognise yours and it shouldn't be confined to Cornwall. All you have to do is look at the site, discuss the ideas the client may have, draw up one of your beautiful plans, cost the materials and the labour and add a percentage for the originality and uniqueness of your skill. And don't undersell yourself. What else is there?'

'The type of ground, acidic, alkaline, neutral, sandy, clay.' I muttered. 'What will grow and whether it's appropriate for what you have in mind. It's not straightforward.'

'Well, we'd leave that sort of expertise to you of course. So what do you say?'

'I suppose I could have a look, but ...'

'But what Simon?'

'Where exactly are the Malvern Hills?' I said.

I'd left Mrs Latchley, soon to be Lady Flinton, and stumbled back to Maggie's kitchen in my socks, slipping a bit on the floor tiles. I was in a state of shock but Maggie was suitably impressed by my news. Finally I couldn't help confiding in her that I'd hate being away from Clare.

'If my daughter knows what's good for her she'll support you every inch of the way Simon. This is an opportunity you should take. Something good could come of it. When are you seeing each other next?'

'The weekend, I hope.'

Maggie sat down with me at the kitchen table and looked me over compassionately. She was a sweet woman, I thought, with her auburn curls and green eyes. Not much like Clare in looks but a lot like her in good sense and level headedness.

'You're quite serious about my daughter aren't you Simon?' she said.

'I'm nuts about her.'

'Have you told her?'

'No. I mean, she obviously knows that I like her a lot. We get along really well.' Blimey, I couldn't tell Clare's mother what we got up to in our rare moments of spare time.

'Well, go along and see what this all means. I gather Flinton Hall is only a couple of hours straight up the M5, more or less. It could be the start of something for your future.'

When I spoke to mum and Gramps they gave similar encouragement and when I caught up with Sam he gave me generous advice.

'Go for it mate. Aunt Flick has given you some good ideas to think over and I can spare you for a couple of weeks or so. You could either use your holiday entitlement or take time off unpaid to do it. Just make sure you charge Sir Hugh enough to cover your wages and things like your travelling time and fuel. His pockets are deep and he can afford it. And don't worry, there's still plenty of work for you when you get back here.'

At the weekend I was grateful to be able to talk it all over with Clare. We were babysitting Grace and Tom again, and fortunately Grace had gone to bed and stayed there.

'It's the paperwork though Clare. I don't have a business, I don't have a clue where to start. And I'll need to write stuff up in an invoice or something and present Sir Hugh Flipping Flinton with a bill. How do I do that?'

Clare had ideas though. 'I've handled invoices and orders at the vets. And there's advice for new businesses and examples of things on the internet or from books. I'm pretty sure we could work it out between us. And you should bill him in stages to keep your cash-flow going and to inform him of how the work is progressing.'

Amazing woman, I thought as I looked at her. She was making it all seem possible but even better it felt as though she was with me, at my side, every step of the way. 'You're fantastic Clare. Have I told you that? I feel as though I could do anything with you helping. But what should I call myself? What's my business name?'

'Easy. "Simon Sherwell Designs" and "Landscape Designer to Posh Toffs" in a curly font underneath that.' She giggled.

'Who only does gardens for wealthy clients who own stately homes.' I added, suddenly aware that was more or less the truth. Hold on though, I told myself. It hasn't happened yet.

I hugged her and held her and kissed her until we were both breathless.

I wasn't due to go up to Flinton Hall until the end of October so there was time to sort things out. Clare went on the internet and ordered a book about starting your own business. It was an eye opener and I realised that I'd have to rethink the way I carried out what I called my casual work. All the information about national insurance and pensions was starting to make sense in a scarily grown up way.

With the Flinton wedding imminent Sam had me sprucing up the area around the old chapel. It was a lovely, secret sort of place, built into the side of the old Tudor building. Its position had allowed the original users to enter from the house, particularly useful on wet days in Cornwall. Sam and I had moved a couple of heavy old urns to a more advantageous position and I was planting them up with trails of white edged ivy to enhance the approach to the chapel when a husky voice called my name. I would have known that soft Scottish accent anywhere.

'Miss Frazer, what are you doing here?'

Fiona Frazer was Daniel Pencraddoc's lady. He of the self-made IT games dot com millionaire fame. I didn't play them myself, but he'd made a fortune in the business. Everything he touched turned to gold or so it seemed to me. Daniel had come home and effortlessly swept up the sexy Fiona before anyone else had noticed what was happening. Fiona had taught me at an adult education art class a few summers ago and then helped me get onto the computer design course. The year they'd got together I'd worked with Andy Hauxwell, a builder I knew, renovating Daniel's house. Now Daniel and Fiona were living there, with two small children. And still not married as my mother liked to point out.

'Daniel, I'm feeling the spirit of the place and getting ideas for some new paintings.' Trelerric House was enjoying a moment of fame since it had all that media coverage over the summer. 'I want to capture and express some of the mystery of these lovely buildings now that the crowds have gone. Jane Latchley has given me permission to roam about.' Miss Frazer was looking around as she spoke, her thick dark red hair in a plait over one shoulder. She was wearing a sage green jumper over rusty red jeans. Despite having two children now she was still as slender as when I'd first met her although I thought her bust looked fuller.

I nodded, understanding what she meant about the spirit of the place. I was back in Walter's world with the spriggans and that feeling of everything being alive and subtly connected by energy. Fiona Fraser wasn't the only person of my acquaintance who shared a Celtic understanding of what are known as the "thin places", where both the present and the past collapse and merge in a strand of spiritual sympathy. Not necessarily religious, but profound in a way difficult to explain. I'd felt it when I first saw Trelerric House, but I'd also experienced the feeling up on Bodmin moor at The Cheesewring, those places where there is magic in the air.

'Jane Latchley is Sam's mum. Sam is my boss now. She's nice, she let me park my van up here in the summer, I was helping with the event. We were so busy it was mental.'

'So you are here full-time now?'

'More or less, but I still look after three holiday cottages in our village.' The news of the request to visit Flinton Hall was at the surface of my mind though. 'And I've got a possible garden design job at Flinton Hall, which is partly thanks to you.' I explained the details and Fiona offered some helpful suggestions. We were deep in conversation when another voice cut in. It was Sam's mum.

'Hello Fiona, I wanted to invite you in for a coffee if you've time.' Jane Latchley looked from Fiona to me and back again. 'Do you two know each other?'

'We do.' Fiona said. 'Simon has taken care of my brother's garden in the past and of Bel, my horse. But we're old friends.'

I liked the way Fiona said that. She made me feel included and equal. Not just the humble gardener, but then Fiona was an unusual and very lovely person.

Jane Latchley gave me a look. 'Simon knows some very interesting people. I've taken your advice Simon, if you remember that conversation we had weeks ago. I got in touch with Sally Evans at the Liskeard museum and she's coming over to talk about the Latchley Book and Chronicle research.'

'Oh, I know Sally as well.' Fiona said. 'She's unearthed some interesting facts about the history of my man's house up on the moor.'

'Oh really.' Jane said. 'Now, have you seen the bee-boles in the old orchard wall? They are a few hundred years old and have a charming history of their own.'

I watched them walk away chattering. Women. Fascinating creatures.

SIX

As it was a family affair I wasn't needed at Trelerric House on the day of the Flinton wedding so I took the opportunity to put some time in at the holiday cottages. I also decided to put my fees up a couple of pounds because I was getting increasingly serious about finding my own place. I reckoned the owners could afford to stand me a pay rise, all these places were second homes and I knew that one of the owners, the owner of Pondside Cottage, was something in television so he had to be loaded. I'd scouted around and checked the local paper, but so far none of the rentals had appealed either due to price or location.

Since it was a beautiful autumn day I got the jobs completed to my satisfaction and decided to get showered and changed and surprise Clare from work. She was doing the afternoon and evening shift so I knew she'd be leaving around seven. I'd spent the day thinking about us and how I felt about her, finally coming to the conclusion that we should talk about putting our relationship on a serious footing, one with a future. I thought hard about how to approach the idea. My mum's bodice-ripper romances had taught me that I should set the scene, one with flowers and a nice bottle of something bubbly. Somehow our favourite table at The Wheal didn't seem appropriate so I decided I'd ask Sam if he could recommend a special restaurant.

The lovely day had turned rapidly into a murky evening with a snarky little wind blowing as I drove into the car park and into a corner parking slot. I could see into the vets because the lights were on and a couple of late customers were at the reception counter. There was a pretty blonde girl dealing with the customers and I saw the vet who had given Ginger the once over go into the office behind her. Then I saw Clare, just her head visible as the windows to the treatment rooms were set quite high. She was doing something, last minute tidying up I guessed, when a young dark haired man, one I'd never seen before, came into the room behind her. He was wearing the sort of professional top the vets wore and I could see him smiling and speaking. Clare turned and all I could see was the back of her head, then the lights went off, just leaving a square piece of light where the door to the corridor was open.

They were in the room alone together.

My blood went cold and I stopped breathing.

Then I saw them leave the room and close the door and I let out a long slow breath, my palms had gone clammy and I could feel the dull thump, thump, of my heart against my ribs.

I was aware that the customers were leaving, the man was carrying something, a dog I think, and the woman was fussing at their car with a blanket and only a street light to help her see. Clare came out with the blonde girl, they were laughing together under an outside light and seemed to be dawdling. For some reason I didn't make a move, so I saw the young man come out. He spoke to Clare and the blonde and then gave a casual flick of his wrist and something beeped and flashed in the carpark. It was a newish car, a boy racer tart-cart if ever I saw one. Just the sort of wheels I would have liked. All three of them got in and he drove away. And I just sat there, feeling my dreams and hopes melting to ice and running dreadfully cold down my spine.

At work the next day Sam was late and when he did turn up his mind wasn't on work. He was bright eyed, absent minded and very pleased with himself. A complete contrast to me, dull eyed, leaden and exhausted from not sleeping. Eventually he spoke.

'I've got some news Simon.'

I looked up from what I was doing, a boring job brushing some clay pots clean. 'Oh yes, what's that then?' I did my best to appear normal.

'I've asked Lucy to marry me. I asked her last night. She said yes. The darling girl said yes to taking me and Trelerric on. Isn't she the most fantastic and gorgeous woman ever?'

I looked at him with a moment of bitter envy. He was good looking and had everything to offer a girl. What woman would refuse him? But he was a good bloke, he'd been born to comfort and plenty because that was the way the cards had been dealt.

'Wow.' I said. 'That's great. Congratulations.'

'And I'm going to get the old cottage on the cherry fields site renovated.' Sam was still seeing his dreams taking shape and not looking at me. 'I found the old door key there earlier this year when I was poking around. It was still on the ledge above the front door. Must have been there, undisturbed, for sixty years. I thought it was a good omen so I gave it to Lucy for her birthday yesterday and promised her a home of our own. We've decided to call it Cherryfields Cottage.'

I looked at Sam, lost in his vision and with a slightly dazed look on his face. The lucky, lucky bastard.

'You're a lucky sod Sam. When's the wedding then?'

'Just before Christmas. Barely a couple of months away. It's best, Trelerric is closed and it's our quiet time. And I didn't see any point in hanging around. I've met the woman I want to be with and Lucy feels the same about me. We'll have known each other a couple of weeks short of a whole year.' He gave a surprised laugh.

'That old cottage won't be renovated in time for you to live in it.' I cut into his happiness with a cold dose of reality. 'It hasn't got a roof on or electricity connected. And the septic tank will need investigating, if it's got one.' Mentally I was back working with Andy the builder, listing all the jobs, working out a plan, costing all the work. I'd learned more from him than I'd realised. 'And you'll need to get permission from the Council, plans will have to be drawn up and submitted.' As I spoke I compared the work of the builder with the work I was going to do, if all went well. Garden design had to be easier than building houses.

'I know, I know. My brother-in-law knows a good architect, the guy who sorted out The Lodge for him and Alice. But now I need to find a builder I can work with.' Sam looked as though his feet were starting to connect to the earth again.

'I know one. You want Andy Hauxwell. He did Mr Pencraddoc's place. He's good and he's a sympathetic renovator.' I fished my mobile out and looked up Andy's details. 'I can ping you his number. Tell him I work here with you now.'

Sam thanked me and wandered off leaving me to the mundane tasks, his mind full of more important things. After finishing the job I was doing I went for a walk round to try to clear my head, and found my feet heading for the old Tudor house. It was my favourite place. There was no-one around although there were signs that a wedding had taken place. The chapel was locked and old Mrs Latchley, now Lady Flinton, was probably halfway to London with her bridegroom. The very idea of two old people falling in love like that seemed peculiar to me, although Clare had said they'd known each other most of their adult lives.

I noticed that confetti had been thrown but on closer examination discovered that it was flower petals, biodegradable and not likely to cause Sam annoyance. Nothing for me to clean up then. I walked round the house and across the terrace at the front, pausing to look over the little private gate to the Japanese-style courtyard I'd designed and built. The courtyard had a peaceful air so I clicked the latch and went in and sat on the little rustic bench I'd put in there. I'd chosen it because of its simplicity, it was old and obviously hand-made by a previous gardener. With its age, patina and a little bit of lichen growing on it, the bench met a concept of honesty the Japanese called *wabi sabi*.

Despite the beauty of the space my mood didn't improve. I felt awful. I couldn't be sure about just what had gone on last night between Clare and the unknown young vet, but my confidence was so low that I assumed the worst. I'd imagined every scenario possible whilst unable to sleep. I'd seen her laughing and flirting with him, imagined her being driven about in his nice car, going places and making plans together. She could have a bright future with a young professional like him.

Vets earned good money and he would have prospects. Finally I'd imagined how she would give me the elbow and dump me. I felt like crap, tired out and thoroughly fed up. For the first time since I was a little kid I wanted to cry and I sat forward with my head in my hands.

There was a faint click as a door opened and a small huffing noise as a little body trotted out and across to me. It was a pleasure to pat Coco, the little dog that belonged to Lady Flinton. It meant that Lucy must have opened the door. I looked up and sure enough she was standing there looking at me.

'Hi Simon.' Lucy was still looking at me and I felt her gaze like a searchlight sweeping through me. 'If you don't mind me saying, you look as though you've not slept. In fact you look rougher than a badger's bum. Can I ask what's up?'

She was so friendly and calm. I knew she'd been a nurse and was good with people. Sam was lucky to get a girl like this.

'I don't know Lucy.' I paused. 'I think I saw Clare with someone else last night.'

'Oh.'

'She had a colleague, another girl with her. But there was a young bloke from work with them.' I felt my face creasing. Shit, I really did want to cry.

'I've just made some tea. I'm on my own. Come inside and talk to me.'

I told her everything. All my doubts and fears came pouring out. Lucy was such a good listener that I told her all about me; my absent dad, my jobs, my ex-girlfriend, my feelings for Clare and my hopes and plans. Lucy listened and nodded and didn't offer any explanations or make any judgements. There was a small period of quiet and then I remembered my manners.

'Lucy, I'm sorry. I've dumped all this on you and I've just realised I've not said congratulations. I saw Sam this morning and he gave me the good news. I'm really pleased for you both. You're a great match and he's crazy about you.'

Her face lit up and I saw the joy she was feeling. 'Thanks. Yes, it's amazing. I can't quite believe that he asked me. I keep pinching myself.'

'Weren't you expecting it then?'

'No, not really. I hoped but then I didn't think I was good enough.'

Well, that was a surprise and it must have shown in my face.

'It's a long story Simon.' She gave a happy laugh. 'But since you've told me yours I'll tell you mine if you like! And let's have a proper drink!'

Hers was an interesting story. Later, feeling much calmer although still very tired I got in my car and went home. Lucy said she'd clear it with Sam and said that I needed some personal time. She spoke to me like a friend.

Mum was home from work when I got in, her hours had her up and out at dawn but the benefit was being at home for the best part of the afternoon. I gave a brief resume of events and said I needed to get some sleep. Mum, however, was brusque.

'Give Clare the benefit of the doubt before you come to any false conclusions my lad and make a mess of your future. You don't have anything concrete to go on but your own unfounded doubts and suspicions, and I really thought there was more to your relationship with her. I thought you trusted each other.'

At that moment my phone beeped. It was a text from Clare.

"Y so v quiet 2day! RU finishing off the wedding wine over there? Fancy pics Thurs nite? Clare xxx"

'She wants to go to the cinema on Thursday night.' I said to mum.

Mum gave a faint smile. 'All is not lost then. Remember, faint heart never won fair lady. Pull yourself together and make it a date. Then find out who this other guy is and kill him. We'll dump his body in the Tamar at midnight.'

Thursday night couldn't come soon enough and I really made an effort to look decent. I was early and her dad opened the door. He was tall and slim, skinny really, dressed in jeans and a very clean dark blue sweat shirt with the sleeves pushed up. I noticed a small tattoo of a crab on the side of his neck. Clare had told me he was a car mechanic and I knew he worked for one of the up-market marques outside Plymouth. He didn't look like a man you should mess with but he gave me a friendly grin and invited me in.

'Nice to meet you at last Simon.' He noticed me noticing the tattoo. 'Yes, it's a crab. My birth sign is Cancer. I got mullered one weekend with some mates, long before I was married, and had it done as a bet. Now my mates all tell me I caught crabs in Plymouth. Never fails to amuse them the dopey idiots.'

I asked him about fishing, it was a safe subject since he enjoyed it and I'd done a fair bit with Gramps in the past.

'You should come out with Ed and me, that's Clare's older brother. Taught him everything I know.'

Maggie appeared and ushered me into the sitting room. 'She won't be long I'm sure. What are you seeing tonight?'

'There's a choice between something with vampires in it, something with guns and violence and another thing with violence and the end of the world via all sorts of omens and disasters.' I said. 'Lots of blood in all of them I suppose.'

'Christ.' Clare's dad said. 'Give me sport any day.'

'Or we could just go to a nice pub.' I said.

Clare appeared and my heart flipped. She was looking lovely in a pale pink top with a squishy blue padded jacket and blue jeans. Her long dark hair was shiny and she'd fastened one side up and back with a clip. The little gold mice were back in her ears. 'Ready?' She asked, beaming up at me.

'Ready.' I confirmed. There was nothing in her appearance or attitude that was any different. She kissed her mum on the cheek, said cheerio to her dad and thumped him affectionately on the arm and I followed her to the door.

'You look smart tonight Simon.' She commented as I paid for the tickets. We were going to watch the end of the world thing which should have suited my mood but actually I couldn't have cared less about what we were seeing. 'Hunky in fact.' She took my hand as we went to walk in. 'Are you okay? Only you seem a bit quiet.'

'Fine. I'm fine.' I just didn't know how to ask her about the other night. It started something like "I was sitting in the car park outside the vets spying on you and ..." I didn't pay any attention to the film and half-way though she poked me in the side. 'What?' I whispered.

'It's rubbish. Bad choice. Shall we go somewhere else?'

Outside the air was cool and a bit crisp. The lights from the cinema adverts played over her face, pink, green, blue, yellow. 'Where do you fancy then?' I asked, trying to read her mood and failing.

She didn't know so I took her back to the car and drove us down to Hoe Road, as near to the sea as possible. Clare tucked her long hair inside her jacket and pulled the collar up. She didn't complain about my choice and walked beside me with her hand tucked into my arm. In the dark the sea was something you could sense rather than watch. There was a feeling of massively indifferent strength, inviting and terrifying at the same time. The sea has always drawn me but at the same time I find it repellent. I can sail happily in the daylight hours but I wouldn't want to be out there at night. It's such a powerful thing. We must have walked for twenty minutes when Clare stopped.

'What's wrong Simon? You haven't spoken a word to me all evening.'

'We were in the pictures.' I said lamely. 'And I was just thinking about the sea.'

Clare made a small sound, a hiss of breath. 'There's something wrong. I can tell. You weren't even watching the film. What is it? Is it something I've done? Or said? Or not said? Tell me.'

I was bewildered. Clare never talked like this, she wasn't this sort of combative person. Then it dawned on me, she's working up to a fight so that she can tell me it's over, so that she can go off with Mr Flashy Car and have a comfortable future surrounded by dogs and cats and chickens. All the things she'd love to have but couldn't afford. That I couldn't afford to give her. She took a deep breath, getting ready to challenge my silence. Here it comes, I thought, and I tensed.

'Is it, is it that you want to do something different, with someone else. Don't you want to be with me any more?' She said in a small, hurt voice.

'What?' I couldn't believe what I was hearing.

'Are you, are we, is it over between us?'

'What?' I said again. 'What on earth are you saying?'

'Well why aren't you talking to me? You've not said a word in the car or out here, and we always talk. What's wrong?' She sounded passionate.

It all came blurting out. 'I came to pick you up the other night, to surprise you. I waited in the dark and you came out with your friend and then you drove off with a bloke. A vet.'

'What?' Now it was her turn to be astonished.

We were staring blindly at each other in the darkness, the only sound the sea swelling and heaving a few yards away. It sounded like an animal getting ready to pounce and tear my heart out.

'I saw you in the room together, he came in and switched the light off.'

To my surprise Clare started laughing. 'That was Tony. He's new and a bit of a prankster. He wanted to ask Emily out but didn't know if she'd accept so he asked me if I'd come along as well, just for support as though it was three friends taking a drink after work. If it all went well the plan was that I had to leave them after the first drink and take myself home. Which is what happened.' She took a deep breath. 'So you saw three of us drive off in his car if you were paying that much attention. Not just him and me. And,' Clare paused for emphasis, 'you might have noticed that I didn't get in the front and sit beside him!'

'So what was the thing with the lights?' I was starting to feel embarrassed.

'Like I said, he's a prankster, he fools around. Does funny voices. It was nothing.' She seemed really hurt.

The sea splashed and sighed behind me and I suddenly realised it was getting cold. I grabbed Clare and pulled her to me. The cold made my eyes water. Or that's what I told myself.

'Clare.' I said her name. 'Clare.' I said it again. I could smell her body lotion and shampoo, I loved the way she always smelled so good.

She put her hands against my chest and pushed me away. She was angry now. 'What did you think I was doing Simon? Do you think I'd be so low as to cheat on you and mess you about? What sort of person do you think I am?' She punched my chest hard with her fists. I hadn't realised she was so strong and I grabbed her wrists.

'Clare, listen to me. I was in a state. I'm sorry I read it all wrong. The thing is, I think I love you.'

SEVEN

Romance is great isn't it? One day you're in the dumps, the next you're in orbit. You tell your girlfriend that you love her for the first time and end up celebrating by eating chips together out of a polystyrene container. She told me she loved me too and I've no recollection of walking back to the car, but I do know I promised her flowers and champagne one day. Falling in love and discovering that the feeling is mutual is like being bathed in splashes of light, it sends you a bit mad but in a nice way. Our relationship had moved to a different footing and I wanted to make it official. Sam had warned me once that a pretty girl like Clare was going to get noticed and snapped up, and that smart young vet had put the frighteners on me, I didn't want him or anyone else elbowing in on the action. My savings were healthy and I decided I was going to buy her an engagement ring as a surprise. Christmas wasn't far off and that seemed a good time to do it.

Meanwhile there was a lot of excitement about Sam and Lucy's wedding and Sam told me he'd called Andy Hauxwell.

'He's coming over to meet me tomorrow morning, early, at Home Farm. You're coming with me since you know him.'

I was agreeably pleased. Sam also asked me about Clare. I knew Lucy had spoken to him.

'I was too caught up in my own good news to notice that you were a bit down the other day Simon. How's it going between the two of you?'

'It was nothing. I'd got the wrong end of the stick. Clare was cross with me but we sorted it out.' That was all I was prepared to say although I did ask him if he could recommend a decent restaurant for a special occasion.

As I was leaving that evening I saw Lucy getting out of her Mini.

'Lucy, do you know what the birthstone is for May?' I asked her. Lucy knew about these things.

She paused and narrowed her eyes as she thought. 'May, er, I think is emerald. Yes, I'm sure it's emerald. Dare I ask why?' Lucy smiled at me.

'I think I might be looking for an engagement ring.' I confided. 'But please, not a word, not even to Sam. It's a secret. I'm not even telling my mum.'

'Mum's the word then.' Lucy laughed. 'Lovely stone, lovely colour, it would suit a very pretty girl with greenish eyes.'

I was up almost as early as mum and told her about meeting my builder friend Andy Hauxwell at Home Farm with Sam.

'Trelerric's doing well out of you then, recommending Sally Evans as well as Andy. Let's hope your good turn gets paid back. These things have a way of happening.' She said.

Andy's pick-up turned into the Trelerric roads just behind me so he followed me in to Home Farm.

'Thought I recognised that car!' Andy said as he got out. 'How are you doing mate? Good to see you.' He slapped me on the back.

As we stood talking the farmhouse door opened and Jane Latchley was standing there.

'Don't tell me Simon, a friend of yours? Sam's already here, do you all want coffee before you go over to the ruin?'

Andy pulled a face and made jokey noises about it not being a job for him then. 'You need an expert for ruins, I'm just a builder.' He introduced himself to Mrs Latchley. I couldn't help noticing that although dressed casually, he was looking pretty neat and his thick foxy coloured hair was well cut. Another idea for me to take on board; dress to impress your client. I hadn't been in Home Farm since the end of August, when the summer event had finished. It was a lovely place. Andy stood looking around with an appreciative eye. 'Very nice. Seventeenth century origins with a few later additions I'd guess Mrs Latchley?'

'I think so, although when we did some alterations when the children were little the builder unearthed evidence of an earlier building. We like to think this is the site where the first Trelerric House was built, which would make it earlier than the Tudor house. But there are no records that we know of so we can't prove it.' Mrs Latchley said.

'What about Cornwall Record Office? They might have something.'

'No idea, but a friend of Simon's might be giving us some help there.' Jane Latchley nodded at me with a slightly amused but wry expression. I watched Andy's expressions of interest; smart, intelligent and complimentary. I was learning so fast.

The coffee smelled good and we sat down while Sam finished eating. 'My second breakfast but don't let Lucy know. She thinks I've only had a bowl of healthy muesli. Mum gives me man-food.'

'Just tell her that planning a wedding is knackering and you've got to keep your strength up.' I said, my mouth watering at the smell of the bacon and eggs he'd finished.

'I'm not having to plan anything. I just turn up and say yes and sign the register. That's all there is to it.' Sam grinned.

Andy sat looking around the kitchen whilst enjoying the banter. I'd forgotten what a good bloke he was, with a mad sense of humour, genuinely funny without being a dickhead. The sort of man who lifted the atmosphere. I saw his eyes rest on a dark old carved side table just across from where Sam was sitting.

'That's a nice piece. Contemporary with the old house is it?' Andy pointed to the table.

'We call it the Latchley table. It's certainly very old, but I don't know what the wood is.' Jane Latchley said. 'I expect Simon knows someone who'd be able to tell us.'

I was about to say I did, Steve Bradley, the carpenter who'd worked with us at Darleystones a few years back, but I closed my mouth without saying anything. After coffee we all walked over to the site, which was across the lane opposite Home Farm and down an unmade track alongside a small field.

'It really is a ruin then.' Andy said, standing back and looking at an area where the roof had collapsed. It was picturesque with an old wisteria climbing up the wall.

'You're about to do that builder thing aren't you,' Sam half joked. 'You know, the one where you suck the air in through clenched teeth and say it's going to cost a fortune.'

'Actually I was about to say it's a pretty place, lots of potential.' Andy replied mildly.

Lucy joined us, she'd walked over from the main house with Coco on the lead. 'Did I hear the word "potential" just then?'

Sam introduced her to Andy. The words "my fiancee" hung in the air. I could see myself saying the same thing about Clare before too long. The idea made me feel dizzy. It was interesting seeing Andy in action again and listening to what he had to say in terms of planning the job. Sam said he had access to equipment which he could use to clear around the site before any building work started. They talked about using existing stone and slate where possible and Andy mentioned a good reclamation yard he knew in Devon.

Lucy drew me to one side as they disappeared round the building, pushing nettles and overgrown buddleia aside as they did so.

'I gather you're okay, you and Clare?'

'Yes, more than okay.'

'Funny how a misunderstanding can clear the air and make things much better isn't it?' she said.

I didn't have to explain anything to Lucy.

The guys reappeared and I could hear Sam educating Andy about mazzards. 'An old Cornish term for cherries, black and sweet. I'm going to reintroduce them here on a new dwarfing rootstock. Bring a bit of history back to life and give the cottage its name.'

'Very nice.' Andy said. The nearest thing he recognised as an edible plant was a chip. Anything that could be deep-fried or roasted was fine but fruit and vegetables weren't something he viewed with enthusiasm. 'Are you going to be working on this project with me then Simon?' He asked, looking from me to Sam.

I shrugged. 'Dunno, depends what the boss wants me to do I suppose.' But I was thinking about the ever closer appointment pending at Flinton Hall. I needed to ask Lucy what she knew about the place, where exactly it was, and what on earth should I wear in the presence of Sir Hugh and Lady Flinton.

From Lucy I learned that Flinton Hall had staff. A live-in couple who took care of the house on a cook/housekeeper maintenance/handyman basis, and a full-time gardener.

'They've been with Sir Hugh for ages. He gets a local caterer in when he has a lot of guests, to take the pressure off Mrs Marriott. He's a very wealthy man I think. Don't be afraid to charge him a bit more than pocket money for your services Simon.'

Lucy had run her own business once and gave me some good advice about what sort of percentage to charge. But the thought of staff and a full-time gardener was making me nervous. I told mum about it. 'They'll see straight through me mum. I can't give orders and boss people about. I don't know how to. I'm the one who gets given orders.'

'Just be yourself Simon.' Mum said calmly. 'Tell them what you think, remember your manners and don't be afraid to ask for advice. And if you really don't think the job's for you then say so and walk away from it. But this is a chance for you to do something special. I'd like you to give it your best.'

Finally I asked Clare to go shopping with me and explained the look I was going for. 'I like the way Sam's dad rigs himself up. I like the waistcoat and tweedy jacket with the cap.'

'Oh, you're looking at the huntin', shootin', fishin' brigade.' Clare said. 'You'll want corduroy trousers and brogues with huge woolly socks next. One of the senior vets likes those clothes. But you'd be better with the on-trend young fogey look rather than the rich old fart. Let's go to Truro then.'

She could have been talking martian for all that I understood her. But I was worried. 'Oh crap, I don't hunt or shoot. And the only fishing I've ever done is on a boat out at sea with Gramps, not on, or in, a river. I'll look like a fraud won't I?'

Clare made soothing noises. 'We'll find you something. I shall make sure you look okay.'

Well, it started with shirts. I learned about Tattersall and Oxford patterns, Prince of Wales check, casual gingham and more formal pinstripe. Did I want button down collars or casual? For a bloke who usually wore t-shirts, jeans and fleeces it was all something of an eye-opener. Then the trousers, a bit easier, I settled on one each of cord, moleskin and chinos. I found I couldn't wear anything with wool because it made me itch.

'You soft girl.' Clare giggled, but the guy serving us was sympathetic and talked about the understandable popularity of man-made fibres for trouser material. He was also very happy to be kitting me out.

'Is this a special wardrobe, sir?' He asked.

'It's my only wardrobe.' I said.

'Then let's do our best shall we. With your fresh colouring and your blue eyes these shades are most suitable.' I was handed shirts, gilets and jumpers. 'Cashmere sir? Since the wool is slightly uncomfortable?'

'Nice try.' Clare muttered under her breath. 'Wool or a natural fabric mixture would be okay since it's worn over a shirt I think.' She said in a louder voice.

Bloody hell, where did she learn this I wondered, my head inside a half-zipped country-wear item which caught my ears. Then we moved on to shoes. A pair of loafers with very thick ridged soles caught my eye and a pair of brogues. I just liked the punched patterned leather and Clare agreed, rejecting something she described as brothel creepers. Honestly I was learning a lot about this girl.

There were some really chunky nice ankle boots but the price was astronomical. The sales assistant gave me a knowing look.

'Come again in the sales, sir. There are bargains to be had if you like the boots.'

We finished with what the assistant called accessories and I got my much desired cap. He then offered socks, belts and ties. Reluctantly I bought a plain woollen tie but I was worn out. And terrified about what I'd spent. Clare had to help carry the bags but half way back to the car she dragged me into a cafe, the trendy sort that have little pots of flowers on the tables and seven types of coffee. We were both in need of sustenance so I treated her to a late lunch, noticing that the waitress called me sir as well. It must have been the effect of the serious amount of shopping surrounding me.

'Am I mad Clare? Have I done the right thing buying all this stuff?' I was suffering from galloping guilt following this unaccustomed self-indulgence.

'Well, it'll keep you going for years. I mean that.' Clare was serious. 'And I liked the way you looked in the clothes. You've got lovely shoulders. It's funny what clothes do. When I put my uniform on people pay me attention.'

'Clothes make the man and all that.' I said. 'Naked people have little or no influence on society. Even when they streak.'

'Oh. Wow. Yes that's right I suppose.' Clare said, looking at me the way she had that night I drew the dandelion clock for Grace. 'Did you just think that up?'

'No. It's something Gramps says. He says it's Mark Twain. He reads a lot.' I added by way of explanation. 'Mark Twain didn't say the bit about streaking though.'

Clare didn't know what I was going on about, but then streaking was something people did in Gramps generation, not ours. I just sat looking at her, loving the way she was smiling in anticipation of her coffee and a posh sandwich, the pulse in her throat beating. I wanted to kiss it. The thought of naked people made me want to kiss all of her, every bit. I tried visualising something else to calm me down.

'Funny things tattoos.' I said, thinking of the one her dad had on his neck. 'I've never wanted one myself. I read once that sailors used them like a language in the old days. They could tell if a bloke had gone south of the equator by what tattoos he had.'

'I quite like them, some of them anyway.' Clare said. 'I've got a small one of my own.'

'Really?' I was surprised. 'Where?'

'You might find it one day.'

Was that an invitation or a challenge? I started feeling hot again, wondering what she'd got and where it was. I'd really got to do something about getting a place. With the way I was feeling about her it would be so nice to get a place of our own. Something to discuss, very soon.

Later, at home, I spread everything out in my bedroom and looked at it all. Mum came up and quietly touched and felt a few things. I expected a terse comment but she looked thoughtful.

'Reminds me of your dad. He liked quality things too.'

I was really surprised. She never spoke about my absent father. I had a sudden thought.

'I haven't got a decent suitcase mum. How do I take all this to Flinton Hall?'

'I've got some of those clothes protector bags, those zipped things. I've seen people use them in the backs of their cars when I've been out delivering the post. People go away for a few days with one of those because you can put everything on hangers. Practical really, stops things getting creased in a case.' She looked at my face. 'It's okay Simon, men use them as well as women.'

That was a relief.

The next relief was Lucy calling me to say that she had to go up to see Flick, as she called Lady Flinton, and would I like to go up to Flinton Hall in the Jag with her.

'For two people and our overnight cases it's a very comfortable ride,' she said. 'Pack for a couple of nights though.'

I was happy to accept. I'd had my jalopy serviced but I wondered how much longer it would last. And with the way I was spending money on my appearance it seemed I'd never be in funds to replace it. The last thing I did before setting off with Lucy was to arrange a gift for Clare. I ordered a dozen long stemmed red roses to be sent to her. Hang the expense.

EIGHT

I tried counting how many times I'd been outside Cornwall in my life, not silly things like trips to Plymouth, which everyone knows is just over the Tamar in Devon, but up country, and concluded that I was a bucolic Cornish bumpkin. Lucy handled the big car well and I was fascinated by the countryside as we drove up via the M5 through Devon, Somerset, Gloucestershire and into Worcestershire. We stopped at a service station for refreshment and she wanted to know about my time working with Andy so we talked building renovation and timescales. Basically she was trying to work out when she and Sam would be moving into their own home.

'It'll be summertime Lucy. Everything has to get worse before it gets better with jobs like Cherryfields,' I told her. 'And the planning and so on will delay things for starters. But it will give you time to concentrate on how you want the place. Mr Pencraddoc made all sorts of changes and additions to Darleystones as the job progressed, that was the biggest job I've done with Andy. I learned quite a bit. And don't forget to look at how the land lies, take a compass reading and decide where you want your sun terrace and if you get a nice view from the kitchen sink.'

'Yes, I suppose there will be lots of decisions to make.' Lucy murmured, her thoughts taking her miles away.

Back in the Jag I lapsed into silence and she put the radio on. I wasn't paying attention to the music, my mind was on how I was going to approach the task ahead of me. Lucy had already complimented my appearance. I'd been to the barber in Liskeard and told him I had a very special date so he'd paid attention to the cut. I was wearing the fawn cord trousers with a blue shirt and a sleeveless gilet in a greenish blue flecked fabric. It had a blue cord collar which Clare had said suited my eyes. The new tan brogues and a tan leather belt completed the look. I'd folded my shirt sleeves back twice over the cuffs, showing my tanned forearms. I'd noticed Sam's dad wearing his shirts like that and had asked Sam why he did so.

'Dad says workmen show their elbows, gentlemen don't. He was taught that at the school he went to. Fortunately he didn't send me there. I'd have hated boarding school.'

Finally Lucy took an A-road and then along increasingly little roads before turning into a long curved drive at the end of which stood a pretty house, almost like a child's drawing of a perfect doll's house, symmetrical but with more windows than usual and a steeply pitched roof. A man was driving up and down long lawns at the front on a ride-on mower, my first sight of the full-time gardener I guessed, but I couldn't make him out clearly. A movement caught my eye, it was Sir Hugh striding out of the poshest garden room I'd ever seen and coming down some wide graceful steps to greet us.

'Lucy my dear,' he kissed her on the cheek. 'And Simon. What a pleasure.' He shook my hand and then gestured towards the man on the ride-on who was disappearing into the distance. 'That's Hartley. You'll meet him tomorrow. He's hoping it's going to be the last cut of the year since we're almost through October. We get frost and snow here, unlike your place on the other side of the Tamar.'

That was generous of him, I thought, making me look like an equal. 'Yes, I'll still be cutting grass up to the end of December, and starting again in January. The moors get a dusting of snow but it never settles at Trelerric.' I smiled.

Sir Hugh ushered us in, he'd taken Lucy's bag out of the boot but a quiet man had appeared and whisked it away almost without moving the air. I carried my own stuff, wondering if I should take my shoes off once indoors but Sir Hugh didn't bother so I followed his example.

'Leave your things in the hall here Simon, Marriott will see to them. There's a cloakroom along there if you need it, we're in the garden room when you're ready.'

There was a flurry of activity, a woman passed me carrying a tray and gave me a brief smile and I could hear Lady Flinton's voice. I opted to use the cloakroom, I needed to wash my hands. In privacy I checked my appearance and looked into the mirror. Blue eyes, tanned face, ordinary features, hair still a little bit sun-bleached even though it was the end of October and the clocks were about to go back. We'd had a lovely autumn. "This is it boy, this is it." I told myself. "The future starts here." Following the sounds of voices, sinking into thick carpet and noticing gilded mirrors and sombre oil paintings on the walls as I walked, it felt unreal. I was actually sleeping here tonight as a guest. And these were real paintings, not department store prints. This house had age and history, what was the word Sam used about Trelerric? Provenance. But it had a very different feeling to Trelerric, there was something slightly brittle in the atmosphere, it lacked softness.

Lady Flinton was standing talking to Lucy but she turned as I walked in and gave one of her peacock like cries and a dazzling smile. 'Simon dear boy, welcome to Flinton Hall. So good of you to come.'

Momentarily I was taken aback by her friendliness, well it wasn't exactly an invitation to come and stay was it. More like a summons. I wondered why they were treating me like a guest rather than just a man with a skill they might like to use. Lady Flinton didn't kiss my cheek or anything but she did take my hand, briefly, and gave the fingers a little squeeze. I mumbled something about how nice it was to see her again. And how well she was looking.

'Refreshments. Simon, what will you have?' Sir Hugh was handing a glass tumbler of something to Lucy and I looked at her for ideas.

'I'm just having a virgin Mary.' Lucy said. I was none the wiser. 'Like a Bloody Mary but without the vodka, just the celery salt and a dash of tabasco to spice it up.' She explained.

It sounded vile so I asked Sir Hugh what he'd recommend. 'Any of the usual spirits with a mixer if you like, or a soft drink if you prefer? And I think we have some cold beer in the kitchen.'

That made beer off limits somehow, as though it wasn't a polite option and I thought soft drinks were for girls. I was already out of my depth, and part of me was kicking myself for not saying something appropriate and congratulatory about the wedding or the honeymoon to Lady Flinton. Then I thought that might have sounded too personal, after all, I was just a gardener. I realised that Sir Hugh was still waiting for my response, and had a sudden memory of Sam's dad at the party they'd had at Home Farm last August.

'A G&T would be fine right now.' I said as casually as possible, knowing that I would have preferred a beer or a glass of cider.

'Ice and a slice of course.' Sir Hugh responded and I found myself nodding in agreement. Spirits had never appealed and mum said gin was a depressant. I watched closely as Sir Hugh selected a heavy glass tumbler, ice from a silver container frosted with condensation, a slice of lemon from a dish and poured a hefty measure of gin into the glass, topping it up with tonic water. His hands were deft and practiced.

'Your health.' He handed me the glass. 'Felicity likes the same so you're in good company.'

Ye gods, I thought, he's talking about his wife as though we're on first name terms. Then I thought, oh shit, it's a girl's drink. I've fallen at the first hurdle. But no-one seemed bothered. Lucy took a plate and helped herself to some small snacky things which the lady with the tray had brought in. She had a professional opinion about the catering and was saying something complimentary so I followed and got a few things myself. Something black and squishy on a tiny biscuit. I put the whole thing in my mouth and was assailed by salt and a slightly bitter flavour. Hastily I chewed and swallowed. It was awful.

'Tapenade.' Lucy said, smiling at me sympathetically. 'Such a lovely flavour from the black olives isn't it.'

So that's what it was. I gave the plate a wide berth and selected something recognisable with a prawn, which was okay, and another biscuit with cheese on it and a little red strip of something. Everything looked inviting but it was a minefield of flavours to navigate. The cheese was nice but the red thing turned out to be chilli. My mouth was on fire so I took a gulp of G&T. Big mistake, not refreshing like a long pull on a beer. After I'd finished coughing and spraying crumbs everywhere I sat down, it seemed the safest thing to do.

'Went down the wrong way darling? So sorry.' Lady Flinton was speaking. 'Mrs Marriott is a marvel with hors-d'oeuvres. Mmm, the tapenade compliments the gin don't you think?'

'Horses doofers, we used to call them when I was little.' Sir Hugh laughed. 'Sets you up for the main event later. What's Mrs Marriott cooking for us tonight Felicity?'

There was some food discussion which could have been in a foreign language. I was longing for crisps and peanuts, knowing myself to be a simple soul. I'd have to ask Clare's mum what all this posh stuff was about and how you should deal with it when I next saw her. She was Lady Flinton's housekeeper back at Trelerric so she'd know. I really wished Clare was sitting there with me. She'd have loved this experience. I looked over at Lucy who was chatting away with the Flinton's like they were family. I remembered her own story which she'd told me that miserable afternoon when I thought I was losing Clare. Lucy had described Sir Hugh as her second cousin. Funny how Lucy sometimes reminded me of Clare. I think it was the thick straight dark hair.

I found that if I sipped the G&T it went down okay and resulted in a pleasantly fuzzy feeling. The chairs were comfortable, the ladies were smiling, the light, falling fast outside now made me appreciate the internal proportions of the garden room. It really was lovely. Sir Hugh switched on a few lamps and we were surrounded by soft shadows, an intimate gathering in a little pool of warm light. Sir Hugh handed me another G&T and I accepted it happily, not realising I'd finished the first.

'Pity about the light going Simon, time of year of course. We'll make an early start after breakfast tomorrow while the girls are discussing Felicity's business. Hartley will be joining us since he knows the garden inside out. I gather the forecast is for a dry day so you should be able to take measurements and photographs and whatever else it is that you need to do.'

I tried to look serious and attempted an understanding nod, but my head felt as though it was wobbling about like one of those annoying dog toys you sometimes see in the backs of cars. Lucy caught my eye and smiled.

'Clare would love this.' I said it to her before I realised that my mouth had engaged.

Lady Flinton looked at me, a searching silvery-eyed look that could see inside me. Sir Hugh sat forward attentively. 'Really?'

'Clare Palfrey. Maggie's daughter. I'm going to buy her an engagement ring for Christmas. Clare that is, not her mother.' I smothered a small giggle.

'Fascinating.' Lady Flinton breathed and exchanged a look with Sir Hugh and then she got up. 'I need to change and prepare for dinner darlings,' she said to the room in general. 'I expect our guests would also like to freshen up. Shall we meet again in the drawing room in an hour?' She was about to leave and then turned and smiled down at me. 'How silly of me. Lucy, could you show Simon his room. He's next door but one to yours.'

I finished my drink and stood up. How I managed not to fall face first onto the floor I'll never know. Lucy casually took my elbow and guided me. 'This way Simon, we're in the guest rooms to the left at the top of the stairs.'

Giving her a foolish grin I allowed myself to be guided. Once out of earshot she spoke again.

'There's a flagon of water in your room Simon. Drink the lot because you're as pissed as a newt. It's why I never accept afternoon drinks from Sir Hugh, his measures are lethal. And you are not used to drinking gin like that are you. And if you want to be able to function tomorrow take my advice,' she said as she steered me into my room. 'Only have two glasses of wine and do not, I repeat do not, start on the after dinner brandy. Sir Hugh can take it, he's used to drinking. You aren't. You'll be slaughtered.'

Lucy left me standing inside the door to my room. She'd switched the light on, which had illuminated the space from wall lights. No boring old single ceiling lightbulb in this house. I looked around, it was all done out in cream, black and gold, with a black and gold bedspread. The smartest bedroom I'd ever seen. There was no sign of my things, but I opened a wardrobe and there they were, all hung up.

A door was invitingly half open on the other side of the room and I walked over to find a well appointed bathroom with a fancy looking shower. There were lots of knobs and dials and two sprays, one overhead and one for the hand. It looked capable of time travel. Soap and shower gel and shampoo and shaving equipment were all provided as well as a towelling bathrobe. 'Bugger me.' I muttered. 'I don't even have to unpack my soap.'

Taking Lucy's advice I drank the water and then had a shower. The next dilemma was wondering what to wear for the evening meal. I'd only got my new chinos so I put those on with a clean blue and white striped shirt, cuffs fastened this time, and that bloody tie. I'd last worn a tie at school and felt like a prat putting it on, but it would have to do. There was a tap on my door and Lucy was standing there, looking very pretty in a dress, pearl earrings and with her hair pinned back.

'You look nice.' I said. 'Will this do? It's all I've got and I don't know what to wear anyway.'

'You're a guest and you'll be accepted for yourself. It's good manners. You look fine, and anyway this is the twenty-first century.' Lucy said helpfully.

That didn't make me feel super confident but we went downstairs together and Lucy took me along to the drawing room. It was nicely furnished, graceful and comfortable in shades of faded rose, dark blue and cream. There were sofas facing each other across a vast low table next to an equally vast fireplace in which a fire was laid, but not lit. Lamps cast a comfortable glow across expensive looking rugs and I was surprised to notice a modern iStation from which music was playing softly. Sir Hugh escorted Lady Flinton in and I immediately felt inappropriately dressed but Sir Hugh was charming.

'Excuse us for dressing, I realise we're old enough to be your grandparents so you must indulge us for clinging to outdated ways.' He went straight to the drinks tray and poured something for Lady Flinton then turned at looked at Lucy enquiringly.

'Nothing for me thank you. I shall enjoy a glass of wine all the more for it.'

'Or me thanks. I've not got a head for mixing the grain and the grape too close together.' I said.

Sir Hugh actually laughed. 'I admire a man with the good sense to know his limitations Simon.'

Dinner was nothing like the minefield of the hors-d'oeuvres. Mrs Marriott brought us tiny flaky pastry parcels of finely sliced mushrooms in a flavourful sauce to start. Lucy identified a dash of brandy in the sauce and thought she detected a hint of truffle oil. Then we had some sort of a chicken dish flavoured with herbs and bay leaf, which I could identify, followed by apple tarte tatin with chantilly cream. Sir Hugh had chosen a beautiful white wine, a Vouvray from the Loire. It was gorgeous but I did as Lucy had instructed and stuck to two large glasses. Finally there were cheeses served with a quince jelly and oat biscuits. It was divine and I moaned with pleasure.

'Simon I believe you're quite the epicure at heart.' Lady Flinton said. 'I do love a man who enjoys his food. Appetite in all things is a marvellous thing for a man to have.'

We made polite talk about how the apples and quinces grew in the gardens and what wonderful things Mrs Marriott did with them. I made a mental note to suggest planting quinces at Trelerric. Sam would like that. After dinner we retired back to the drawing room for coffee and someone had lit the fire. It was like a life I'd read about in mum's historical romances but I'd never experienced anything like it. Lucy and I both declined the brandy and she started talking to Flick, as she called Lady Flinton. Sir Hugh invited me over to a large desk at one side and produced some rolled up maps from a rosewood cabinet.

'These are old, original drawings of the garden when it was first laid out in the time of Queen Anne. Here's what was a walk, somewhere for the ladies to promenade their finery on a pleasant day. It's now a neglected rough area and I'd like to reinstate it for my wife.' He positively glowed with pleasure at the phrase. 'But I'd like a new interpretation, a modern twist, something beautiful and unusual within the confines of the space. It will be interesting to see what you come up with Simon.'

I looked at the old map, the fine execution of line and colour depicting what places and areas should be used for. There was perfect tiny writing, I traced it with a finger tip; croquet lawn, Ladies Walk, roses. The intent of the designer touched me across the years and I felt moved. 'This is beautiful. I'll have to think very hard to come up with something which compliments it.' I said.

Sir Hugh nodded. 'Yes indeed. A challenge I think. Sleep on it.'

I went up to my room replete and contented. I'd sent Clare a text earlier to say we'd arrived safely, now there was a response. She'd sent a photograph of the roses, including one of her grinning with a rose between her teeth. She was so photogenic and pretty. She'd written one word, *"Beautiful"*. I texted back, *"You certainly are."*

And with that I flopped into bed.

NINE

I slept like a log and breakfasted like a king back in the garden room. Lady Flinton didn't put in an appearance and Lucy only ate a small bowl of muesli before disappearing. Apparently they were popping out for a couple of hours. Sir Hugh seemed pleased to have someone to eat with and made some easy small talk.

'I love this room, it's the best thing I ever did here and we use it all the time. It's built on the site of a sunken garden my late mother had put in once she'd handed me over to a nanny. I don't think I saw her again for about ten years. Anyway, in the winter it was waterlogged and in the summer the ground used to crack. The gardeners hated it. Hartley was glad to see it go. And thinking of Hartley, he'll be here any minute so let's finish our breakfast and get a move on.'

I was wearing the new brown moleskin trousers with a light blue shirt and a dark blue v-necked cable knit jumper of Clare's choosing. The weather was dry and colder than yesterday so I added the gilet and my new cap. Mum had provided me with an ancient leather satchel for my drawing materials. It also held my iPad, useful for taking decent photographs. Thus equipped I picked up my gardening boots, which had been subjected to a thorough clean and with liberal quantities of dubbin applied and went downstairs in my socks. There was a passage leading to a side door and boot room which had been pointed out to me earlier and I could hear male voices. I put my boots on and stepped outside. Sir Hugh made the introductions.

'Simon this is Hartley, who keeps this place looking beautiful for us.'

I stuck my hand out to a slim, wiry man with a lined face and short iron grey hair. His dark eyes were guarded and his handshake was crushing. I couldn't guess his age, anything from a prematurely aged mid forties to a well preserved man in his sixties. He was about my height.

'Jeff Hartley. Pleased to meet you Mr Sherwell.' His eyes flicked over me and lingered on my boots.

I crushed his hand in return. I'd not worked as a labourer for nothing. 'Simon Sherwell.'

'Well then, let's walk over to the site and take a look.' Sir Hugh said, taking charge. He set off and I walked slightly behind him, Jeff Hartley walking slightly behind me. The feeling of hierarchy made me feel uncomfortable so I stepped to one side and then resumed walking next to Jeff Hartley.

'How long have you worked here Mr Hartley?' I asked him, trying not to notice the bright pink but very scruffy jumper he was wearing under his waxed jacket.

'Twenty-five years. Started under the old gardener when I was near thirty. Had an industrial accident and couldn't work for a bit. They paid compensation and this came along. Saved my life.'

'Had you been interested in gardening before that?'

'Always, but out of necessity. We grew our own veg at home, I still do. Just peas and onions and potatoes. Tastes better. But I like flowers.'

The path was taking us through and under a long sturdy pergola still festooned with roses. There was evidence of pruning and tying-in. It was all very neat. I stopped and cupped a late rose in my hand, a crumpled petalled velvety red damask. The scent was lovely and a few petals fell.

'Old, that one. Not sure of her name. Doesn't get black spot.' Hartley commented.

Sir Hugh was waiting for us at the end of the pergola. 'Some of these roses were put in by my grandmother. My mother was a great believer in dahlias. Horrible mop headed earwiggy things in vile clashing colours. Hartley took them all out the minute the old bat died.'

I saw a flash of mirth on Jeff Hartley's face but Sir Hugh spoke again.

'Here we are then Simon, this area along here. The Ladies Walk.'

The pergola had ended in graceful flagstoned steps leading up onto a long wide bank with a flattened grassy top which curved off round a well tended lawn, shown as the croquet lawn on the old drawings. Various shrubs were growing in the sides of the bank adjacent the lawn and several small trees, including a couple of self-set silver birch I suspected, were growing on the other side, which fell away to a small orchard. There was also a tight clump of evergreens towards the end of the bank. I slipped a compass out of my pocket and checked the directions. Anything growing on the lawn side of the bank was sheltered from wind and that side got sun all day. The views from the top of the long bank were lovely, the house to one side, the Malvern Hills in the distance to the other, great vistas of green to the cold north east. It was a fabulous place. I could feel something taking shape in my mind, serpentine, uncoiling, alive and breathing.

'What's the soil like?' I asked Hartley.

'Stony loam for the most part. God knows what's under here though.' He indicated the bank with the flat of his hand.

'Rubble and rubbish I imagine.' Sir Hugh said. 'When mother's sunken garden was created they had to put the spoil somewhere. I think they added it to an existing natural feature and built this up. Thus the original plan for the Ladies Walk was vandalised.'

I nodded. It made sense but I was in awe of the amount of labour, all done by hand and wheelbarrow. We continued to the end of the bank which sloped uncomfortably down to the side of the croquet law and a pretty little pavilion, painted white. The creative thing moved in my mind again and I felt it flex and extend a leg, or a claw. The pavilion sat by itself, unconnected and unused between the bank and the house. It needed to be included in the design and settled more firmly into the landscape. I visualised a circle running from the boot room, through the pergola walk, along the Ladies Walk, down to the pavilion and across to the house. Within that was the half circle that I needed to work on, linking everything with new steps down to the pavilion, hard landscaping connecting it to the house and an existing terrace so that Lady Flinton could get the daily exercise she needed without get wet or muddy feet. A picture so complete emerged that I almost gasped. My fingers tingled and I needed paper and ink. Instead I reached into my satchel and pulled the iPad out.

'I need to take a few photographs Sir Hugh, and I also need to talk to Mr Hartley about what's growing here if that's okay.'

'Absolutely. I'll leave you chaps to it. I think lunch is at one today Simon.' He strode off.

'He's a good man.' I said, framing a couple of shots.

'A bloody good man. Considerate and bloody clever with it. If you click with him and do a good job he doesn't let you down.' Jeff Hartley replied. 'Now then Mr Sherwell, what do you need to know?'

'Please, my name is Simon.' I looked Jeff Hartley in the eyes. 'I'm twenty-four, I work at Trelerric House for Lady Flinton's nephew. I've been gardening since I was ten years old and we also grow fruit and vegetables at home because they taste good.' I paused, he was still staring at me. 'I designed a courtyard garden in a Japanese-style for Lady Flinton. It was just a small job but I must've done something right because they asked me to come up here and look at this. It's my first proper job away from Cornwall and my first chance to do something special.'

'Knew you were genuine when I saw your boots.' His face cracked into a smile. 'And I can see you've already got some ideas. Just don't make it high maintenance, I've got enough to do.'

I took photographs and measurements and looked closely at the existing shrubs. We talked about drainage and light, wind direction and weather, pruning and planting. We shared ideas about what grew there and then shared his flask of tea. I apologised for taking up his morning and his drink but he shrugged.

'No problem. A few hours doesn't mind and Angela will refill my flask.'

'Angela?'

'Angela Marriott. Cook-housekeeper here. Known her and Ian, her husband, for years.'

Lunch was another leisurely affair centred around cold poached salmon served with thinly sliced cucumber and a horseradish mayonnaise which was delicious. I found we were staying another night so I asked for a few hours by myself in which to sketch some ideas I'd got and retired up to my room. There was a desk suitable for my needs which I could use and I made good progress.

'I thought a cold beer might be acceptable this evening Simon.' Sir Hugh flipped the cap off and handed me a long glass and the bottle. 'I'm having one myself, it's beef tonight and this prepares the stomach as it were.'

I looked at the bottle. Japanese label Asahi beer. Gorgeous and so welcome. Mrs Marriott had again provided snacks. Lucy was calling them canapés. 'Can of peas?' I teased her. Lucy went into gales of laughter and Lady Flinton smiled.

'You're as daft as my girlfriends.'

There were cheese things again and a mackerel pate but no tapenade. And salty mixed and roasted nuts which I enjoyed. The ladies went off to freshen up but this time Sir Hugh and I stayed behind and had another beer. He was very easy to talk to, full of funny stories and interesting experiences and I felt relaxed in his company. So I wasn't expecting a change in conversation.

'Tell me about your young lady, Clare, Mrs Palfrey's daughter. You said you were getting engaged this Christmas if I recall correctly?'

'I hope so. I haven't asked her yet. I'm not sure how to go about it. I mean, do I buy a ring and surprise her? Or do I ask her and then take her to buy a ring?'

'Hmm, I see your dilemma.' Sir Hugh looked amused. 'Depends on the lady and on the circumstances I think.'

I was none the wiser.

'What does your instinct tell you?' He asked.

'Buy the ring, take her to a special place for dinner, and spring the surprise.'

'Well, that's both romantic and commendable. I take it you're pretty sure she'll accept then?'

I looked at him in surprise. It hadn't occurred to me that Clare would refuse. 'Yes, she loves me. She said so.'

'Splendid.' Sir Hugh sat back and crossed his long legs. 'And what are your plans following the engagement, if you don't think it presumptuous of me to ask.'

I frowned. 'I don't know yet. I've been saving for years but houses get more and more expensive every year and always just beyond my range. I guess I'm hoping that with two wages we'll be able to afford something together.'

Sir Hugh was silent. This is surreal, I told myself. The bedroom I'm in here is bigger than the floor plan of mum's little house. This man is probably as rich as Daniel Pencraddoc, they both own a property in London. And Sir Hugh owns a boat as well. That was a thought, the idea of living on a boat appealed to me.

Lady Flinton appeared at the door. She was wearing a long layered dress in shades of turquoise with what looked like beaded fringes. On her slim frame it looked stunning, on anyone else it would have made them look like a drag queen. 'Aren't you changing darling? Lucy and I are already down and with no company.'

Sir Hugh made his apologies and said that he wasn't going to bother changing if nobody objected. He would dine in his day clothes. I had a feeling it was to make me feel comfortable.

We were waved off after breakfast with instructions to pass Lady Flinton's love on to everyone at Trelerric. 'We'll be down for the weekend next Friday, remind Jane won't you Lucy.'

Sir Hugh and I shook hands and I thanked them both for their hospitality, saying that I hoped to have something on paper to show them when they came down. Lucy drove us away and back into the real world.

'I think that went okay Simon.' Lucy glanced at me before turning right out of the long drive.

'I think it did.' I was deep in thought and didn't say much on the drive back.

It was odd getting into my old car after the comfort of the Jag, but I drove home in good humour after texting Clare at work to say that we were back. I had enough new things to talk about to mum to keep her interested for weeks, but it was Clare I wanted to see and I was taking her out to The Wheal that evening. I wanted to ask her about her thoughts on moving in together.

Clare met me at the door and almost jumped into my arms. I hugged her, delighted that she was so pleased to see me. I was wearing clean blue jeans with the blue cable knit jumper Clare had chosen and she noticed. I was far more interested in her.

'I've missed you, it was only two nights but I've bloody missed you.'

I called a hello to Maggie but Clare was already dragging me back to the car.

'What's up, are you starving?' I laughed at her.

'Yes, no, I just want to be with you,' she replied. 'I've got you something.' She was bursting with excitement.

We got into the car and Clare opened her tote bag. 'I've got you a present Simon, oh, and thank you for the roses. I've never had anything like that before. They're in my bedroom.' She leaned over and kissed me. 'Would you like the present now, or in the pub?'

'Oh, in private I think. But let me move the car to a quieter place. Up to the car park at Minions, it's on the way to The Wheal.'

This was one of our special places, pitch dark at night but with fabulous views to Dartmoor in the daytime, wonderfully romantic under a star filled sky. We'd done a lot of kissing and a bit more up there in the summer but now it was getting cold at nights. Definitely time to get my own place. Or our own place together, I thought with anticipation.

The car crunched slowly over the potholes and stony ground. It really was dark, with a cloudy sky promising rain later. I flicked the light on and turned to Clare, smiling at her lovely face.

'I've missed you.' I said again. 'I've got loads to tell you but the most important thing to say is that I've missed you.' I was in danger of coming over like a stuck record.

'I missed you as well. I was thinking about what you were doing and I got you this.'

Clare handed me a flat parcel. She'd wrapped it in red and gold paper with a thin shiny gold strip tied round it and ending in curly coils. Pretty, girly stuff. It made me smile.

'Wow. It's all wrapped up.' I said, feeling the thought and care she'd put into it. 'But it's not my birthday or anything.'

'Open it.'

I carefully picked at the corner and slid my thumbnail along the paper. Yikes, she'd bought me a book. I turned it over in my hands and examined it. It was all about designing and making Japanese gardens, in English, full of colour photographs and black and white drawings.

'Wow.' I said. 'This is seriously good. Sam doesn't have anything like this.' I looked at her, my heart turning over at the happy expectation in her face. 'Clare, this is, well, I don't know what to say. It's wonderful.'

'Is it okay? I mean, will it help your work?'

I nodded. 'I should say so. It's brilliant. You're amazing.' I couldn't find any sensible words so I kissed her, lots. Until my stomach rumbled.

We talked non-stop over lasagne with a side order of chips to share and I told her all about the trip.

'Crumbs, an ensuite room and dinner two nights running with Sir Hugh and Lady Felicity. I've sort of met him a few times, when he used to visit Mrs Latchley as she was then, when I was helping mum at the house. Her nickname is Flick.'

I was thoughtful, I wanted to say that he asked about us, about my intentions. Odd that he'd been interested in an almost paternal way. I dismissed the thought and judged it appropriate to pursue what was really on my mind.

'Clare, I've been meaning to ask you something.' I took her hand across the table, the pub was fairly quiet now and the log burner was casting a warm rosy light into the room.

Clare looked at me with wide eyes, all her senses alert. She reminded me of a little cat, focussed on something just beyond her reach. 'What, what do you want to ask me?'

'Well, I'm thinking of moving. Not from Cornwall,' I added hastily, seeing a flash of alarm on her face. 'I want to find my own place, somewhere we can be together perhaps. What do you think?' I was vaguely aware that I hadn't quite found the right words. Did this sound as though I was making a declaration of love and intent and asking her to move in with me? Not quite.

'Oh. Well, yes I can understand that.' Her eyes studied something on the table and I thought she looked disappointed.

There was a strange feeling that the happiness and expectation were draining away.

'Would you help me look for somewhere?' I said lamely.

'Yes, of course. If you like.' She excused herself and went to the ladies room.

Shit. I don't know how, but I'd bungled it.

TEN

To say I was grumpy was an understatement. The rest of the evening had fallen a bit flat. It certainly hadn't gone how I'd wanted it to and Clare had asked to be taken home. She'd been very polite, saying she was tired and to be fair it was late, I'd talked all evening and the time had flown. But I'd driven back to mum's with an odd sense of failure. It was tricky stuff, this dating game. There was no point in telling mum about it, she "didn't do relationships" as she put it. I was quite pleased to get a call from Gramps the next day which took my mind off things.

'Simon, can you pop round when you've got a chance? We haven't seen you for a while and there's something I want to speak to you about. Something you might be interested in.'

A mystery, Gramps wasn't usually so reticent. 'Sure, after work this evening if you like.' I told him.

Gran and Gramps lived at the other end of my village in the terraced house they'd lived in since the year dot. They'd rented it as newlyweds and then managed to buy it from the owner. They were as much the house as the house was them. Their hands were familiar with every shape, curve, edge and surface. Gran always seemed to have a cloth in her hand, the house shone with years of rubbing and polishing. I loved it.

Gran produced cake and tea, her fall-back at any time of day or night when a visitor called and she fussed around me, interested to know how I was and what I'd been up to. I told them about the trip to Flinton Hall and my experiences there, seeing Clare's pretty face in front of me as I used the same words and descriptions. Finally I ran out of stories and asked Gramps what had prompted him to call me.

'Well, it's about your campervan outside.'

'Oh?' I'd kept the old van parked at the front of their place for nearly four years. It was probably time to find somewhere else to keep it. The van hadn't been moved since the summer when I'd used it at Home Farm for a few weeks. When Clare had started spending her spare evenings with me.

'Yes, there's a fella interested in buying it off you.' Gramps interrupted my memories. 'Knocked on the door a few days back, when you were away up country. Said it was a classic and he'd be interested in discussing a fair offer if the owner was wanting to sell. Got his name and phone number here.'

Gramps handed me a piece of paper.

'A classic?' I echoed. Since getting the van from another of my gardening clients who'd become too old to use it, I'd kept it clean and had a bit of work done by the garage in the next village. I recalled they'd said it was a decent vintage, a 1978 T2 Devon Camper. I thought back to the old boy who'd let me have it. I'd a feeling he'd passed on now, but vaguely recalled he'd said something along the lines of "look after her son, she'll see you right one day".

'Can you remember what you paid for it Simon?' Gramps was asking.

'About five grand I think.' I saw the expression on his face. 'Was I ripped off then?' It had seemed like a good idea at the time, I was just twenty then and had imagined myself swanning around the lanes of Cornwall all summer, visiting beaches and saving money by camping in field gateways. In fact I'd hardly used it, I was always working.

Gramps started laughing. 'Amazing. This fella, he suggested a price more than twice that. He was serious.'

I felt my jaw drop.

Gran was looking pleased. 'That's a nice little nest egg then,' she said. 'I always knew you were going to be lucky Simon. Your stars are good.'

Gran had always been deeply into the hocus-pocus of horoscopes so before she could get going about what the stars foretold I made my excuses and left. I needed to get on the internet and do some hard cold research.

What I found was amazing and had me searching for the paperwork the old boy who'd sold the van had given to me. There was a folder full of receipts for work he'd had done and I'd just assumed it was general maintenance and old MoT certificates. What was it a teacher had once said in a moment of classroom sarcasm; "Never assume anything Mr Sherwell, it makes an *ass* out of *u* and *me*". He'd even chalked it up on the board so that my mates could have a good laugh at my expense. Thank god I hadn't thrown the folder away. After some careful reading I added the few receipts for the maintenance I'd had done and then sent the guy a text. It was pretty late so I didn't expect a response and went to bed with my brain buzzing, a windfall like this would be a really healthy addition to my savings and to what I might be able to offer to Clare.

The following morning my phone beeped as I was having breakfast. The guy was pleased to hear from me and said he was free to visit on Saturday afternoon so I was round at Gran and Gramps early that morning to take advantage of the dry weather, always a bonus in Cornwall, especially in November. Gran hoovered and polished the inside and Gramps and I washed and polished the outside. I left the windows down and gave the van a good airing while we had a pasty Gran had made, and I talked briefly about my plans of finding my own place.

'And what about your girlfriend, Clare is it? Will she be living with you?' Gran asked.

I looked at her in surprise. 'Would you be shocked if I asked her?'

'Not really Simon, your generation doesn't suffer the constraints we grew up with. Life is different for you, there are some things I envy, and some things I don't.' She said.

'Such as?' I was intrigued.

'Well, you can have sex whenever you want, which is nice,' she began. I nearly dropped my coffee cup. 'But I don't like the way everyone has to do more than one job to keep their heads above water these days. And I don't like the drugs and the violence.'

Gramps was looking over my shoulder, out of the window. 'That fella's here Simon. Do you want me to come out with you?'

'No thanks, I've done my research Gramps. I think I can handle it.'

'Bring the gentleman in for coffee and cake when you're done Simon.' Gran called after me.

Trying not to think about Gran having sex I strode out and met the bloke, the folder containing the van's history under my arm. We shook hands and took up our positions in an invisible ring, as though a contest of some sort was starting. First of all he complimented my efforts.

'A guy who cleans like that is obviously interested in making a sale.' He bent down and looked at the tyres. 'Safe and legal to drive on.' He couldn't resist giving one a kick.

'And all MoT'd and serviced.' I said. 'Road legal. I had her out for a few weeks this summer.' I could feel myself slipping into car-talk.

The guy asked to look inside and he climbed all over everything, pulling things out, checking details, sitting on the seats, stroking and feeling and touching surfaces with long, strangely prehensile fingers. Then he looked at the engine and asked me start her up.

'Nice. Starts first time.' He watched the engine for a while with an experienced eye and listed a few things he thought needed doing. I'd been expecting that and wasn't bothered.

'Are you a dealer or is this a personal purchase?' I asked.

The man smiled. 'I scout around for these in my spare time. I'm a hobbyist, a fan of the marque. I've got some friends who are specialists in upgrading and updating these vans, we go to rallies and bore for England on individual merits. We're sad gits really.'

I warmed to him. 'Better than train spotting I suppose.'

'Better class of nerd.' The man said agreeably, looking at the mileage.

'Your dad - '

'Grandad.' I interjected.

'Did he tell you what I was thinking?'

'Yes, I'm interested, but she's got history.' I indicated the folder. 'Provenance.' I thought of Sam using that word about old, valuable items. 'I think she's worth a bit more.'

'Okay. Well I'm not going to insult you.' He said. 'Let's take her round the block and then see if we can find some common ground.'

The guy was keen to buy and we agreed a sum that almost made me do back flips and handstands, so I took him indoors and Gran immediately pounced with the refreshments. I had to shoo her out of the little dining room where we'd commandeered the table for the paperwork. Once we'd sorted out the relevant details he wrote me a personal cheque.

'Bank that on Monday. It should take around six days to clear into your account unless you can pay them a fee to do a speedier service. Call me when it's in and I'll arrange to come round with a mate who can drive the van back for me.'

A question crossed my mind. 'How do you know I'm not going to vanish and sell the van to someone else?'

The man gave me a shrewd look. 'One, you've got an honest face. Two, I spotted the van, she wasn't on the market. Three, I know where your grandparents live. Four, I took a photograph of what I presume is your car outside, so I've got your name and your numberplate. I can find you.'

'Blimey.' I didn't know what else to say.

'That is your car out there then? The old blue Volvo? You didn't say you'd walked here.'

I nodded.

'Interesting. Nice to do business with a man who likes a bit of class.'

I walked him back to his car, an old but high spec and well cared for BMW. As he got in I got my phone out and took a photograph of him with the number plate visible. He laughed, waved and drove away.

The first thing I wanted to do was tell Clare, but this time I wanted to do things right. On impulse I telephoned the restaurant Sam had recommended, just over the Tamar in Devon. They had a table for two free at eight. Then I phoned Clare, she answered her mobile on the third ring.

'Hi.'

'Clare, it's me.'

'I know.'

What is it with women? Affectionate and friendly one minute and blowing a cold arctic wind the next. Gran had said something about Clare being a Gemini, I'd misheard as it as Jedi and cracked up laughing. What made me laugh even more was that Gran knew what a Jedi was. But she and Gramps were big fans of wacky space movies. On the subject of Gemini, Gran had said something about the sign of the twins, being two characters in one body. I'd made some joke about getting more for my money then, two women instead of just the one. Right now I was dealing with the distant, slightly frosty one.

'Clare,' I said again. 'It's not babysitting night so I'm taking you out.'

'I'm not sure I'm in the mood Simon. I don't fancy the cinema or The Wheal tonight.'

'Good, because it's neither of those things. I'm taking you somewhere special for dinner. I'm picking you up at seven, wear your prettiest dress and your nicest perfume. Tonight we're having a date. You deserve it.'

There was a surprised silence, and then a small voice. 'Okay. That's nice. I'll be ready.'

Goodness me, sometimes you just had to take control and be the boss.

She wasn't at the door when I pulled up so I had to knock. Her dad answered and invited me in to the sitting room to wait.

'Have you two had a tiff then? She's been in a funny mood.' He said in a mock whisper.

'Ted!' Maggie admonished him, shaking her auburn curls. 'Don't embarrass Simon. It's not our business!'

We were saved from any awkwardness by the door opening. Clare was standing there in the light from the hall, looking like a dream. She'd put her hair up in a soft arrangement with a few loose strands curling down. I'd never seen it like that and it gave her such a different look, older, sophisticated, elegant. She was wearing a peachy coloured dress with a slanting neckline and a dipped hemline which showed her lovely legs to advantage and she paused, not for effect, but hesitantly. For a moment no-one said anything.

'You look amazing.' The right words came out of my mouth.

'A real picture, my poppet.' Her dad spoke.

'Beautiful.' Maggie made a funny noise and I had a feeling she wanted to cry. 'So grown up.'

'Mum, I am twenty-two.' Clare said dismissively, but I could see she was pleased by our reactions. 'Shall we go then?' She looked at me and gave a little toss of her head.

'Yes milady.' I mimed a deferential touch to my non existent cap. 'This way milady.'

Outside I opened the car door for her and she got in gracefully. Clare was like her mum, always quick and nimble in her movements, but this evening I was in the presence of beauty. In the car I reached for her hand and on impulse I gently kissed the back of it. She was surprised but didn't say anything. Taking my lead from her I said nothing but put the car in gear and drove off smoothly.

The restaurant Sam had recommended was in the countryside, just twenty minutes the other side of the Tamar over an ancient packhorse bridge. That meant parking was easy. A light drizzle had started so I drew up right outside the entrance and before I could do anything a man stepped forward from the doorway and opened the passenger side door while holding up a huge umbrella. 'Allow me to assist madam.' He said nicely.

Clare took it all in her stride and smiled. It was as though someone had choreographed the whole thing; her right was to be escorted indoors to warmth and safety, my task was to park the car.

She was waiting in a prettily furnished anteroom, a fire crackling in the hearth and posh glossy magazines on a coffee table. A middle aged couple were tucking into drinks and hors-d'oeuvres. I had a sense of having gone through all this once before. An image of Sir Hugh swam before my eyes and I caught the eye of the couple.

'Good evening.' I bid them.

They responded politely and I turned to Clare. 'We'll have a drink first shall we, before we order?'

Clare looked at me in wonderment and then the house procedures took over as an efficient waitress attended to our needs. A small dish of hors-d'oeuvres appeared with our drinks - I'd chosen a non-alcoholic virgin Mary, which despite my misgivings at Flinton Hall wasn't disgusting - and I appraised the dish with a worldly eye. 'That's tapenade,' I advised Clare. 'It's okay with gin and tonic and not bad with tomato juice, but I'm not very fond of it.'

'Yes, but what exactly is tapenade?' Clare whispered.

'Olives.' I explained.

'Oh, I love olives.' She ate hers with delight, followed by mine, her eyes beginning to sparkle with pleasure at this new experience. 'Simon, have you been here before?'

'Oh several times. I practically live here.' I kept my face straight and ate a small cheese football, all fluff and flavour with a gooey centre and a hint of chives.

Clare was gazing at me, her eyes wide and lustrous in the flattering lighting. 'Well, you certainly seem at home.' She glanced around, at the magazines laid out and the oil paintings on the wall. 'It's a very nice place.'

'You're a woman who deserves very nice places.' Christ, I sounded like a creep but Clare seemed to like it. She was relaxing into the velvet embrace of comfort, responding to the sounds of subdued laughter and the clink of cutlery. Music was playing very softly, something classical and gentle. I watched her taking it all in. She'd fit in perfectly at Flinton Hall, I thought, this girl was born for the fine things in life.

The evening was a success. The food was gorgeous and even I was sated despite lots of plate showing. Beautifully presented and with stunning flavours; the iron metallic taste of spinach in a wine jus against soft venison, complimented by creamed celeriac left me speechless. Remembering Sir Hugh's discourse on wines on our last evening I'd ordered a bottle of red wine, a Malbec from the Argentine since we'd started with a game terrine and Clare had chosen a beef medallion for her main course. By the time the second *amuse-bouches* arrived to refresh our palates she was completely relaxed and glowing with pleasure.

'Simon, this is fantastic. I've never been anywhere like this before.'

'I've something to celebrate,' I said. 'And you're the person I want to celebrate with.' I'd got a package of things in my head that I wanted to share with her. Before the meal I'd got them all in order of priority and had envisaged myself explaining things in a coherent manner. Now, after two glasses of Malbec, my heart took over my head. 'I've got a chance at an interesting garden design job which will earn me a bit extra. Sam wants me to stay on working with him at Trelerric, so that's a safety net job-wise. I've got my steady bread-and-butter holiday cottages which give me income. And I've been saving for about ten years.'

Clare was looking at me with slight amusement. 'Yes Simon, I know. We've talked about all this before.'

I paused while the waitress poured more wine into Clare's glass and shook my head when she offered me a top up.

'Well. What you don't know is that I sold my old classic campervan today. For more than twice what I paid for it.' I enjoyed using the word "classic" but even better I enjoyed the mental image of the fat cheque securely placed in the top drawer of my bedside table. 'So I reckon I can find us somewhere to live because I can cover key money or whatever securities landlords want, plus a bit extra for the essentials that we'll need to buy.' I stopped talking, checking what I'd just said.

'So you've got money in your pocket and if I heard you right you're suggesting we should move in together?'

Everything in me focussed on her expression, the sound of her voice, the look in her eyes. She had a faintly frozen, slightly wild look and I suddenly had the feeling that she was going to self combust, like a phoenix, and all I'd be left with was a pile of ashes.

'Clare,' I said quietly but with a sense of urgency. 'Clare, I haven't finished.' All my decisions and plans telescoped into a solid bullet of certainty. 'I was going to ask you next month, at Christmas, I was going to surprise you with a ring. I want to ask you to be my fiancee, to get engaged.' I stopped talking. You may as well finish the mess you've made of it you idiot, I told myself. Clare still hadn't moved or spoken but her eyes were huge and fixed on me. I reached across the table and took her left hand in mine. 'Your birthstone is an emerald. I thought you might like to choose an emerald engagement ring to put on this finger.' I said softly.

I waited for the sky to fall on my head.

Clare had turned pale. So, I think, had I.

'Yes. Yes please Simon. Yes, I would like that, very much.'

I couldn't believe my good fortune. What a day this was turning out to be. I wished I'd bought a lottery ticket, I'd have been a millionaire by now. Clare got up and pressed her lips against my cheek and excused herself to the cloakroom. I expected she wanted to text someone with the news. It felt rather good. I sat back, the glass of Malbec in my hand, and grinned foolishly. Then I put it down and drank a glass of sparkling water instead. The waitress, who had been beckoned over to a conversation with the next table, came over to me.

'Was that a piece of special news that was just overheard sir?' She smiled at me. The couple at the next table had heard it all apparently and the man raised his glass to me.

'Yes. Yes, my girlfriend has just agreed to become my fiancee.' At last, I could say it out loud. I felt a bit dazed.

'In that case, may we celebrate the occasion?' She asked. I must have looked confused. 'A glass of champagne for the happy couple, on the house of course.'

It came on a silver tray decorated with a scattering of pink and red foil hearts. Clare was delighted and the waitress used our phones to take some pictures in the approved manner. When our puddings came some clever sod had written the word 'congratulations' on her plate in chocolate. She thought that was something else I'd arranged. I could do no wrong. Since I was driving Clare drank my champagne as well and later we sat holding hands and drinking coffee with *petits four* in a cosy little sitting room. Before we left the waitress handed us a fancy bag.

'You didn't finish the Malbec so I've put the cork back in to take away with you, and there's a complimentary brochure about what the hotel and restaurant can offer. We have a private room for engagement parties and we have a wedding license as well. We like to say that "special occasions are our speciality".' She almost simpered.

On my way to get the car I popped back into the restaurant and asked the waitress for a couple of the little foil hearts as a memento. Clare liked that sort of thing.

ELEVEN

Although my initial plans had gone awry, everything turned out for the best. Clare preferred to go shopping with me for the ring, rather than have a surprise, and it was one of those times when you make a memory, something significant you'll remember all your life. Being Cornish we shopped in Truro, and afterwards went to the same cafe we'd used when I was buying all my new clothes. Clare was already calling it "our cafe". I was just happy to be spending money on her instead of myself. It was a new and special experience.

Meanwhile I'd completed the garden design for the Ladies Walk at Flinton Hall, and was putting in some extra hours at Trelerric since Sam was busy labouring at the Cherryfields site. He'd decided my time would be better spent working for him, rather than for Andy. The Flinton's turned up on Friday lunchtime and I was invited in for tea in the afternoon. I had the preliminary drawings ready in a portfolio and put them on the table in the Chinese room in their suite.

'First of all I visualised a circle incorporating the walk from the boot room at the house, round through the pergola then up the existing steps and over the bank where the Ladies Walk went originally.' I began. 'The bank needs a proper path laying, and you need steps, similar to those already there, but going down the other side to the pavilion.' I drew my finger round the circle. 'The pavilion should be incorporated into the design, perhaps instead of being painted white you might like it painted vermilion - or even black. A touch more oriental anyway. But remember this is an English garden with roses and various shrubs so we don't want to create an uncomfortable parody.' I glanced at them and Sir Hugh was nodding. 'And then I think you need a short path to connect the pavilion round to the existing terrace. It completes the circle, and will provide you with a firm surface. You'll be able to walk without spoiling your fancy shoes in rainy weather.'

'Ouroboros.' Lady Flinton said.

'Sorry?' I thought I'd misheard her, I didn't recognise the word.

'The symbol of eternity, the soul of the world. The endless circle.' She said.

'My wife is talking about ancient mythology, Ouroboros turns up in Egyptian, Indian and even Norse writings, art and carvings. Think of it as a huge serpent curving round to eat its own tail.' Sir Hugh explained.

I must have looked startled.

'Sorry Simon, am I being too unreal for you darling?' Lady Flinton put an elegant hand on my arm and squeezed it slightly.

'No. Not at all. It's just that when I walked the bank for the first time I felt something move under my feet. It was a kind of energy.' I pulled a face. 'I imagined it had scales and claws.'

'Some people are more connected to the soil and land and energies.' Lady Flinton said, quite unperturbed. 'I'm sure that's what whatshisname was going on about when he wrote Lady Chatterley's Lover. Lady Constance was just responding to the raw nature and energy of the gardener. I performed the part on stage in London and got quite splendid reviews.'

I looked from Lady Flinton to Sir Hugh.

'My wife is a wonderful actress,' he said calmly. 'You should read the book Simon, it's by D.H. Lawrence. It was banned in England due to the obscenity laws at the time. But it's sensitive and not at all racy by modern standards.'

'Er, yes. I might do that.' I said. They were the same age as my grandparents. And they all seemed to think about sex. 'Getting back to the design, the top of the bank is broad so the path can be made to wind from side to side a little. That will make it more interesting because I can place some small groups of rocks and incorporate a bench, a simple construction without a back but supported on rocks. That will look more natural and won't spoil the look from the croquet lawn below.'

They were taking it all in and listening to me banging on about shaping and thinning the existing bushes, crown lifting a small tree and so on. I mentioned cloud-pruning, structure and rustic paving, and then talked about the views from the top of the bank.

'The Japanese talk about stealing or borrowing a view, letting the eye go beyond the garden or the path to appreciate what's in the distance. They call it "shakkei", it rhymes with "hay", not "eye".'

'I've heard of that.' Sir Hugh said. 'Well, these ideas are wonderful Simon. Tell me again, how long have you been gardening?'

I burbled on about working since I was ten years old, learning from Gramps and the old men in the village. The old guys who'd been so kind to me, I thought of the campervan.

'And I've always loved the stones up on the moors, the way nature has placed them. They talk, there's no wonder the ancient people built circles and worshipped the stars up there.' I said, enthusiastically.

'And a lot more than prayerful worship, I'm sure.' Lady Flinton murmured. 'Well, I think this is all quite marvellous Simon. I'm more than happy for you to proceed.'

She left us to freshen up for dinner at Home Farm. Sir Hugh poured himself a whisky from the drinks tray and offered me a shot. I declined since I had to drive home.

'If my wife is happy then so am I,' he said. 'But joking aside Simon, you certainly do have talent and I'm impressed by these drawings. I shall have to purchase the originals from you for the garden records of course, so you will need to take copies for your own portfolio. We need to discuss a timescale - pity winter is setting in. Hartley is happy to assist you, and of course you'll need to source your materials. He knows local suppliers for stone and so on. When do you think you should make a start?'

We discussed practicalities and cash flow and I thought some of the groundwork could be done even with winter coming. Then

I got up to leave. Remembering his personal enquiries when I'd stayed at Flinton Hall I paused at the door. 'I bought Clare an engagement ring Sir Hugh. She decided she'd rather choose it than be surprised. It's still at the jewellers though, being resized.'

'Resized?'

'She's like her mum, she has small hands.' I said.

'Ah yes,' Sir Hugh looked past me at the wall and smiled vaguely into the distance. 'Small, soft hands.'

Looking for a rental property was a bloody miserable experience. Together we looked at what we could afford in and around Liskeard, Launceston and Saltash but turned down flats and houses where parking was difficult or downright dodgy. We were also picky. For the first time I really appreciated how hard mum had worked to keep a snug roof over our heads. At a personal cost I now understood. There'd been no holidays, but then mum had asked "why would we want a holiday when we live in Cornwall?"

The places Clare and I looked at were too often cold, badly equipped or unloved and down at heel. Some of them smelled peculiar and some of the rentals required the tenants to carry out repairs. We couldn't see us living in any of them. And I realised I just didn't feel comfortable in suburbia, it was a place where trees got cut down and roads named after them.

Clare could drive but she didn't have a car because she could easily walk from home to the veterinary surgery where she worked. And buying a second car would eat into our disposable cash and her own savings.

'I wish we could find somewhere local to Trelerric,' she moaned in exasperation. 'Somewhere where you don't have to drive for miles to pick me up when I'm on a late shift. And what if you're away working up country on a project? I'd have to stay back home with mum and dad. It's a pain.'

We were already into December and I was beginning to feel desperate. Small places in our villages were all holiday or second homes. Not for the first time I envied Sam Latchley. He'd got three beds in which to lay his head on the estate; Home Farm, the Coach House, Lucy's rooms in Trelerric House, and by next summer he'd have Cherryfields Cottage, all brand new and perfect. I put my arm round Clare's shoulders, we were standing on a wet street in Liskeard looking at rental properties in an estate agent's window. Rain was dripping off something and going down my neck.

'What about that one,' Clare pointed. 'There, top left. I've not seen that before.'

I looked and saw the details for a detached cottage on the side of the moor. 'Two bedrooms, refurbished kitchen, electric oven, woodstove, oil-fired central heating, lpg hob. Sounds perfect, and it's affordable. Let's ask.'

Four hours later we met the agent at the empty property. Outside it was cute, with a stream running along one side of the garden. Inside the kitchen was lovely and Clare breathed a sigh of relief.

'This is perfect isn't it Simon?'

'Let's look at the rest.' I was feeling hopeful. It seemed too good to be true.

'The owner was trying to sell this place but the sale fell through so he thought he'd try letting it at least for the winter. Though I'm sure he might be persuaded to a long term rental if the circumstances are right.' The agent said, twiddling the keys in her fingers.

I felt a small moment of disquiet. 'But we might find ourselves homeless and out on our ears in six months time? Why did the sale fall through? I thought Cornish cottages got eaten up by incomers.'

The agent shrugged her shoulders. 'I don't know, problems within the purchasing chain or with funds usually. I just work in lettings.'

I was thinking back to long conversations with Andy the builder when I'd worked with him. I could hear his voice in my head, his Northern accent. "Effing nightmares some of these old places. No damp course, wringing wet, no insulation, frost on the duvet in the mornings."

Clare was looking anxious. 'Do you mind if I use the bathroom?' She asked, and disappeared.

The living room, where the woodstove was housed in an old attractively wonky fireplace with a huge granite lintel, smelled damp to me. The agent assured me it was because the house hadn't been lived in for a while. There were no carpets, only bare dark stained floorboards which creaked as I walked. Peering at the walls and corners I could see that a built-in cupboard had been removed from the side of the fireplace and tell-tale shine alerted me to a problem. I bent down.

'There are fresh slug trails here.' I poked my finger into the corner where the back wall had been left as a "feature granite wall" so beloved by interior designers. The wall felt damp. My finger touched something soft between the junction of the floorboard and the wall. It wasn't a slug. It was soil.

'This place doesn't have proper foundations in this corner.' I said. 'Is that why it didn't sell?'

Before the agent could say anything Clare appeared looking distraught. 'I'm so sorry,' she said. 'I've been flushing the loo but it won't flush properly.'

The bathroom was downstairs, not uncommon in old properties. I said I'd have a look since the agent was apparently clueless. Clare followed me.

'Simon,' she hissed. 'I had to go, you know, a poo. It won't go down the pan. Oh no don't look, I'm so embarrassed.'

'Don't be.' I flushed and I flushed. 'There's a problem with the drainage here. We're dead flat in a hollow, there's a stream right outside and and I'll bet the septic tank hasn't got a decent fall to it. I'm sorry Clare, this place isn't for us. We can't live here, we'd be constantly paying for the honey-wagon to come out and pump the septic tank, that or forever rodding it. It's a nightmare.'

We left feeling awful and as though we'd nothing to look forward to. We were getting engaged at Christmas and had no place to live. Not even a stable.

A few days later I mentioned it in conversation with Sam. We were pretending to clean things and check our kit in the potting shed since it was sluicing down outside. Sam had done all the ground clearance at the cottage site and we were talking houses and building. I kept our house hunting escapades all lighthearted and made the latest damp slug infested cottage experience into a funny story.

'So what are you going to do then?' Sam asked, wiping an oily cloth round the tines of a garden fork before hanging it up.

'Keep looking. I've left my details with the local agents and begged them to call me the moment there's something decent and affordable. But the good news is I've collected Clare's engagement ring, and I've booked us into the restaurant where I asked her to get engaged, you know, the one you recommended. Since they've got rooms I've booked us dinner, bed and breakfast, so I can drink champagne as well. Not that I like champagne, but you know what I mean.'

'I certainly do old son.' Sam grinned at me. 'You want to have your wicked way the minute you get a ring on that poor defenceless girl's finger. Does she know what she's letting herself in for?'

'At least I've bought my fiancee a ring.' I said, ignoring his crude observations. 'And yes, she's agreed to spend the night with me, it's a lovely hotel.'

'I'll be off on my honeymoon with Lucy by then.' Sam said. 'Two weeks away in the Caribbean. Guaranteed sunshine while you poor lot are drowning in Cornwall.'

'Awesome.' I said. We'd had some unusually wet winters recently. To take my mind off what Clare might look like naked I went back over an idea I'd had. I'd decided to contact the owner of one of the holiday cottages I'd looked after for years and see if there was a chance we could rent that. Called Pondside Cottage, it was a sweet little place that didn't seem to get much use by the owner. Nothing ventured, nothing gained.

Sam asked me about the design I was working on for Flinton Hall and we chatted about that for a while. It was a relief to be able to talk about something ordinary and with someone who knew what I was talking about. 'The soil's not acidic enough for the sort of plants I'd like to use, the sort that grow here without a problem. But I can substitute some things and use what's there already.'

'We're lucky being able to grow Acer and Magnolia,' Sam agreed. 'Do you remember months ago I suggested a pretty walk between the visitors' car park and the Stables Tea Room? I think your idea could be adapted for that.'

'We could call it the Magnolia Walk since there are already some planted along there. Properly grouped rocks could be placed to make the path more interesting.' I said.

'And leave the grass either side to grow into a meadow.'

'Introduce some different Magnolia varieties, to enhance those already existing.'

We were off on garden talk for the rest of the day.

That evening I emailed the owner of Pondside Cottage with my proposal. A day later I got a response from his wife. "So sorry Simon, I've just accepted bookings for Christmas and New Year, and then bookings are already in for Easter."

Shit, I thought. What had happened to the run of good luck I'd been having?

TWELVE

The next time I went up to Flinton Hall I was on my own, Sir Hugh and Lady Felicity, as I'd been instructed to call her, were away in London. They'd put me in the same room as before in the guest wing but this time I ate with Mr and Mrs Marriott in the kitchen, and Jeff Hartley joined us. Angela and Ian Marriott were a professional cook-housekeeper maintenance/handyman combination and in their mid-fifties, like Jeff. They'd got together when they were working for a smart foreign hotel chain and had spent several years working in different parts of the world before coming back home to the UK and landing the job with Sir Hugh. They chatted about his first wife, about Lady Felicity's fame as an actress and about the various marital indiscretions of the Flinton set, as Angela called them.

'As a housekeeper you can always tell when anything has been going on Simon. You cannot disguise bedroom sports from the person who changes the sheets.' Angela said.

I thought that was too much information and got Jeff talking about his life. I remembered he'd suffered an injury at work and asked him about it.

'Toes on one foot were crushed and I lost the two small ones. We'd not been given safety boots to wear so the enforcement people from the Local Authority took them to court. That allowed me to take a private case, but they settled rather than go through Court again. I was put off that sort of work. I didn't like the noise anyway. Can't beat the peace and the pace of working on your own in a garden.'

'Did you always enjoy your own company Jeff.'

'Had to, after the missus ran off with that tosser from the gym she went to.'

I didn't pursue the conversation. Jeff had taken me to a local garden supplier, who in turn had put me in contact with the quarry they obtained stone from. It meant that Jeff and I were going into Wales to see what they had. I was looking forward to seeing more new places, especially because Jeff had decided he'd drive. He had a robust modern Toyota pickup which he said would look more appropriate to do business from than my old Volvo. Being in his car was fun, he liked 1980s power ballads and we sang along to his playlist of Phil Collins, Aerosmith and Bonnie Tyler. He was amused that I knew the songs so I said that he had something in common with my mum.

'She plays this stuff all the time.'

'She likes her music well drenched then. And what does your dad like? Heavy metal I'll bet.'

'Dunno, he walked out on us when I was a baby. Never met him.'

Jeff shot me a look. 'Sorry. That must have been tough.'

'Not really, well not for me anyway. I grew up knowing nothing different. I'm lucky, I've got mum, Gramps and Grandma. And we all get on.'

'Asshole.'

'Sorry?' I said. There weren't any drivers behaving like dorks.

'Man walking out on a little family like that. I never had kids. Always fancied I'd like kids of my own. Pity it never happened.'

The trip had gone well, I'd selected and ordered stone and we'd spent another day dealing with existing shrubs and trees and marking out the simple changes which were going to transform the site. We parted on good terms, pleased with ourselves and with each other. I wouldn't see him again until the New Year, meanwhile it was just days away from Sam's wedding to Lucy, and then I'd be getting engaged to Clare.

We were stupidly busy. A winter wedding is much harder work because the gardens, although lovely in their stripped back appearance, obviously don't possess that lushness and colour expected by photographers. We'd brought on some white Hellebores in the greenhouse and got a nice grouping of those with winter flowering Sarcococca, an evergreen shrub with a tiny white flower which produces a beautiful scent. The inside of

Trelerric chapel was decorated with swags and garlands of pale flowers and ribbons, all provided by Lucy's mother, who it turned out was a professional florist as well as being first cousin to Sir Hugh. Clare and I had received a proper embossed invitation, as a couple, which thrilled Clare to bits.

'I've got this, and that bottle of Malbec, and the little hearts as keepsakes.' Clare informed me.

'Why? It's just clutter and junk.' I teased her.

'It is not. It's things which mean something to us as a couple.'

I held my tongue. I knew my Gran had a cupboard full of bits and bobs like this. Gramps had explained that some women had a need to keep stuff, like magpies. It was something to do with sentimentality. 'Best let them do it, if it makes them happy. But when we croak some poor fool has got to go through it and chuck it all away.' He'd given a wry smile.

On the day of the wedding I sat in the chapel with Clare on one side and Maggie, her mum, on the other. It was the first time I'd had a chance to look inside properly and the atmosphere really got to me. There was more than a sense of occasion, the feeling was one of importance, significance. These walls had witnessed so much over the centuries, so many prayers and wishes, vows of intent and solemn promises that I actually felt emotional. It was a lovely place. My eyes wandered over a few old commemorative plaques fixed to the walls, mostly to various ancient Latchley men and their wives. Sam could trace his genealogy effortlessly back to the Tudor period, when the house was built. Clare nudged me in the ribs. The wedding was starting. I watched Sam, looking handsome in a new suit with a colourful embroidered waistcoat and wondered what I'd wear on my wedding day. I wasn't the only one thinking along the same lines and when Lucy came down the aisle in a simple high necked elegant gown with long sleeves I noticed Clare had tears in her eyes.

The family had got event caterers in and everyone was in a party mood. Clare looked gorgeous with her hair up again and wearing a pale dress, the skirt part splashed with pink, white and teal colours. She wore it with a teal coloured fitted jacket which had a bit of pleated material in the back so that it flared slightly over her bottom. A gold necklace with a small turquoise pendant and matching earrings completed her appearance. I was so proud of her I stuck to her side like glue.

A magnificent Christmas tree hung with white and silver baubles and chains graced the black and white hall at Trelerric House and the Georgian salon had been opened up to reveal its full length and to enable dancing at one end.

'Just like in our day,' Lady Felicity was exclaiming with pleasure. 'This house comes alive for parties.'

Sir Hugh greeted us and he kissed the back of Maggie's hand in a nicely mannered old world way. Maggie blushed slightly and looked pleased. I could have sworn I heard him say "small soft hands".

We joined the congratulatory throng around Sam and Lucy. Lucy thanked me for the gift I'd given them. I'd surveyed the site at Cherryfields and done a simple colour-washed design for a pretty garden terrace for them, in keeping with the appearance of the building, incorporating a small pond with a seating area and room for a barbecue. Clare had giggled, remembering our own barbecue fiasco back in the summer.

'Can you draw people the way you can draw and paint gardens?' Clare had asked me when she'd looked at my design.

'Not really, Miss Frazer showed me how to do figures in a landscape, the way I did that little drawing of the dandelion clock for Grace that night, but my skills are more on the technical side, I'm more a designer I think, not an artist.'

'Well I'm not sure what the difference is, but I do think you're brilliant. And sexy. And ...'

I smiled, remembering that night. Afterwards, Clare had insisted I should sign and date the Cherryfields drawing so that she could get it framed while I was away at Flinton Hall. Now Lucy was smiling at me, every inch the beautiful bride.

'My pleasure,' I grinned at her. 'The other part of the gift is that I expect Sam will have me doing the hard-landscaping and layout on my own while he swans around indoors putting shelves up for you in Cherryfields.'

Sam laughed but I noticed Clare's smile had turned a little bit tight. We still hadn't found anywhere to live. The estate agents said that lettings had dried up now, no-one wanted to be bothered with that sort of thing at Christmas. I took her off to the buffet and we got talking to people, listened to the speeches and toasted the newlyweds and then watched Sam and Lucy take a romantic turn on the dance floor. I couldn't wait to hold Clare close and we were on the dance floor as soon as it was permissible. Clare seemed to feel pretty much the same and we whispered our love for each other. The party was nicely settled when the cake-cutting ceremony was announced, which gave us all a chance to cool off. A bit later Sam caught my eye and waved me over.

'Lucy and I want a private word with you and Clare, so don't disappear yet.'

'Oh, okay.' I couldn't imagine what it was about. Clare was similarly mystified. We were talking to a bunch of relatives when Sam and Lucy appeared hand-in-hand and extricated us.

'We need to go someplace quiet for a moment.' They led us off to Lady Flinton's suite just across the hall. Sam closed the door behind us and we all stood there in the Chinese room.

I squeezed Clare's hand.

'What is it?' I asked, looking from Sam to Lucy.

Sam looked at Lucy. 'Shall I say it Mrs Latchley, or do you want to?'

'Well, we're off on our honeymoon tomorrow,' Lucy began, smiling at the use of her new name. 'But before we go we've got a sort of surprise for you.'

She paused and looked at Sam.

'You're getting engaged at the end of the week, and that's very special. So we've come up with an idea for a present.' Sam spoke carefully, looking from me to Clare. Then he looked at Lucy.

'Go on.' Lucy said.

'I, we, Lucy and I wondered, if you and Clare would like to move into the Coach House?'

I stared at him, not quite slack-jawed but certainly surprised. Clare emitted a small excited squeak.

'We both thought you might like to live in the Coach House while you got something else sorted out.' Lucy said. 'Sam's told me how difficult it's been, finding somewhere to live that suits. There's no rush, it's yours, if you'd like it, for as long as you want.'

'I thought you were going to live there until Cherryfields is finished.' I said.

'No, we're going to live here in Trelerric House, in Lucy's rooms. Our combined junk won't fit in the Coach House. And for once in my life I want all my stuff under one roof. As befits a married man.' Sam grinned at Lucy and then turned to a side table with two keys on it. 'Here's the keys. You've been inside Simon, but don't say yes until your soon-to-be fiancee has seen it.' He smiled down at Clare. 'My stuff is already out. Go and have a poke around tomorrow, or tonight if you can't wait.' He held the keys out to me.

I lifted Clare's hand and let him drop the keys onto her palm. Then I put my hand out and we shook hands, a brotherly handshake. 'Thank you. Thank you so much, both of you.'

I kissed Lucy on the cheek and Clare kissed them both, her eyes bright with tears. They left us alone together and I held Clare close while she pulled herself together.

'Do you want to look now?' I asked, kissing the top of her head.

Clare nodded tremulously. 'I won't be able to sleep tonight if I don't look.'

And Clare and I walked hand-in-hand to the Coach House on a cold December night.

We both loved it. Clare stood there, holding my hand and gazing about.

'I've been coming to Trelerric all my life,' she said in a small, distant voice. 'Mum started work here before I was even born. I've always known it, I've played here, worked here, fallen in love with you here, in a funny way it's part of me. But I've never been inside this building and I never dreamed I'd make a new life by actually living here. It's wonderful. It's not perfect but it's wonderful. We'll say yes won't we Simon.'

It wasn't a question. And I was so bloody relieved I just pulled her close and breathed the sweet warm scent of her hair and skin. 'Yes. Oh very definitely, yes.'

The first thing on my mind was buying a bed, well, maybe not the first thing but then practicalities have to be sorted out. I knew what I wanted, a proper Cornish-made metal bed. Clare paced about, imagining a small table and chairs, a cosy sofa in front of the woodstove. It was loft living at its most basic, all open plan but with a nice little bathroom off at one end. I remembered Sam had used a screen to hide his bed, what I hadn't remembered was that there was a built-in wardrobe against the internal bathroom wall. One less thing to buy.

Back at the wedding reception Maggie was incredulous. 'They're letting you have the Coach House? For nothing?'

Clare was glowing with good fortune. 'Yes. We have to cover all the bills, obviously, but it's rent free. Can you believe that? It seems too good to be true. But that's what Sam and Lucy said.'

'Well my girl, what a Christmas this is turning out to be.'

I saw Maggie's eyes flick across the room to where Sir Hugh was standing with a group of people. He was watching the three of us and gave a little nod, raising his glass in a sort of salute. I felt as though there was something to interpret in the gesture, but other than the usual good wishes I couldn't think what and anyway, Clare at my side was almost incandescent with happiness. I realised we'd both been feeling the strain and the sense of it lifting from my shoulders was pretty fantastic. We danced as though it was our own celebration, which in a way, it was.

It was an odd sensation, having a few days off. Mum helped me move some of my things so that she could see the Coach House.

'Is this what they call loft living? 'Easy to clean and heat I suppose. You two will be able to keep saving then. And it's made Christmas presents very easy this year, you need stuff for your new home.' She walked up and down, looking out of the windows and into the bathroom. 'Very private, not overlooked at all. But there isn't what you'd call a kitchen, just a sink and a sort of cupboard worktop arrangement. Where do you put your washing machine, and I can't see the right sort of wiring for a cooker either.' Mum looked at me enquiringly.

'Sam said the place was originally designed to be a separate office for his mum, not a living space. But she found this too big and preferred working from Home Farm, so it was redundant until Sam took it over as a bolthole. That was when they put the bathroom in. And he took most of his meals at home, or scrounged off Maggie, Clare's mother.' I smiled at her. 'We can't have a washing machine or a proper cooker. We'll have to borrow yours or Maggie's. So you'll still be seeing plenty of me.'

Mum actually snorted, I think with amusement. I could see that she was pleased for me but at the same time I guessed it must have been making her feel strange, her only child finally leaving home. 'Mum, are you bothered about me leaving home?' I couldn't help asking.

Mum gave me a long look before speaking. 'Yes, because I'll miss you. No, because I've brought you up to stand on your own two feet. And it's right that you should be with your girl now.' She ran a finger over the woodstove where a little bit of dust had settled. 'To think, I was already a young mother at Clare's age. But I'm sure you'll manage, it'll be something to tell your own children one day. And I expect I shall be happy to feed the both of you once in a while.'

Preparing to collect Clare to take her to the hotel on the night of our engagement gave me a funny feeling and put me in an odd mood. I was both nervous and full of anticipation at the same time. We were going to spend our first proper night together and as promised on that dark night on Plymouth Hoe I had ordered champagne and flowers to be put in our room. But something didn't feel right. I tried to sort my head out as I stood in the shower. I was pretty sure we'd have no problem making love after the serious cuddling we'd done over the past few months. We both wanted to be together, and she was going to be wearing my engagement ring. Then it hit me just as I got shampoo in my eye. I hadn't worked out when to put the ring on her finger.

Fifteen minutes later I was on the phone to Jane Latchley and after that I called Clare and asked her to be ready half an hour earlier than planned. To mum's surprise I hugged her before I left the house and went to pick Clare up. It felt peculiar, her mum and dad waving us off, but all the parents were content that we'd arranged to have a family Christmas day get together with everyone in one house, as a sort of engagement party.

Clare was looking beautiful. I loved it when she put her hair up.

'What's the urgency then Simon?'

'You'll see.'

Fortunately Trelerric House was on the way to the hotel we were booked into, but instead of taking the turn to the Coach House I drove round the back, on the old, original drive, and parked up at the massive old door to the Tudor House. We both got out and I took Clare by the hand, it was very cold and stars were lighting up the evening sky.

'This way, in here.' The door was slightly ajar and I pushed it open, silently blessing Sam's mum with every world of thanks I knew. I heard Clare's little intake of breath. On the huge old oak table in the great hall a dozen large white church candles were flickering in a shallow water filled tray, their light amplified and reflected by the water. Set back and surrounding the candles were several of the white flower arrangements from Sam and Lucy's wedding. The light from the candles made a private, intimate space in the otherwise dark hall and there was a little fragrance scenting the air.

Clare didn't speak. She stood there, still holding my hand and looking at the candles, her face illuminated by their glow. I turned her to me and looked into her eyes. There was an exquisite moment of trust and love between us.

'I don't know why, but this place has a special feeling for me,' I began. 'Maybe it's because I first saw your lovely face through a Tudor window here. Trelerric is where I fell in love with Clare Margaret Palfrey.' It was so cold I could see my breath in the candlelight light as I spoke.

Taking the ring box from my pocket I opened it. 'This means everything Clare. I love you.' And I slipped the emerald and diamond ring onto her finger.

THIRTEEN

I started calling Clare my "naked tea lady". She had a delightful habit of walking around quite unselfconsciously with nothing on in the mornings and at last I knew where her tattoo was.

'What is it?' I'd asked, examining the tiny shape in the small of her back.

'My star sign, it's the sign for Gemini, although mum says I'm on the cusp and am sometimes a bit of a Taurus.'

'I wouldn't know whether that was a compliment or a complaint. You ought to talk to my Gran, she's an astrology freak.' I said.

'Oh I don't believe in any of it, it's a load of old tosh. But I like the shape. All the girls at college were getting something done, so I chose this.'

Clare had given me her little cat smile. Oh she was a Gemini all right. Next week she would say something quite different and profess to believe in magic mushrooms. Fortunately Gran had said that since I was an Aquarius I'd be fine, I could handle her. I think it meant I had some sort of force field protection or immunity from Clare's bouts of mercurial madness.

We'd taken advantage of the sales and I'd been impressed by Clare's taste, but for me the best thing was the bargain I got on a Cornish metal bed. The company had a cancelled order of a deep red king-sized beauty which made a very comfortable contribution to my new life.

Sam and Lucy, back from their honeymoon, paid us a visit not long after we'd moved in. Clare had hung a couple of framed posters on the kitchen wall depicting arty impressions of summer berries in shades of red and pink but with the deep hues of blackberries and blueberries. She'd chosen a dark heather coloured sofa with a heather and dull green patterned rug, purple seat cushions on the dining chairs at our little table and green towels in the bathroom. Mum had let me have the old yew wood

Windsor arm chair from my bedroom and Clare had put cushions on it in cream fabric with a tiny berry print. With the plain white walls and light wood floor I thought it looked friendly and welcoming.

Living in the Coach House was like upmarket camping and with some restrictions on ordinary things like somewhere to hang the washing we knew we couldn't make it a permanent home. But we were so pleased to be together that nothing could intrude on our happiness until I had to go away. Barely three weeks into January and I was due back at Flinton Hall where I had five days work planned with Jeff Hartley.

'I'll call you every day, and text. I'll miss you but I'll be home by Friday night. Be good for me to get some sleep for a change, what with you keeping me up half the night.' I teased Clare as we kissed goodbye at a a stupidly early hour on Monday morning. It was still dark. Driving away was a wrench, but there was a job to do. The Flinton's were away again doing what they called the London Season, seeing shows and spending time in the bright lights with their smart friends.

By the time I got to Flinton Hall the daylight was a sulky grey with no promise of improvement, but at least it wasn't raining. Jeff, by comparison, was a burst of sunshine. He was wearing a thick primrose yellow jumper which looked as though a tractor had driven over it. Jeans, boots, a very battered waxed jacket and a red knitted pull-on hat completed the picture. Once again I experienced his bone crushing handshake and after a mug of tea with a crispy bacon sandwich supplied by Angela we got to work.

To my relief I found that Jeff had already done quite a lot of groundwork.

'Ian Marriott came out and gave me a hand. Gets a bit claustrophobic in the house in winter and with the boss and his lady away Ian's more than happy to come out here and get out from under Angela's feet. She'll only have the poor sod folding sheets and the like. Tedious stuff.'

I made no comment. The first time I'd experienced the novelty of folding sheets with Clare we'd ended up in the unmade bed. Afterwards I'd joked that we'd wear the bed out in a year if we kept that level of activity going. Not that I was complaining. Clare was gorgeous and she knew it. I was besotted.

'Are you in there today Sherwell? Only I've twice asked which stone you want loaded first and you're not answering.'

I came out of my daydream. 'Sorry Jeff. I was miles away.' I liked the way he called me by my surname.

'I could see that. Now then, make some decisions because I need to keep moving in this cold.'

We toiled for three days moving stone piece by piece up on to the bank and roughly into place. The large stones were a trial, the smaller ones for path edging equally so because I tried moving them in a wheelbarrow which tipped over and spilled them all down onto the croquet lawn. Jeff used the trailer attached to the ride-on mower which speeded things up a bit but the hard physical work gave us both enormous appetites. Angela fed us with home made pies and stews and steaks all week. Ian came out and helped with some of the trickier stones, a bonus since the old injury to Jeff's foot was a bit of a hindrance, although he didn't like to show it.

'Worse in cold wet weather, we've been bloody lucky this week though Sherwell.'

By the fifth day the bulk of the work was completed although I estimated at least another five days would be needed to put the final arrangements together. I took more photographs, satisfied that I had a good record of the job to date. Jeff stood back and studied what we'd done.

'Funny that,' he said. 'Never really noticed the view along the top. I've been up here countless times over the years to strim and not stopped to take it all in.'

'That's the problem with being a gardener,' I agreed. 'You're always looking at the next job. But at least with a path in place you'll have less to strim.'

Jeff was right, with a casually winding cobbled and slabbed path, stones placed to accentuate the turns and movement of the journey, the walk was a pleasant experience and provided the opportunity to stop and look about. I'd left gaps for strategic planting later in the year, the plain bench seat had to be made and work still had to be done to link the pavilion to the house. Jeff and I stood looking at the cuts we'd made into the bank down to the pavilion where the new steps were to be constructed.

'Reckon I can do that. There's a pile of the same old stone slabs still behind the potting shed, the same as them used in the other steps before I even started here. If you want a mirror image I can crack on with that till you come back. Ian will help.'

By now Jeff was used to my exacting attention to detail and I thought I could trust him to follow my plan. He'd also said he would take my guidance on any planting.

'Not because I don't know my plants, I do. Problem is I'm a touch colour blind, bit of trouble with the red spectrum, same as my dad. When I cut flowers for the house Angela sorts them into colours that go together. And Sir Hugh always advises what he wants planted and where. Got a thing about Delphiniums at the moment. Likes the colour blue.'

I immediately decided to add drifts of cornflowers and a clump of evergreen periwinkle to the bank, the latter having a reliable and long lasting blue flower as well as being fantastic ground cover.

Finally it was time for me to leave and face the drive back down to Cornwall. I put Christine and the Queens on to play, because Clare liked it, and headed for the M5. I didn't mind driving, but I resented the lost time and absolutely hated negotiating roadworks. Fortunately it was closed season for holiday traffic and I seemed to pass Exeter in record time. Another ninety minutes and I was in the safe embrace of

Trelerric and the even warmer embrace of Clare. She was impressed with the toned muscularity of my back and shoulders. We couldn't keep our hands off each other.

A day later and the weather broke, up country they had snow but apart from a white dusting on the tops of the moors, Cornwall got rain by the bucket load. Nothing could be done at the Cherryfields site and the greenhouse and potting shed were immaculate so Sam and I made a dash for Home Farm. Grace was there apparently recovering from some imaginary tummy ailment which meant she'd skipped school. Alice had gone to collect Thomas from the nursery in the village. Jane Latchley set out some refreshments, she was the sort of woman who was always prepared for visitors and she clearly enjoyed having her family around her.

'We've got another guest today. Your friend Sally is here Simon.'

Grace decided to be shy with me and preferred to snuggle up against her uncle on the kitchen sofa. I was just accepting a piece of Dundee cake when Sally emerged from the office, just off the kitchen. She was always the same, dressed in skinny dark jeans with a jumper over a t-shirt which somehow accentuated her thin bony frame. Her crinkly dark hair was pulled back off her face, showing fine eyes with sweeping brows.

'Hi Simon.' Sally said vaguely.

I responded with a friendly nod since my mouth was full. Sally seemed distracted and I watched her getting a mug of tea and a slice of Bakewell tart. She barely noticed Alice arriving with Thomas. Once everyone was sitting down Sally seemed satisfied that she had an audience.

'For those of you who don't know me I'm Sally Evans and I'm based at the museum in Liskeard.' Sally began in her straightforward manner. 'I'm a historian and my particular interest is in the fifteenth and sixteenth centuries. I'm currently undertaking research at the Records Office for my PhD, but access to the Trelerric records is giving me a rare strand of authentic and previously un-researched documentation.'

I recalled Jane Latchley saying something about Sally having access to the "Latchley Coffer", which held the private collection of the Latchley papers and documents, including what the family called the Latchley Book and the Latchley Chronicle. The former listed births, marriages and deaths of estate workers and their families over the centuries, the latter covered the private lives of the Latchley family itself. I caught Jane Latchley's eye and got the impression that she hadn't expected the delivery of this formal summary to a captive audience.

'We know the established facts about minerals leaving Cornwall and we have a whole industry telling wildly romantic and inaccurate tales of wreckers and smugglers, but what I want to do is tease out what benefits came to Cornwall as a result of the mineral trade.' Sally was getting into her stride and her dark eyes were shining. 'Cornwall is a sea-faring nation, its many coastal ports and natural harbours have always made it easier to trade by sea than to try to cross the moors up into England. And in order to make a profit a ship was never run with an empty cargo hold.'

I fell into a meditative lull of my own, remembering the ominous power of the sea in the darkness, that night Clare and I had our first tiff and then declared our love for each other. Sam grinned at me across the room as Sally continued for a few minutes, talking about seeing the bigger picture and what made Cornwall attractive as a trading partner.

'The detail is what interests me', she said. 'Not just the statistics regarding how many cords of wood, bushels of wheat and bales of hides, but the needs of the people who lived here. What did they want, what could they afford, how did the power and wealth of the landed families influence trade?'

'And what about fashion? In clothes, furniture and so on.' Alice was fascinated.

'Yes, it's about human interest.' Jane Latchley added faintly. I guessed she was thinking about what to make for dinner and mentally listing all the other jobs she had to get on with in running the farm and the estate.

Sally looked pleased at the response and glanced around the kitchen. Her eye lighted on the dark carved table against one wall, the one Andy had noticed, and a small frown line creased vertically between her eyes.

'That's a lovely old table Mrs Latchley.'

'It's a very heavy old table,' Jane Latchley replied. 'It's been here for ever. It used to be in the entrance hall but I got it moved in here.'

'And nearly gave me and dad joint hernias.' Sam remembered, pulling a droll face at me. 'I shall probably be unable to father children.' He held up a crooked finger suggestively and I couldn't help it, I guffawed. A loud and positively vulgar laugh. Embarrassed I put a hand over my mouth, but the more I tried to apologise and control myself the more I laughed. Sam just had a way of reducing me to hysterics sometimes. The mood in the room was broken; Alice wanted to get the children home and Jane said she had to get on with her own work. Sally was unperturbed and still looking at the old table.

'Simon, does that remind you of anything?' She asked me.

With an effort I composed myself sufficiently to give her my polite attention although I still had a big silly grin on my face. 'I'm not sure. What do you mean?' I said.

'The newel post on the old staircase at Darleystones, Mr Pencraddoc's place on the other side of the moor.'

'Oh yes, you're right. The same dark wood and similar carving.' I could remember now, the discussions between Steve Bradley and Daniel Pencraddoc. Steve was a superb carpenter and he reckoned the staircase was older than Mr Pencraddoc's house.

'Acanthus leaves with some scrolls,' Sally murmured. 'I wonder if there's a link between Darleystones and Trelerric House.'

'I've never heard of one.' Jane Latchley said, busily clearing up plates and cups. 'I've met the Pencraddoc's, they're friends of Simon's, as are most people around here. Fiona has been to Trelerric in recent months to sketch and photograph. She was quite inspired by the old buildings, not just the Tudor part but the old round barn with the horse-whim. She rides and is rather fond of horses.'

Sally wasn't listening. 'Do you mind if I take a photograph?' No-one answered so she took some anyway in the bustle of people leaving.

Sam and I knocked off early, the daylight had gone and I wanted to go home and make things ready for Clare. Home, such a magical word. She was on the evening shift again and I wanted to get the stove lit and everything warm and comfortable. One of our engagement presents had been a slow cooker which was worth its weight in gold. Clare had produced an endless variety of delicious casseroles, chilli and curry and was worried that she'd end up the same shape as the cooker. I'd made her laugh by pretending to take a solemn vow to keep her well exercised and fit. What was it Gran had one said? "Sex, it's wonderful, for the first six months you could eat it. And after that, you'll wish you had." I simply couldn't imagine what she meant.

FOURTEEN

Sam put a hired mini-digger over the ground between the visitors car park and the Stables Tea Room and we made a start on what we were calling the Magnolia Walk. Once again it was my trademark serpentine path with lumps of granite grouped in odd numbers and placed to enhance their shape and appearance, incorporating simple benches and with a new idea of a stacked slate built seat. Cold on the bum but very handsome to look at. Sam had ordered several different Magnolia so the walk would shade from white to pink to a deep wine red colour. He'd also got plans for a screen of evergreen Camellia with a dark red flower to protect some Enkianthus which had a pretty pale flower cluster reminiscent of Lily of the Valley. It was going to be an enchanting addition to the garden especially when the path was actually laid. We were doing a complicated but rustic mixture of old granite setts, reclaimed granite slabs and reclaimed slate cut and positioned edge upwards. Similar surfaces were to be found around the old stables and the Coach House, surfaces once traditionally used to help coaches gain purchase on the ground and to help prevent horses slipping. We were working there one day when my phone started ringing. It was Sir Hugh Flinton.

'Simon my dear boy, how are you? Well, I trust.' He wasn't giving me time to answer. 'We're most impressed with the work you've been doing here, Hartley's completed the new steps.'

Sir Hugh paused long enough to allow me to make a pleased mumbling noise. I knew anyway because Jeff had sent me a photo and a text saying *'Up to your standards then Sherwell?'* I'd replied that he'd done "a proper job", as the Cornish liked to say.

'The reason I'm calling is because something has come up. A venture which I think might be worthy of your attention. Lucy is coming up to see Felicity on Thursday, can you come with her? Just for the one night. There are some people I want you to meet. Best explained when you get here.'

Sir Hugh wasn't going to discuss details over the phone and he left me mystified. Sam couldn't shed any light on it either.

'Who knows what it's about? Anyway I'm more concerned that you're going away with my wife for another night.'

'No worries.' I said. 'I'm only in it for the dinners at Flinton Hall. Angela Marriott is an ace cook.'

Clare was ambivalent. 'Just the one night? I'll stay at mum and dad's that night then and use mum's washing machine. But you'll have to make it up to me, doing mundane jobs while you're being wined and dined by the gentry.'

I promised I'd do whatever was in my power to give her pleasure. And a lot of happiness.

Lucy and I chatted on the journey up. My birthday was only a few weeks away and I told her that Gran and Gramps had booked a table for the five of us down at the Royal William Yard in Plymouth. Lucy was so easy to talk to. I mentioned my Gran's interest in birth signs and horoscopes.

'That alone will keep Gran and Clare talking half the night, although Clare says it's rubbish.'

'I tend to agree with Clare, but then it seems silly to dismiss something that has been almost mathematically worked out over hundreds of years by civilisations older than ours.' Lucy said.

'So why isn't it taught in school then?' I thought I was being smart. 'Why aren't people's birth charts drawn up at birth and their lives mapped out for them, you know, likes, dislikes, talents, types of people they would be compatible with. Seems like a roadmap for achieving happiness and fulfilment and ending loneliness.' And if that idea had been applied to my family, mum would never have bothered with my dad because they would have known they had nothing in common, and I would never have been born.

Lucy glanced at me. 'Good question and I don't know the answer. It could be that the established church thought it was all witchcraft and banned it. And the best way to knock a subject on the head is to denounce it as ridiculous or execute the practitioners. Village wise women who understood the medicinal uses of herbs and maybe a bit about the influences of the stars were persecuted, many were burned to death only a few centuries ago.'

I'd heard of things like that, the old gardeners who'd taught me had mentioned the trouble people experienced over ancient beliefs to do with companion planting and the times, according to the moon, about when things should be planted. I kept an open mind but didn't go with it myself. I'm very much a pH, water and light-availability gardener. 'But it still keeps popping up. People are still interested.' I said vaguely.

'It seems so, Flick likes to read her horoscope. But it's more complicated than that. What are you Simon? Aquarius? So under current thinking you were born under the sign of the water carrier. An air sign oddly enough. But think of the zodiac like a clock face, twelve signs, but each sign holding its own mini clock face version of the twelve signs. According to the month and day you were born on you're under the sign of Aquarius but another sign is rising on the clock face at the time of your birth. That means you could be Aquarius with Leo rising, or Scorpio or whatever. So you're not the same as the Aquarian boy sitting next to you at school because he might have Pisces rising for example. That's why you don't have the same likes, dislikes and interests. Do you follow?'

I nodded, her explanation sort of made sense but I didn't really get it. 'What do you mean about current thinking?'

'Well, there's all that faff with the changes in the calendar in the mid eighteenth century, which must have cocked things up no end for astrologers.' Lucy continued. 'You know, the change from the Julian to the Gregorian calendar.'

I stared at her blankly. 'Nope, no idea what you're talking about.'

There was a pause while Lucy concentrated on driving.

'Well the continent adopted the Gregorian calendar in the later half of the sixteenth century, but it took Britain about a hundred or more years to agree to introduce it. I think it was a popish directive as well so maybe we, as a predominantly protestant country, felt a bit awkward about it.

'Well that's nothing new is it, we never see eye to eye with Europe do we? But I'm not with you on the cock-up.' I wasn't sure I was that bothered, but it seemed polite to keep talking since I'd introduced the subject in the first place.

'From an astrologers point of view it added ten days into the calendar.' Lucy smiled wickedly. 'It drives Flick nuts when I point this out to her.'

I stared out of the window at the passing landscape. 'Clare mentioned something about her being corn on the cob, I mean, born on the cusp.'

'Oh that's a whole new ball game.' Lucy laughed at my joke and we stopped talking while she negotiated a set of cones and traffic management on the motorway. Once we were clear I spoke again.

'Talking of being born,' I began. 'My mum said I was born with a caul and veil. Have you heard of that.'

Lucy nodded. 'Of course, I was a nurse once but I've never seen it. It's quite a rare thing I think. There's a bit of old midwifery folklore, something along the lines of you seeing no evil if you were born with a veil. And the caul was thought to mean that you couldn't drown at sea. Sailors used to pay a fair price for a dried caul, they'd wear it close to their bodies as a good luck talisman.'

Gran had told me all about it but I was interested that Lucy knew the old stories. She glanced at me again.

'It explains a lot though Simon.'

'What do you mean?'

'It explains why you're such a lucky person. A caul and a veil are unusual. They are said to bestow special gifts and good fortune I think.'

'That just what my grandma says. But I'm a Thursday's child, I have far to go according to the old rhyme.' I added, just to confuse things.

Lucy didn't bat an eyelid. 'Well I certainly think you're going to go far.' And she turned the Jag into the drive up to Flinton Hall. Maybe I was about to get lucky in some way.

I had to wait until the evening before Sir Hugh would reveal his reason for inviting me up. Lucy spent the afternoon with Lady Flinton discussing the business she ran for her, and I sought out Jeff. He was easy to find, I just followed the sound of singing to the greenhouse where he was tending his lilies and alstroemerias. I could see that he was quite an expert on temperature control and growing conditions, able to bring them on early for the house. A brief grin illuminated his face when he saw me and he stopped singing. He was wearing an orange jumper with holes in the sleeves.

'What was that you were murdering?' I greeted him.

'Foreigner. "I want to know what love is", don't you know it?'

I shook my head. 'Don't think I recognised it, the way you sing Jeff.'

'I could play it for you but you've come up to swan around and enjoy the fine dining haven't you?'

'Strictly elbows off the table tonight.' I admitted, and admired his work in the greenhouse. This man knew what he was doing but there was genuine passion for the task. The greenhouse was spotless.

'Pity you don't present yourself as well as you do everything in here.' I couldn't help saying it.

Jeff was startled. 'Cheeky sod.' There was no further discussion but we went out to look at the Ladies Walk together. The weather had been awful for a few weeks in this part of the country, as Jeff explained "it blew something awful over from Wales", but the new path surfaces were settling in and had already lost that raw, new look.

'The boss had some visitors in the other day and showed them all this. I was watching from the orchard just below, doing some winter pruning. They seemed to like it, lots of arm waving and walking up and down.'

It turned out that was what Sir Hugh wanted me for. The same visitors were guests at dinner and Sir Hugh made the introductions during pre-dinner cocktails in the garden room. He fancied himself as a mixologist and had given me what he called a Lynchburg Lemonade, his choice, not mine. Half way through it I realised I was drinking a sizeable shot of whisky.

'Nigel, I'd like you to meet Simon Sherwell, the talented young garden designer whose work you were admiring the other day.'

I shook hands with an ascetic looking man of indeterminate age impeccably dressed for the evening. 'Nigel Reid-Ross.'

He had long white fingers, very dry hands and wore a monogrammed signet ring on his little finger. I was glad I was wearing a new jacket which Clare had spotted in the sales at what she now called "Your special outfitters". The same assistant had served me and recognised us. The jacket was a dull blueish brushed material, not velvet and not cord. I'd got dark trousers on and a very pale blue shirt but I couldn't compete with his bow tie, in fact I'd chosen not to wear a tie. I'd talked to Clare about my sartorial fears but she'd dismissed them.

'Just be yourself Simon. You're the one with the talent and that's what they want. Don't even try to dress like them, they've gone through life having to dress for occasions and they all look like they've got pokers up their bums. You're free of all that, and anyway, look at that television gardener, Monty Don. He wears the same old clothes wherever he goes, he looks like the man coming to mend the boiler. But he's the one with the star quality. And so are you.'

Nigel Reid-Ross gave me the quick once over and introduced me to his wife, a plump brunette wearing a satin evening blouse and midi skirt ensemble with ruffles and pleats. 'My wife,

Cecily.' Whilst he was a man of few words his wife made up for it.

'Mr Sherwell what a pleasure it is to meet you, I saw your garden drawings the other day, your work is exquisite, it comes right off the page. I gather you designed for Lady Felicity before she married Sir Hugh. And I understand you've been engaged to do another design at Trelerric House, I visited last summer and saw Lady Felicity's exhibition there. Quite magnificent. I can see at once that you have artistic qualities ...'

It was like standing under a warm fountain, her words cascaded around me and bounced off the floor and all I had to do was look interested and nod my head. Lucy interrupted with a cocktail for Cecily and calmly indicated the table holding canapés. Lady Flinton glided past me. 'I think she likes you Simon,' she said softly while Cecily was distracted by the food and then, in a louder voice, 'Ah, our other guests have arrived.'

Another couple were introduced, an enthusiastic moustached man with a pump-action handshake, and his wife, a slightly taller woman with nicely cut grey hair and some flashy jewellery. Jeremy and Catherine Stewart. There was lots of friendly chatter going on, these people all knew each other and Lucy drew me to one side to keep me company.

'Do you have any idea who these people are and why I'm here?' I asked her.

'Best let Sir Hugh have his fun I think. It's meant to be a surprise, although it's also a bit of a challenge.'

Before I could ask her what she meant Sir Hugh called for attention.

'Everyone, I'd like to thank Simon for coming up from Cornwall at such short notice, however this is urgent business. Simon,' he turned to me, glass in hand, every inch the gentleman. 'Jeremy is CEO of Western Counties Events, and Cecily is Head of Shows.'

I had absolutely no idea what he was talking about and wondered how much whisky I'd drunk.

'With a team of talented people they are responsible for putting on the Moulton Shows at the Western Counties Showground. That's horticultural, agricultural and farming interests represented. The RHS is involved in the horticultural side of things of course.'

At last, I understood something. He was talking about the Royal Horticultural Society, the gods and gurus of gardening to the likes of Sam Latchley and me.

'The thing is Mr Sherwell, we have a vacancy for an emerging garden designer for the show in May.' Cecily interrupted. 'Normally candidates go through a submissions procedure and the slots are all filled before a given deadline. Unfortunately one of the candidates has had to withdraw for personal reasons, very unfortunate circumstances, health reasons.' She paused and collected her thoughts. 'I'm looking for a replacement, we can't disappoint the public who pay to see show gardens and emerging talent. When I saw your drawings and the work you've started here I thought you might be a good candidate.'

I had the feeling that I was standing at the other end of the telescope and seeing things with a peculiar perspective. From what little I knew, I suspected that strings were being pulled, influence was being brought to bear, and that rules were being very slightly bent. They were all looking at me expectantly.

'Tell me more.' I said.

Angela had served us with a stunning beef wellington and Sir Hugh was, as usual, generous with the wine. 'I'm trying this, a Shiraz Carignan from South Australia. See what you think. My wine merchant recommended it.'

Three glasses later I was feeling very happy. Why wouldn't these nice people want me to design a garden for their show? I'd talked classic cars to Nigel and impressed him with the mark-up I'd made on my campervan and I'd talked about roses to Catherine. There was something about food and wine by candlelight which was utterly charming and I hadn't spilled the soup down my shirt. I'd also discovered a trick to good manners, by politely waiting for other people to start I could observe the correct selection of knives, forks and spoons. I fancied the imperceptible delay gave me an aura of sophistication and respectability. But then again, the alcohol intake might have been giving me ideas.

Much later, after the guests had gone and the ladies had retired upstairs I sat with Sir Hugh warming a venerable brandy between my hands. Sir Hugh had been explaining that he was going to act as my client for the show, sponsor me and also cover any fees and that I'd just got to get on with the application and garden design submission.

As he talked part of my alcohol-fuzzed brain was grappling with a question and not for the first time either. Sir Hugh had given me a handsome payment by cheque, insisting that this was solely payment for the garden design concept and drawings and nothing to do with the physical labour involved in building the garden, labour that Jeff was helping me with. I remembered him raising his glass across the room at the wedding reception, the night Sam and Lucy gave us the keys to the Coach House. And now this. Why was he being so damn nice to me?

FIFTEEN

I asked Clare the same question on Valentines Day. Clare had no idea either. 'Mum always said Sir Hugh was a decent man. He's getting on though isn't he? Perhaps he's going through an altruistic phase in his dotage, wanting to give things away before he croaks. Although he's got a son who will inherit.' She was delighted with the news though. 'But you're right, it does seem like a bit more than a stroke of good luck.'

We'd gone to an event at The Wheal and while we were at the bar before the meal I was able to introduce her to my friends, Andy and his girlfriend Marie, Steve and Liz Bradley, Rob and Su Williams. The builder, the carpenter and the blacksmith, well, they were three characters you'd meet if you were about to tell a joke in a pub wouldn't you. And they were all getting together to do work on Cherryfields Cottage for Sam and Lucy. The place was packed with couples and I noticed my ex-girlfriend Chloe Baxter with a man I didn't recognise. Chloe smiled across the room at me and I saw her eyes assessing Clare.

'Old friend of yours?' Clare murmured, not missing a thing and placing a slight emphasis on the word "old".'

'Old schoolfriend. We dated for a while, that's all.' If that's what you could call that hot summer of long walks over the moor and sweaty al fresco fumblings.

'Was she special? Only she seems quite interested in you now.'

'We were just kids. And I didn't like her extensive collection of dolls and teddybears.' That was true, the one time I'd gained access to her bedroom when her folks were out I'd been put off by all those little beady eyes watching me.

'Is that her father she's with? Only he seems a bit old for her.'

'Are you being catty Clare?' I was amused. 'Anyway I've no idea. She went away to uni. Been gone quite a few years now.'

'Well she's not wearing a ring.' Clare said, and casually placing the hand showing her engagement ring on my neck, pulled my face down and gave me a gentle but lingering kiss.

We spent the evening enjoying each other's company and the outrageous sentimentality of the occasion. The landlord, or more likely his wife, had decorated the pub with red hearts and pink streamers and there were red candle holders on the tables which were scattered with tiny red foil hearts. I loved being out with Clare and showing her off, watching the sparkle in her eyes. You could see everyone checking out other peoples' partners; I was more than pleased with mine and we left the pub with our fingers entwined. I thought life could hardly get any better.

My birthday was two days later and Gramps drove the five of us down to Plymouth in horizontal rain. I'd begged them not to make a fuss but Clare had ignored me and I had to sit in the chair with a ridiculously large black and gold happy birthday balloon attached to it. At least it was masculine colours. I'd also asked them not to spend money on presents, explaining that a small contribution to our savings would be best as we were now putting everything we could into a house fund. Clare had designed a spreadsheet listing outgoings, essentials, incomings and so on. She was an efficient money manager and I teased her about her counting house system.

'The rhyme should say that the queen was in the counting house counting up their money.'

'And eating bread and honey.' Clare responded quickly. 'The queen always gets that. But what does it leave you with Simon?'

Gazing at her lovely face I felt myself going soppy. 'You, it leaves me with you. That's all I want.'

Mum and Clare insisted we had a glass of champagne to start the birthday celebrations. Gran got all giggly before she'd even had a sip.

'It's so nice to have an opportunity to celebrate as family.' Gran said. 'First you and Clare getting engaged, now your birthday, and it's Clare's birthday in May. Although I expect you'll want to celebrate with your own family Clare, we can't have you all to ourselves, much as we'd like to.'

'And there's Simon's other news mum, that's worth a bottle of bubbly, or preferably something else. Champagne is funny stuff, a bit on the dry side for me.' Mum was sipping from her glass and pulling a face.

'What other news is that Simon?' Gran asked, peering at me over the menu. 'We've not seen much of you since Christmas.'

That was an understatement, being so busy I'd not seen them at all. I talked briefly about the Moulton Show submission and they were impressed. 'So I'm lucky that I could do all the paperwork while the weather is crap and all my outdoor jobs are on hold. It came along just at the right time.' I concluded, making it all appear so easy.

During the silence which followed as we studied our menus I thought back over those few weeks and reached for Clare's hand. It had been a strange experience. I'd never felt such pressure or been under such strain. Coming up with a design for a show garden, even one for a small space, wasn't as easy as I'd expected. I'd sat in the Coach House for a day, flicking through the book she'd bought me, filling the waste basket with paper and becoming increasingly irritated with my lack of imagination. Eventually I'd gone to collect Clare from work and she'd immediately noticed the tension.

'Simon, you're as twitchy as a bag of fleas and I've seen enough of those in the small animal clinic today. It's not like you at all, what's up?'

All my frustration had poured out and as I talked to her it immediately became obvious what I was missing.

'I really need to stand in a place and see it, and feel it. With this it's just a paper exercise. A blank sheet, and I feel blank inside. Does that make sense?'

Clare agreed. 'So you need to find somewhere outside that's about the same size as the small garden you have to design, pace around in it and imagine what might look good there.'

She'd hit the nail on the head and I said so. 'I just can't do it with my arse on a chair, I have to feel the ground under my feet first. Going up to Moulton is out of the question but they've given me a plan of the showground and where my plot is. I need to orientate myself, I need a decent map.'

After dinner we'd spent an hour using her laptop and looking at the terrain on Google maps. The following day I'd gone into a corner of one of the sheep fields at Home Farm and worked things out. At last there'd been that rush of ideas with the curious falling sensation I'd experienced on my other designs. As though I was looking from above and flying down to settle in the completed picture. Mentally I described it as "Clare's flying dream", anything connected to her seemed to work.

'And Sir Hugh Flinton personally invited you to go up there and meet these people? That's extraordinary and very generous of him.' Gramps said out of the blue, having made his choices. 'What dates are the show?'

Clare and I glanced at each other. We'd already had this conversation. 'It clashes with my birthday, but we'll find a way round that.' Clare said lightly. 'It's exciting and very important for Simon, so I might go up for the day and visit the show anyway. Simon gets a couple of tickets as a perk.'

'We could go up together Clare, and share the driving.' Mum said. 'I've got to see what my boy is doing, it's a very special occasion after all.'

I sat there, enjoying their lively faces and watching Gran and Gramps watching them. The sense of family closeness was tangible and I got a lump in my throat. Taking a swig of champagne didn't help, I sneezed, coughed and choked simultaneously but it made everyone laugh.

Over dinner Gramps changed the subject. 'I've got some news of a different sort that might interest you. We've been going to the local history group, they do talks at the village hall once a month over the winter and cover all sorts of topics, mining, farming, architecture, stuff like that.'

'But all of it with a local flavour, for us here in South East Cornwall.' Gran interrupted. 'Go on Bill, tell them what you discovered.'

Gramps rolled his eyes. 'I will if you'll stop your nattering, wife. Where was I? Oh yes, your Sally Evans has had some input. Very nice lady she is. Liz Bradley, that's Steve the carpenter's wife isn't it, well, she contacted Sally about local family research ...'

'Oh get to the point Bill, you're going all round the houses.'

I smiled, this was perfectly normal behaviour.

'Well, between them they've come up with family records from before 1841.'

'What's so important about 1841?' Clare asked.

'That was the first census date, started just after Queen Victoria came to the throne,' I told her. 'Carried out every ten years ever since. Gramps has traced our family, the Sherwell's, back to that date. Before 1841 you have to go into parish records and find what the local priest recorded. Something like that anyway.' I looked over to Gramps. 'So what did you find out then? We're not Cornish after all?'

Gramps shook his head. 'Dunno about that, but I found that our name was different. The 1841 census has us down as Sherwell, but your Miss Evans found the same Christian names in a parish birth register, but the surname was spelled as Sherill. She said it was all to do with phonetics.'

'I thought Cheryl was a girl's name?' Mum said, confused.

'It's about the way words are spoken or how they sound.' Clare said, she was fascinated. 'Dialect and stuff.'

'Exactly,' Gramps agreed. 'She said we could be recorded as Sherill, Sherrill, Sherrille, Showell.' He counted and spelled the various alternatives on his fingers.

'Oh I see, that makes sense.' Mum nodded. 'We get misspelled letters at the sorting office all the time, names and roads have to be deciphered. Which reminds me Clare, your surname is unusual. Do you know where your dad's family come from?'

Clare smiled her little cat smile. 'Palfrey, it's a special sort of horse, ridden by ladies in medieval times. My dad's family came down from Worcestershire generations ago, they were ostlers and horse traders I gather. I think I get my love of animals from them. Anyway they married Cornish girls and stayed here.'

'Moulton is in Worcestershire.' I smiled at her. 'You should do some family research of your own while you're up visiting the show. You should ask your dad if there's anything to see or any place to visit.'

Clare shook her head. 'I'm seeing you, your garden and the show, that's all that interests me.'

Mum had been thinking. 'Can I ask something?' She had that "mum" expression on her face. 'How are you going to build a show garden, you can't do it by yourself Simon. You need a team of people.'

For once I was way ahead of her. 'I've got help. Jeff Hartley, he's Sir Hugh's gardener, Ian Marriott, that's Sir Hugh's man of all work, and Sam Latchley. My boss at Trelerric House.'

There were gasps from everyone but Clare, she already knew.

'Your boss is going to help you build your show garden? A landed Latchley?' Mum was astounded.

'I always knew Simon was born lucky. He's got Jupiter well aspected in his chart.' Gran giggled into her glass. She raised it to me. 'Cheers Simon, and well done. Happy Birthday.'

In fact Sam had offered almost immediately when I'd given him the news about the show garden. I suspected Lucy had already known something and had told him, but he was as excited about the opportunity as I was.

'Brilliant Simon, I can get to stay at Flinton Hall as well, ravish Lucy in the evenings in that four poster bed she sleeps in and get to eat the marvellous grub you've been raving about.' Sam grinned wolfishly. 'And then there's all that other stuff going on with the show, meeting the other gardeners and building stuff. It'll be great. Trelerric is terrific but sometimes you need to see something else. It'll be like a holiday.'

'A busman's holiday.' I said. 'But yes, we can have some fun, I hope.'

'What are you calling the garden? They have to have names these days don't they?' Sam asked.

'I'm calling it "The Space Beyond". There's a book I've got, Clare bought it for me and it describes the Japanese style of garden as "the space beyond the everyday world" I liked the description.'

'Not bad.' Sam agreed. 'Poetic.'

I glanced at him sharply but he wasn't taking the piss.

'What plants are you using.' Sam was definitely a plantsman, whereas I was discovering I was a more of a landscape man. It was why we were such a good team, our skill sets complimented each other. It was a bonus that our humour clicked as well.

'Plants to reflect the colours in Clare's dress.' I replied absently. 'It's a garden in light shade.'

'Come again?'

'I'd got the design and the reasons for it sorted out in my head but I was having awful trouble working out the planting and the task had gone into the evening, which I don't like because Clare's home. It's not fair to expect her to sit quietly, especially when she loves to talk about her day to me. Anyway, I was lost for inspiration and Clare was sorting her things out in the wardrobe. Have you noticed how women do that sort of thing?'

Sam smiled. 'Nesting behaviour.' He commented. 'The sign of a contented woman. You must be doing something right old son.' He didn't snigger or pull a suggestive face. Some things were sacred after all.

'Well, Clare took the dress out she'd worn the night we got engaged and I was staring across the room at her, remembering how she looked ...'

I was watching Clare looking through her clothes and laying things out on the bed. She took the dress out she wore the night we got engaged. 'Hold that up,' I said. 'No against you.' She did as I asked. 'It's lovely, all those golds, reds and heather colours and a little bit of black. Lovely against your dark hair and your colouring.' I was fascinated by the play of light over the fabric, like the first sunlight of the morning glinting through ... 'That's it, I've got it!' I had my eureka moment.

Pulling myself back to the present I explained it to Sam.

'Stipa gigantea grouped with Verbena bonariensis, that's the gold and purple, underplanted with black Ophiopogon nigrescens and Japanese blood grass, so that's a touch of red, plus a group of red Canna lilies. Bronze Heuchera, and Hakonechloa Macra Aureola to add some golden green light.' I was counting the plants on my fingers. 'Jeff already has the Verbena coming on early in his greenhouse and the grasses are easy to source. And there's a guy down near St Austell who has promised me the Golden Oats, the Stipa, if I list him as a plant supplier. And he says he will have some lovely golden edged Hostas as well. Oh, and I'd like to borrow that little twisted white Pine that I pruned, the one in the pot.' I grinned at Sam. 'Look what working with you has done to me, I sound like a bloody textbook.'

'And that's all inspired by the dress Clare wore at Christmas?' Sam said and gave a long drawn out whistle. 'Mate, you are streets outside my league. But I love the restricted palette. Very arty.'

That was what I hoped the judges would say. Judges, my blood ran cold. What the hell was I thinking of? Privately I was seriously worried that I was going in way too deep, running before I could walk, the cliches were endless. And I desperately didn't want to come out the other end looking like a complete and utter prat.

'So tell me about these other guys who are going to help you build the garden. Who are they?'

I was sitting in the kitchen at mum's house and she was curious about what I was doing. Funny how I no longer thought of the place as home. I told her about Jeff and Ian, explaining that Ian was happily married to Angela and that Jeff's wife had left him for another bloke several years ago.

'Shit happens.' Mum commented without rancour.

'Mum.' I said. 'Mum, tell me the truth. Has it been awful for you? I mean, it wasn't a barrel of laughs with my father buggering off when I was a baby. I know you've worked hard and there've been compromises. But you're a pretty nice looking woman. You don't look your age. Why haven't you found someone else after all this time?'

'Who's to say I didn't?' Mum replied evasively. 'And thanks for the compliment.'

I was all ears. 'Did you? I mean, have you?'

'There was a man I was soft on, a few years ago now. He was very attractive. I liked him a lot. Told me he and his wife were having difficulties, she'd met up with an old flame at a school reunion apparently.'

'What did you do?'

'I had some hopes for a while and then I dumped him. If he could cheat on his wife he could cheat on me. He was doing precisely that in fact.'

'How did you come to that conclusion?' I was fascinated, seeing a side of my mum I'd not seen before.

'I went to the pictures one afternoon with my friend from the tai chi class. You were about sixteen, old enough to be left to your own devices. You were seeing Chloe at the time. I'm glad you didn't stay with her, I always had a feeling she'd take after her neurotic bitch of a mother. I never liked her when we were at school together. Anyway, he was two rows in front of me and breathing down the ear of a redhead, not his wife.'

'Bastard.' I said, part of me wondering why she didn't care for Chloe's mother. 'How did you know it wasn't his wife?'

'No man behaves like that with his wife in public unless they're just married, and he'd been married ten years and with two kids. I was disappointed Simon. I've never said it before but your dad couldn't keep it in his trousers either.'

'Well, you did once say that he still wanted to play jack-the-lad as well as being married.'

'Oh, he didn't want to be married. We only got married because you were on the way. To be fair he tried, for a bit anyway, to get the hang of marriage and fatherhood. But he wasn't suited. And when he left he never asked for a penny of what he'd put into the house. He left us with a roof over our heads even though it was a struggle for me to pay for it.'

'Where did he go?' It was a question I'd never asked before.

'I don't know. He vanished. I've never heard a thing from him or from his father. I got no support whatsoever.'

I remembered her saying once that my paternal grandfather had been a widower and gone off with another woman.

'But you've still not found a guy to be with.' A thought occurred to me. 'Mum, I wouldn't be offended. I'd rather you had company and happiness. You bloody deserve it.' To my surprise I found I was getting emotional.

Mum squeezed my hand briefly. 'I shall remember that. Now, let's get on with business shall we?'

I'd almost forgotten the reason I was there. Clare and mum had decided that in order to appreciate their trip to Moulton it would be a good idea to find a B&B to stay in since it was clear that the Flinton's expected me to stay at Flinton Hall with them and with Sam and Lucy. I'd wondered if that invitation could include my fiancee and my mother but they had both said a very emphatic "no" to the idea.

'Don't even ask, don't suggest it, please. I couldn't bear it, I'd be so nervous Simon. I'm sure they're very kind but they're toffs and it wouldn't suit me or them.' Mum had been adamant.

Clare said she felt the same. 'I'd rather be independent and relaxed, and anyway I get on with your mum. It'll be nice for both of us to have an adventure.'

Mum and I spent some time on the internet looking for suitable accommodation, but everywhere we found was either already booked or they refused, understandably, to take a booking for one night. It was too much work doing a room change and better for business to take bookings for a number of nights. I hadn't realised that the show was so popular. Dispirited we gave up.

'Lucy has some connections in the area,' I told mum. 'Let me ask her if she's got any ideas.'

Before I could contact Lucy I got a call from Jeff Hartley, he was sorting out a delivery from the same rock supplier we'd used previously and needed a particular contact number for the show ground. Things had to be ordered well in advance, in precise amounts and delivered at specific times and to the right location. He was a brilliant organiser and I thanked him.

'Wish you could do the same for Clare and my mother, we're having awful trouble finding a place for them to bunk down for a night. The show clashes with Clare's birthday as well. It's a pain.'

Jeff's reply surprised me. 'They're welcome to stay at my place. I've got a three-bed semi with a downstairs loo as well as the bathroom upstairs. And I've got the ensuite on my floor so they wouldn't be intruding.'

I was so surprised I didn't say anything. To be honest I had horrible visions of my house-proud mother and my equally fastidious fiancee stepping cautiously over Jeff's discarded underwear and disreputable jumpers. Sometimes it was a curse having such a vivid and creative imagination. There was a chuckle over the phone line.

'Surprised you have I Sherwell? Let me put it like this, you've been in my car and you've seen the way I keep the greenhouse. How would you describe them?'

'Surprisingly clean and tidy,' I answered. 'Worryingly and obsessively neat if you want the truth.' I found myself smiling into the phone.

'That's how I live boy, shipshape and decent. Only my working clothes don't come up to your poncey standards you cheeky beggar. Anyway, I mean it, they're welcome to stay over as long as they like. They won't be disappointed in the facilities. But I'm not what you'd call a cook. They'll have to self-cater.'

'Thanks Jeff, appreciate it. I'll let you know pronto.'

Mum had sat quietly, earwigging the conversation. 'That was very kind of him.' There was a look of profound amusement on her face.

'He's a nice bloke. We get on okay. What do you think?'

'I think we've not got any other option. If Clare's up for it then so am I. It might be fun. I just hope he hasn't got a dog.'

Of course, mum was a postwoman, dogs were not her favourite beasts.

To my relief Clare was okay with the idea. She was snuggled up against me on our little sofa, the woodstove was glowing and we were finishing the bottle of wine we'd shared with our pasta. I'd discovered I really liked home made pesto swirled into the sauce, sprinkled with flakes of parmesan cheese and enjoyed with a hearty red wine.

'Can't be any worse than camping can it? I hate camping. At least there'll be hot water and a flushing toilet.'

She was such a practical girl. I texted Jeff with the answer. *"Expect invasion of curious Cornish females. Be prepared, they miss nothing!"*

He replied. *"Gottit. Chuck out the crap, de-louse, all will be ticketyboo".*

I laughed out loud.

A couple of days later Sam and I were busy on the Magnolia Walk again. I was pleased with the shape of everything and Sam had made a rustic backless bench out of planks to fit into a couple of suitably placed stones I'd selected. I'd already been impressed by his handiwork in building the slate seat and learned a lot. It was really helping, like doing a practise run for the Moulton Show.

'How did you do that?' I asked him, running my hand over the curves of the wood.

'I used Steve's jigsaw. He'd left it all set up in the cottage, the work there is cracking along. He did give me a lesson beforehand, it's just a couple of manky old scaffolding planks I found in one of dad's barns. Recut, shaped and sanded they've got a new life now.' He'd protected them with a few coats of clear matt yacht varnish.

'That's just what I need to finish the job at Flinton Hall. Got any more unwanted planks?'

We used it as an excuse to walk over to the barn and have a rummage. Honestly, there was all sorts of good stuff in there, discarded old machinery and garden items like a lawn roller, things that were now becoming trendy and sought after. I was nosing about like a ferret down a rabbit hole when a voice called from the open door.

'Boys?'

'Yes mother dear?' Sam responded in a high pitched voice.

Jane Latchley waited until we appeared from the gloom and she laughed at the sight of us. 'You grubby little horrors. I don't want to know what you're doing in there.'

Sam and I looked at each other, he had a really big cobweb down one sleeve and something on his hair. I guessed I must look the same. We gave each other cheesy grins.

'What can we do for you Mrs Latchley?' I asked.

'It's Sally, she's called to say she's found some interesting facts and would like to tell us all about them.'

'Oh no, not another lecture.' Sam groaned. 'There's a limit to how far I can go with bills of lading and bushels of bollocks.'

'It's family history Sam, you should be interested. But this involves Simon too, apparently. She's asked if you could both be there, and the Pencraddoc's are invited as well. I'm expecting you to bring Lucy and Clare. Saturday at two o'clock. There will be snacky things so your blood sugar won't nose-dive Simon.'

That evening I told Clare. 'Remember those three wishes you were talking about in the back garden last summer? One of them was about being able to see into the past. Well we're invited to Home Farm to do just that on Saturday afternoon. Sally Evans apparently has something to tell us all.'

'Why us? We're nothing to do with the Latchley family.'

'I know, but she wants us there. It's an invitation to us as a couple.' I added, seeing her dubious face.

'Oh, okay. Well, unless we go we won't know.'

SEVENTEEN

Sam's father, Tim Latchley, opened the door to us when we arrived at Home Farm. It was quite nice, walking up together from the Coach House, holding hands and feeling like we belonged.

'Ah, the young lovers. Welcome, nice to see you Clare. Are you comfortable enough in the Coach House? If there's anything needs doing you must tell me, or Sam. On reflection it's best to tell me since Sam's got his head full with the rebuilding of Cherryfields Cottage.'

We both made polite noises and were ushered into the sitting room. Sally was talking to Alice Marquand, Sam was holding little Grace's hands and walking about with her feet on his, making her squeal a bit, and Alice's husband Jon was sitting down with their toddler, Tom, on his lap, who was clutching a toy tractor and looking wide-eyed at all the adults. I heard a vehicle pulling up outside and looked through the window, Daniel Pencraddoc was getting out of a blue Audi Q7 and I saw the lovely Fiona busily unstrapping their children. I greeted them as they came through the door to join us.

'That's a beast you're driving these days Daniel, managed to find something with attitude that takes the whole family then?'

'Once an Audi man always an Audi man Simon. Good to see you, how's things these days?'

We shook hands and I introduced him to Clare, telling him of our good news. She smiled up at him shyly. It's not everyday you meet a millionaire whose face appears in the Sunday supplements.

'Engaged, well congratulations. I hope he's worthy of you Clare. I still haven't worked out how to do that yet. Fiona and I have two children now, we're too busy to even think of getting engaged, let alone married.'

I noticed Clare looking at their children, Fiona was holding a baby boy on her hip and jiggling him up and down and Flora

Rose was a heart-stoppingly pretty little girl with her mother's mahogany coloured hair and her father's chocolate brown eyes. She and Grace were standing solemnly examining each other in the middle of the room, then Grace took Flora's hand and they left the room, clearly intent on more important things. Alice didn't miss a thing and went off to check what they were up to. Apparently that involved putting Jane's jewellery box somewhere out of reach.

Daniel was interested to hear that the old gang were now working on Sam and Lucy's new cottage and said he occasionally saw them in The Wheal. 'And have you heard that Rob and Su Williams are finally going to be parents? They've had some bad luck and I gather Su opted for IVF. She's being very careful and Rob is treating her like a piece of fine china, but, crossed fingers, she's going to be okay this time.'

I told him I didn't know. 'Clare and I were at the Valentine's night at The Wheal, we saw them there. They didn't say anything.'

'Probably being cautious.' Daniel replied. 'God, I sound like the village fishwife gossiping about the hatched, matched and despatched.'

'You're obviously in touch with your feminine side,' Clare said. 'But perhaps we won't let on that we know or that you told us.'

Daniel was smiling at Clare and there was a lot of friendly buzz. Tim was handing out tea and coffee, Clare opted for a diet Coke, Jane was saying something about stronger refreshments later. I looked around at all these comfortable people and wondered where and how I fitted in. Apparently it was up to Sally to tell us.

Everyone found a place to sit, Sam opted for a cushion on the floor and leaned against the chair Lucy was sitting in so I followed suit where Clare was sitting on the sofa with the Marquand's. It meant I wasn't looking directly at Sam, which was good because I didn't want him to crack me up again. Sally had brought a dining chair in to sit on by the fireplace so that she could address us all from a position of authority. Once again she introduced herself, even though we all knew who she was and where she worked. It was an academic thing, and it set the scene as we all fell quiet.

'Thanks for coming. The Trelerric papers are proving extremely interesting as I'm going to reveal.' Sally began, checking some notes she was holding.

She went on to talk about palaeography and deciphering Tudor English. 'I'm fine with what's known as "secretary hand" and I'm familiar with the abbreviations or word contractions which they used to save space on precious parchment or expensive velum. But English language wasn't standardised until the 18th century and words and names were often spelt phonetically, as they sounded.'

Like my surname, I thought, remembering what Gramps had talked about at my birthday meal. I felt Clare squeeze my shoulder, no doubt she was thinking the same thing, and I surreptitiously moved my arm and squeezed her ankle in return.

'In fact names were mis-spelled even into the nineteenth century.' She was getting into her stride. 'For instance my own three times great-grandmother's first name was Martha, but I eventually found her in the first census listed as Murtha because according to her Nottinghamshire dialect that's how she pronounced her own name.'

There was a little bit of shuffling and Fiona's baby yawned and gurgled. I saw Sam drop his head comically sideways onto Lucy's knee and she tapped him warningly on the shoulder. Sally began talking about developing the bigger picture and not just recording the detail for her PhD. She said she was referring to documents lodged at the County Record Office where she could glimpse the people behind the history and she began to get quite animated.

'So it's more than the information we have here in the Latchley Book and Chronicle.' Jane Latchley said meaningfully, looking hard at Sam.

'Yes. But before I discuss the people, there's a small mystery which I think I can shed some light on which concerns Daniel and Fiona's property, Darleystones. If I'm right Daniel, the exact age of your house isn't established and it was, until recently, incorrectly assumed that the staircase dated the property.'

Daniel nodded, his senses all focussed on Sally.

'The staircase, for those of you who have never seen it, is a rather fine dark wood with a newel post carved with acanthus leaves and the side panels below the bannisters carved with scroll work. To the trained eye it's clearly of the Tudor period, but that ran from 1485 to 1603 so there's over one hundred years to play with. Darleystones has date-stones incorporated into the original build which place it at more than one hundred years later than the end of the Tudor period.'

'1733 is the first date.' Daniel confirmed, for everyone's benefit.

Sally nodded. 'In the kitchen next door there is a dark wood table, identically carved. I took some photographs and made some measurements of the scroll work and sent them to Daniel, and to a colleague of mine in London who specialises in Tudor period furniture. He's pretty sure they're linked, perhaps by the same hand. Of course we'd need a dendrochronologist to identify and date the wood. But at Darleystones, where Daniel and Fiona have had quite a lot of renovation done, there was a feeling that the staircase was not an original fixture.'

I was interested, I'd been involved in that renovation about four years ago and enjoyed my time working there.

'And during my research at the Cornwall Record Office I came across a document, quite by chance, because I'm not looking at the Georgian period, which detailed a transaction in 1815 between a Mr Edward John Latchley of Trelerric and a Mr

David Penive of Darleystones in which a fine oak and French walnut staircase was purchased.'

'David Penive was my ancestor on my mother's side.' Daniel said. 'He came into money when minerals were found beneath his land. There's an 1812 date-stone showing his marriage, which is when we think he extended and improved his property. That makes sense then Sally, he obviously bought my staircase from Trelerric. But why was it taken out of this house?'

'The Georgian period is when Trelerric House was extended and updated.' Sam said. 'I guess it must have been a redundant item.'

'But of sufficient quality and worth to recycle.' Alice added. 'Fascinating, I'd like to see it.'

'You must all come over, the house loves having people in it.' Fiona said. 'It tells us stories.'

Jane Latchley looked both intrigued and mystified but I smiled, that was a typical Fiona take on things. She could see beyond the everyday and mundane.

'What's so special about French walnut?' Clare asked.

'A very good question.' Sally nodded at Clare approvingly. 'I later found some very faded and rather worse for wear documents relating to the importation of French timber for the Manor of Trelerric by one Johannes de Lachele.'

There was a change in the atmosphere. The Latchley's all reacted as though Pan the Piper had blown a string of notes only they could hear.

'Go on.' Tim Latchley breathed.

'Lachele imported oak and French walnut in the year 1545. Henry the Eighth died in January 1547 if you need to put that into context.'

'So de Lachele, our ancestor, was building Trelerric House in the mid-sixteenth century then?' Sam said, rubbing the bridge of his nose between his index finger and thumb. 'Funny, I always had the feeling it was a bit earlier than that.'

'Well, Johannes de Lachele didn't build Trelerric House.' Sally said, her eyes sparkling. 'It already existed.'

'What?' The Latchley's spoke in one word.

'Thomas Trelerric built Trelerric House. That's why it's called the Trelerric lands in some of your documents.'

'The prefix "Tre" means a settlement or homestead in Cornish.' Alice said. 'So Trelerric means the "home of Lerric" or something. I've always wondered why it wasn't called Lachele House, or Manor, or Hall.'

'So who was Thomas Trelerric?' Sam asked. 'I've never heard of him. In fact who was Lerric? And did he have a sidekick called Lernie? Will we ever know?'

Tim groaned at Sam's pathetic attempt at a joke but Sally ignored it.

'Well, I can tell you that Thomas Trelerric was a successful merchant, trading out of Plymouth. He's also your ancestor. So your connection with this piece of land goes back a little further than you thought.'

'Been there, experienced that.' I heard Daniel Pencraddoc say to Fiona.

'No way! How come?' Tim Latchley thumped his fist down onto his thigh.

'Because Johannes de Lachele married Elizabeth Trelerric, the daughter of Thomas and his wife, Joan.'

'My god. Lachele was a bloody fortune hunter then.' Tim Latchley choked with laughter.

There was a moment of badinage and banter while Sally let the news sink in. Alice was particularly thrilled because she'd called her son Thomas.

'I must have known somehow, that the name Thomas was right for the house.'

'Coincidence darling, just coincidence, but a nice one.' Her husband Jon was patting her thigh.

'Well, I must say Sally, you've found out some very interesting things. We didn't know this because the Latchley

Chronicle which records the Latchley family birth, marriage and death details starts in the very early seventeenth century, with the first use of the Latchley name. I'm guessing it might have been de Lachele's grandson, the Chronicle starts with a reference to "our esteemed ancestor Johannes de Lachele" but this is the first time I've heard the name of his wife or of her parents. And I've always thought it curious that there are no gravestones or any records that I know of to indicate where they are buried.' Tim said, leaning back and stretching his legs.

'The study of burial sites is something I can't help you with.' Sally said. 'I'm vaguely aware of old burials having new burials placed above them, it's why some churchyards have walls around them and are higher than the road outside. Graves lose definition over the centuries and of course de Lachele might not even have died here. He could have died at sea or in another port.'

'That's left us all feeling very grave about the subject.' Sam lightened the atmosphere and earned another cuff round the head from Lucy.

'So Thomas Trelerric was a local merchant? How interesting.' Jane said, thinking out loud.

I got the impression that Jane thought the revelations were over, but Sally clearly had more information to impart. I don't know about everyone else in the room but I was feeling ready for a Saturday afternoon cider. To Sally however, her subject was more sustaining than food or drink. She raised a hand to call for attention.

'I haven't established how far back your ancestor Thomas Trelerric actually goes, and that's not really part of my PhD anyway. Perhaps that's something to be pursued by a genealogist in due course. I do know that he traded out of Sutton Pool, which is the Plymouth harbour area, and that he had a house in Plymouth, a suitable base for business I suppose, being nearer the quays and docks and warehouses.'

'Sutton is still a constituency isn't it?' Jon said to no-one in particular. I recalled Sam once saying that Jonathan Marquand fancied himself as an MP.

'We once owned property in Plymouth then?' Tim Latchley said. 'Probably lost that in death duties as well!'

'So we have Thomas Trelerric building this place, Johannes de Lachele marrying his daughter and importing French walnut to make improvements to the house, what else?' Sam summarised.

'The walnut was valuable, it was to make furniture, possibly as a wedding gift for Elizabeth, we'll never know.'

'I don't think I would have been happy with a table as a wedding gift from Tim.' Jane laughed. 'Although it is a lovely table. I shall look at it with new eyes.'

'I'm just looking forward to seeing it.' Daniel rolled his eyes. 'But didn't they grow walnuts on the banks of the Tamar? I thought I read once that barrels of walnuts went as voyage provisions for the sailors.'

Sally shrugged. 'What I do know,' she continued, 'is that de Lachele was also a merchant. There's a description of a ship he invested in, it seems he traded in spices, cloth, anything he could obtain from the continent which was rare or high value and worth a lot of money in England. This is where my PhD comes in. I have reason to believe he traded all along the south coast of England, back across to the French ports, along to the Netherlands and back again, probably into London, before repeating the process.'

'A coaster.' I muttered. 'A coastal trader. My Gramps has talked about it, when I was a boy out fishing with him. He used to tell me stories, I thought he'd made them up.'

'Quite.' Sally said, while Sam turned and grinned at me.

'And think about his name for a moment.' Sally was still talking. 'The name Johannes is common in the Netherlands. Whereas his surname, de Lachele, suggests perhaps a Norman-French origin. It could be that this was a highly intelligent bilingual or trilingual man, speaking and trading in two or three languages. He would be successful, educated ...'

'Quite a catch for Elizabeth.' Lucy said. 'Sounds pretty sexy.'

'So when he married Elizabeth Trelerric, did he settle here or carry on trading? Apart from his name, we know nothing about him.' Jane asked.

'I rather suspect he might have settled here and started a family, investing his time and money in the Trelerric lands. Perhaps he'd had enough of trading and being at sea. Seaports were dangerous places, breeding grounds for illness. Records clearly show that infection often spread from ports. They were often where the sweating sickness or plague began, I think it's one reason why London was so vulnerable because traders could sail inland up the Thames. They were unhealthy places, full of pestilence and disease. The last major outbreak of sweating sickness was in 1551.'

'Poxes, fluxes and fevers.' Lucy murmured thoughtfully. 'The joys of life in the good old days.'

By now even Sally could feel the general sense of information overload in the room. She looked at me pensively and began again.

'To conclude then, de Lachele had a trusted man, an employee in our terms, who seems to have been involved in de Lachele's business although the records so far are sketchy.' Sally looked down at her notes. 'There's a touching reference in a fragmentary document, rather worse for wear through damage by what looked like mice. But I quote, using modern English, "To Will Sheryll, my faithful and beloved servant, my gold ring with the green stone for his bride. And the gift of one palliasse with a feather bed over and quilt of fine wool and sarsenet."

EIGHTEEN

Clare gasped and Sam and I looked at each other in astonishment.

Lucy laughed with delight and Fiona stared at us, fascinated.

'My ring,' Clare was saying. 'Simon gave me a gold ring with a green stone, he put it on my finger by candlelight in the great hall just before Christmas. It was the right place to be for both of us.'

'I'm confused,' Jon said. 'Who is Will whatsisname?'

I started laughing, I couldn't help it. I could see Sam understood and obviously Clare and Sally knew, but I did my best to explain it.

'Sally has been doing a bit of work with the local history society in my village.' I said. 'She told my grandad about our family name and its earlier pre-census forms of spelling. I'm Simon William Sherwell, but my surname has been spelt as Sherill, and possibly has other variations.'

'So you might well be a descendant of Will Sheryll, de Lachele's faithful and beloved servant.' Sally finished for me. 'Simon William Sherwell, phonetically it sounds similar.'

'The initials WS are scratched into the door between the chambers, you know, the rooms behind the great hall.' Lucy said musingly. 'There are lots of initials and dates, we spent quite some time looking at them one day didn't we Fiona.'

The room erupted and Sam rolled over onto his knees and leaning over he shook my hand. 'That explains why I had a strange moment of déjà vu when I first met you Simon. Obviously you were my manservant once, and I probably still owe you money.' He crowed with laughter.

Fiona was delighted. 'Déjà vu is the nearest we come to knowing something else exists at the limit of our understanding without falling about laughing with embarrassment at the idea.' She said in her husky Scots accented voice.

'My beloved is going all fey. I need a drink.' Daniel said, touching Fiona's arm affectionately. 'Let's take a look at that table Fiona. See if I can offer Jane a price she can't refuse.'

'In your dreams Mr Pencraddoc.' Jane Latchley responded.

'A drink is a very good idea.' Tim got up and headed for the drinks tray as everyone else moved and stretched. 'Orders please, one at a time.'

Clare sat forward and folded her arms around my shoulders. 'A gold ring with a green stone for my bride.' She whispered in my ear.

I kissed the back of her hand and turned on my cushion to look up at her. Her little cat face was glowing with pleasure. 'Looks as though history will be repeating itself doesn't it.' I said, enchanted by the expression on her face.

'Yes, yes it does.' Clare replied.

Bloody hell, I thought, I've just proposed.

Later, when the couples with children had left, Sam and I sat talking in the sitting room. Lucy and Clare were in animated discussion in the kitchen with Sam's parents.

'So my ancestor seems to have gifted what could be your ancestor with a ring and a bed then, probably as a wedding gift.'

'It's spooky isn't it. Like you letting Clare and me have the Coach House while we get ourselves sorted out. But de Lachele was obviously a cheapskate Sam, giving the happy couple a straw mattress. That's what a palliasse is isn't it?'

'That's what Sally said, although it would go on a bed frame, and then the feather bed on top of that with the quilt-thing over. Seems like quite a decent present to me. Very snug. And they used to give beds and clothes and cooking utensils to people in their Wills in those days.' Sam replied. 'Possessions like those were important.'

'Well, you can keep your crazy collection of mugs in the potting shed. I don't want them.' I joked half heartedly. The afternoon's revelations had left me feeling odd, as though on the edge of a memory I couldn't quite grasp.

Sam was on the same wavelength. 'Simon, do you feel some kind of a connection with Trelerric?

'In a funny sort of way yes I do. There was a sense of familiarity when I started work, after that day with the college, when I first met you and I was a bit cheeky and you offered me a job. But it could be just that I like old buildings and it's a beautiful place. I don't really know.'

'And what about Clare? Does she feel anything?'

'I know she likes it here. She's been coming since she was a baby. And getting engaged that night on our own in the great hall was pretty special, thanks to your mum. It really meant something to us both.' I wondered where this was leading. 'What about you and Lucy?'

'Well, I belong here, I was born here on the estate, a home birth. I couldn't imagine living anywhere else. And Lucy loves it, but she has no ancient connection with the place.'

We sat quietly, pondering the strange turn of events of the afternoon.

'Look,' I said. 'I'm not coming over pathetic or emotional, but ...' I hesitated, searching for the right words. 'Would you think I was bonkers if I said you felt like a brother to me?'

Sam didn't fool about or even look offended. 'No, friends can have a brotherly love. Why not.'

Again we sat quietly, being manly and drinking our cider.

'Funny how life seems to repeat itself. There are patterns aren't there, if you look for them.' Sam mused.

'What do you mean?' I asked.

'Well, the déjà vu thing for starters, sometimes having the feeling you've met someone before or having that odd sense of recognition when you visit a place for the first time.'

I nodded. 'There was an old guy in the village when I was a kid, his name was Walter. He taught me lots of things, one was to keep an open mind. He was convinced that he'd live again in some way because he said everything had a cycle. Bulbs created new flowers every year, seeds spread and flowers reappeared in different parts of the garden. He said everything renewed itself given the chance.'

Sam stared into the fireplace, lost in thought. I wondered if I'd said too much and finished my cider.

'Have you ever noticed how Lucy and Clare sometimes look a bit similar?' Sam said out of the blue. 'Although they've got different eye colour.'

I glanced at him. 'Just once, in the early days in winter, from a distance I thought I was looking at Clare in the garden but it was Lucy, before she had her hair cut. They've got similar thick dark hair.'

'Yes, yes they have.' Sam said. 'Maybe that's it.'

I finally asked a question that had occurred to me several times over the months. 'Sam, how come you never asked Clare out yourself? I mean, she's been around here all her life and yours, and there's only seven years between your ages.' And, I was thinking, she's just as pretty as Lucy.

Sam unconsciously recrossed his legs. 'Um. I suppose that when I was fourteen she was seven, and not in possession of the interesting feminine attributes I was noticing in girls at school. And then a couple of years later I went off to Writtle College in Essex for a few years. When I came back she was at the Duchy College doing her veterinary nurse course. Our paths never really converged.' He was quiet for a moment. 'And I think there has to be that spark, that indefinable something that makes you focus on one special person. I felt it when I saw Lucy, that's all.'

Sam didn't say any more.

Clare was still bubbling when we walked back to the Coach House. I was looking forward to eating the chilli she'd made in the slow cooker, enjoying the special little touches she'd learned from her mum, a generous pinch of cumin with the onion, garlic and chilli flakes, a pinch of paprika and a hazelnut sized lump of dark brown sugar to counteract the acidity of the tomatoes. Clare's mind wasn't on food though.

'Well, that was thrilling wasn't it. What will your grandad say when you tell him that story? It's so exciting. I wonder who the girl was that Will Sheryll married? The girl who got the original gold ring with the green stone. I wonder what she would have made of mine with the diamonds either side. I wonder if we'll ever find out her name?'

I listened to her excited chatter and smiled. 'That's a lot of wondering, but I'm thinking more or less the same things. There might be something in the Latchley Book, the one where they recorded the estate births, marriages and deaths.'

'Oh yes!' Clare stopped walking. 'Why didn't we think of that? We could have asked Mrs Latchley, Sally Evans could have deciphered the words. Damn, shall we go back?'

'No. Another time. It's the weekend, it's our time together since you're not working. Let's just be us, on our own together.'

What I really wanted was time to reflect and think about things, I don't know why. It was like half remembered dreams swimming about but not quite surfacing. I was thinking about mum telling me I was a Sherwell right through. And then I wondered, rather fancifully, if seeing Clare's face through a window the day I started work at Trelerric House had been a re-enactment of a previous life in another time. Had Will Sheryll first seen the girl who would become his bride through a mullioned window? I shook my head at the notions I was entertaining.

In fact it was Gramps who came with me to Home Farm one wet afternoon to see the Latchley Book, which turned out to be several books recording the estate events over the centuries. Jane Latchley had laid them out on the big dining table in the kitchen and supplied us with white gloves to wear at Sally's insistence plus a cushion to place them on when they were opened.

'I hardly dare touch them myself these days.' She said.

In turn Gramps had given her a bunch of flowers. 'To say thank you for your kindness Mrs Latchley.' I was proud of the old man and Jane Latchley was touched.

'Take as long as you like with the books.' She advised us. 'I'll give you tea or something later, once the books are closed. Can't risk spillages you see.'

The books were of varying sizes, the early ones leather bound over boards and with metal clasps. They gave me a funny feeling. All their records were redolent with emotion, marriages made from love or from necessity, grief over the loss of loved ones or perhaps relief that someone unloved had finally gone. Babies born and babies lost. Children growing up and gone away, to fight wars or to start new lives overseas. The pages were full of whispers, laughter and sorrow, tiny summaries of lives once lived. And they all had an odour from years of storage in the purpose made oak coffer.

At first they were difficult to read but slowly our eyes became accustomed to the cramped writing and the shapes of the names. We found an early reference saying "To Richard Sherill, son of Thos Sherill, a son Richard Wm Sherill". There was no mention of the wife or mother's name. Gramps made careful notes in a notebook he'd brought with him using a pencil he'd sharpened with the pocket knife he always carried. I could see the cut marks at the end of the pencil as he wrote. And then we found a few more sons listed over the years, called Thomas, Edward and Stephen. Then a daughter, named Joan Margret, and another one, called Elizabeth Anne. Various Sherill/Sheryll/Sherrill names cropped up for a couple of decades but then petered out. It seemed they'd left Trelerric and gone elsewhere, but to go through all the books in close detail would have taken weeks and we only had a few hours.

Of Will Sheryll and his bride there was nothing. They'd slipped away quietly into the past. Gramps was a bit disappointed, but I wasn't. In my mind I was sure of a connection stretching through time.

NINETEEN

'Jeff, have you got a dog?' I was back at Flinton Hall for a couple of days finishing the Ladies Walk and I remembered mum's fears.

'No, had some fish once, in the garden pond. Then I realised I preferred them fried in batter, why?'

'Oh, just that mum's a postie, she's not that fond of dogs. And she doesn't like what she calls "dogpong" in houses.'

'Right. She's a character then your mum? What did you say her name was?'

'Her name is Gwenna, she knows what she likes and dislikes. We've got a cat, Ginger. He just moved in and adopted us one day. But even he's learned to wipe his feet when he comes in.'

'Well you can give my place the once over tonight, see if it's suitable and report back to the women.'

Jeff was finding my anxiety hugely amusing and had decided to allay my concerns by inviting me to stay with him instead of being a guest at Flinton Hall. It was a relief to be honest, the Flinton's had got guests staying, some friends of Lady Flinton's from her acting days. I wouldn't have fitted in at all.

We had worked well together, the pavilion now fitted into the design and we'd linked it to the existing terrace with a neat stone-slabbed path. Jeff was pleased because it had eradicated a muddy patch of grass and made the croquet lawn look fit for purpose. He'd also liked the style of the plank bench I'd pinched from Sam. I'd decided against putting rain-chains at the corners of the pavilion, they would have looked naff in that setting, especially because Lady Felicity had requested the building should remain painted white. Since Jeff liked flowers we were going for clumps of Canna lilies in shades from pink to deep purple. They fitted in with the existing planting and would look lovely with the reshaped bushes, a couple of which I'd cloud pruned.

There was no doubt in my mind, Sir Hugh had made things easy for me but then the Ladies Walk hadn't been a difficult task. I'd used original materials already available on site and incorporated a lot of the existing plants into the design. The only purchase had been the Welsh rocks. Jeff was already a salaried employee and that simply left payment for my own time so I charged a little more than Sam was paying me and included my travelling expenses. Sir Hugh had already paid me quite handsomely for the original designs plus extra for the design concept.

Meanwhile I was thinking about the forthcoming show. The month of March had long gone and April with all its softness and promise was already warming up. As far as I could see everything was organised and ready for the Moulton Show. We all had a week in which to build our gardens and then a week for the show, plus the dismantling at the end of it. The rules were that the showground had to be returned to turf. I guessed it was going to be a tough and intense experience. Clare had suggested I should get some new working clothes and I'd gone to the local farmers' supplies warehouse near Liskeard because they stocked decent jeans and working shirts. I straightened up from the task I was completing and looked over at Jeff.

'How long did you say you'd been on your own Jeff?'

'Long enough. Why?'

'It shows, if you're going to work with me at Moulton you're going to have to smarten up a bit. I don't mind the vibrant jumpers but we're going to be on view to the public and the rules say to be smart at all times. Time for some new gardening gear, a new pair of jeans and a couple of decent shirts I think.'

'Cheeky sod.'

He grinned and I smiled back at him. 'Can I ask you something Jeff?'

'Depends on whether it's another cheeky question Sherwell.'

'It is a bit, er, well ...'

'You can ask what you like, but I don't have to answer. No offence of course.' Jeff said.

'Well, I've wondered how come you never found another woman. I mean, dating's hard enough or at least that's what I've found. But you're a decent looking bloke.' I stopped speaking before I dug a hole big enough to put both feet in.

Jeff gave me a long look. 'I was in a bad place, being dumped after you've walked down the aisle and made vows to someone is a shitty thing to experience. Then I had the injury and was hurt physically as well as mentally. Dunno why, I didn't seem to get back into the swing of things. I see my mates, they're all mostly married, as are their sisters. Some are happy, some aren't. And the occasional woman I've met or been introduced to hasn't come to anything, probably because I can't be arsed to cope with their emotional baggage and because I don't want a new set of relations.'

I nodded, it didn't seem necessary to say anything more so I stayed quiet. I was surprised then when Jeff spoke again.

'I dunno Sherwell, I wonder what life is going to be like the older I get. I'm in my mid-fifties. I'm fine with my own company but sometimes I do wonder. And Sundays can be a bit cruel when you're on your own.'

Jeff stopped talking so we packed up and surveyed the results of our hard work. Doing the work at Flinton Hall and the Magnolia Walk at Trelerric House had been good mental and physical exercise for the main event looming on the horizon. I now knew what skills my team had and that they wouldn't let me down. I just hoped I wasn't going to let them down. As we drove to Jeff's house he asked me how I was feeling.

'Bricking it.' I told him. 'I don't know what I've let myself in for.'

'Treat it like a one-off, just an experience. It'll be a chance for a good laugh and we'll all work it out together. I'm looking forward to it. I've been to the show quite a few times, it's a good place. And at least it's not Chelsea, you ain't got to curtsey to Her

Majesty.' Jeff laughed. 'Now then, what shall we have tonight? Curry, Chinese, Pizza, fish and chips or beans on toast? As you can see I'm not a culinary wizard. Eggs and bacon is all I can cook.'

'So why do you grow your own veg then?'

'For the Sunday roast of course. Potatoes, peas and onions go with roast chicken, it's the one thing I can do.' Jeff laughed. 'But my gravy needs some work.'

'You should talk to my mum, she makes fantastic gravy.'

We opted for curry. And quite a few beers.

The three of us were sitting in mum's back garden. Ginger was stretched out on his back in the sun, blissfully warming his tummy. He'd playfully attacked one of mum's backdoor clogs, wrapping his front legs around it whilst kicking with his back legs and then sticking his face inside the clog and inhaling deeply like a dope addict. He didn't know that he was in the doghouse for bringing a mouse indoors.

'Can you put a cat in the doghouse? It sounds like grounds for cruelty.' I said to mum, who wasn't having any of it.

'He brings one more timorous beastie in and I'll have his guts for garters.' She said firmly.

Clare was wearing the first shorts of the season. She leaned forward to pick up her drink and I was treated to a glimpse of smooth skin below the waistband and the little tattoo. It was a rare moment of family peace, Easter had been early this year and Sam and I had worked hard making sure Trelerric gardens were ready for visitors. Initial reactions to the new Magnolia Walk had been encouraging and Sam had got his mum to do a laminated information sign advising that we would be appearing at the Moulton Show in the guise of Simon Sherwell Designs. It even had our photographs on it. I'd felt a bit spaced out seeing it, as though a dream was becoming reality. That wasn't on my mind now though, I was telling them about Jeff.

'His place is really neat mum. But don't laugh, his semi is on Hornyold Road. Jeff says people keep pinching the road signs.'

Clare giggled. 'A great name for a bachelor pad. Is his place old or new?'

'It's quite old, I think he said it was about 1890s. Jeff grew up there and inherited it from his parents. He moved back after his wife left him, it's got three storeys and he has his own floor. He looked after his parents as they got older and because he invested his own money into modernising the place after his divorce, his folks put his name on the deeds as a joint owner.'

Mum was interested and I could see her mulling that over. 'Sensible idea.' She commented. 'So what's it like inside?'

'Don't worry, you'll be fine. Jeff's house-trained and you'll like it.' I said and left it at that. I liked Jeff a lot I realised. He was good company and he lived an uncluttered life. The house was quite old and with enough period detail to delight the most blasé estate agent. There were sanded, stained wooden floors with modern rugs, lots of natural fabrics and muted colours, very few ornaments but he liked modern chunky ceramics. One basement room was devoted to music and he had a small keyboard, but his instrument of choice was the guitar and there were a group of friends he played with most weeks. Just enough to give credibility to getting together for a few beers as he described it. I'd been surprised that there'd been almost nothing to remind him of his parents apart from a few framed photographs.

'They live up here,' Jeff had tapped his head. 'This is my house now. I always was a plain sort of man, my ex-wife wanted frills and chintz with flowers on everything. She had ghastly taste, enough to give a bloke a migraine. I like things straight and I like to see what I've got.'

It had made me think about what it would be like for Clare and me to have our own house. I'd never had to make choices before. I knew that the interiors at Flinton Hall and Trelerric House were way over the top and not my style. Home Farm was comfortable but Sam's sister's place, The Lodge, was my favourite. I could see myself living in a Victorian house with Clare. I remembered the pleasure she'd shown when we'd bought our few new things in the sales after Christmas. Jeff had tapped me on the arm.

'Did you want another beer? I've asked twice already only you've got a daft expression on your face. You're away with the fairies.'

I told Jeff I was thinking about Clare.

'If you're as mad about her as that Sherwell, just make sure you tell her. Never leave it to a woman's imagination. They need telling otherwise they get all sorts of silly ideas.'

I wondered if he was giving me advice he'd learned the hard way.

Sam and I went up to Flinton Hall in his Land Rover and at last I was able to introduce him to Jeff and to Ian Marriott. Right from the start there was an atmosphere of excitement and anticipation. We felt like four boys let out of school to go off and have an adventure. The night before the start of the build we went to the local pub for a bit of bonding, this was not going to be a week of fine dining with the Flinton's.

'I want each one of you to play to your strengths,' I told them. 'We can all dig and plant and move heavy things about, but this has to be a smart and neat job and followed exactly to the plan. We're going to be assessed from day one, so every day I want to see the site looking pristine and no mud or anything spilled or sloppy where the public or the judges will be walking. Tarps to be used to protect the ground when we're moving things please.'

God, I sounded like my mum, I must get my neatness genes from her.

'Okay sergeant major Sherwell. Got the picture. Does he boss you about like this down at Trelerric?' Jeff said to Sam.

'I don't need to,' I said before Sam could answer. 'Sam's almost as much a neat freak as you.'

'Well I shall just do as I'm told. I've had years of experience and I'm very good at it.' Ian said wryly.

We worked incredibly hard. We hardly saw the Flinton's and at night I revised everything we'd done and listed the next set of tasks before texting Clare and collapsing into bed, sleeping like a log, getting up and doing it all over again. Ian's wife Angela supplied us with what Sam dubbed "the posh picnic" every day. A hamper filled with sandwiches; cheese and onion, cheese and coleslaw, egg and cress. There were little quiches and savoury vegetable tarts, cold apple turnovers in sweet pastry and hearty wedges of fruit cake. Nothing got wasted. The guys on the site next to us called us "The Palace Plot" and occasionally begged a morsel.

'Have you noticed there's no meat or fish in these picnics?' Jeff said one day. 'And it's all so tasty that you don't miss it.'

'She doesn't want to poison us.' Ian explained. 'I'm not joking, she's done her food hygiene training and won't pack anything she thinks might incubate some nasties since it's not refrigerated.'

'Lucy's the same.' Sam said. 'She was a nurse and then she ran a cake business for a couple of years. She has a thing about personal hygiene and fresh cream.'

We all fell about roaring with laughter and made predictable speculation about his private life.

'This is a very merry band of workers.' A posh voice sounded behind me. It was Cecily Reid-Ross wearing a very tweedy pleated skirt and matching jacket in maroon with a wine coloured velvet collar, red wellingtons and pearls. Somehow she pulled the look off. It was like seeing the Queen in her headscarf, almost unbearably frumpy but with such a natural dignity and authority you just accepted it.

I got to my feet and rubbed my hands against my jeans but before I could speak she introduced herself to everyone. 'I'm just taking a sneak preview. Have you got everything you need Mr Sherwell? Have your deliveries been getting through on time?'

I assured her that all was going to plan. The plants from the nursery at St Austell were due that afternoon. We'd already got the rocks placed, the path laid, banks contoured and the shallow pond made and filled. The water was still cloudy but it had three days in which to settle before I placed some pristine white river cobbles. Our efforts passed scrutiny and she moved on to the next garden.

'Is she a judge?' Sam asked.

'I don't think so, she's Head of Shows.'

'A big giant head.' Jeff said. And we all started laughing again.

Finally the garden was built. Ian was glad there was no grass in the design, he'd personally ensured that the grass surrounding our plot was cleaned of any speck of debris and kept smart, a fact appreciated by our neighbours.

'Funny thing isn't it, they don't feel like competitors, any of them.' Ian had observed.

They hadn't, people had borrowed tools, offered labour and given a helping hand whenever needed. We'd reciprocated and got along particularly well with the teams either side of us and struck up a good working relationship.

'That's gardeners for you. We've all got our feet firmly on the ground. It's about the plants, not about the personalities.' Sam commented, hugely satisfied with the work and flexing his aching shoulders. 'And anyway, every garden is individual. I don't see how they can compete, I'd hate to be a judge.'

'Judging is about meeting the brief you've submitted, assessing if what you've designed actually comes across in the flesh.' I was beginning to get the jitters. I almost didn't want to go back to Cornwall for the night, even though I was looking forward to seeing Clare. If I'd had the campervan I would have stayed on the showground and if possible slept next to the garden, it felt so precious to me.

Knackered after a series of eighteen hour days, I plonked myself down on an upturned plastic bucket and stared at the garden in amazement. In my tired mind there seemed to be a reflection of my life, it was more than just a garden, it was a summary of all the things I'd learned and been taught by people whose lives had touched mine. It was a way of saying thanks to all of them.

'Did we just do that?' I said in surprise.

TWENTY

We were thrilled to see each other. Clare wrapped herself round my neck and I held her close, breathing in the sweet warm scent of her. She was looking gorgeous in cropped jeans and a pink top with playful dangly coloured earrings in the shape of a bunch of purple grapes.

'Wow aren't you the loveliest thing to come home to. I've missed you something chronic.' I told her, kissing the top of her head and the side of her neck. 'But you were there with me all the time. I've built the feeling you gave me the night we got engaged.'

Clare pulled back in my arms and gazed up at me. 'That's the most romantic thing anyone has ever said.' She ran her hands up my arms and over my shoulders. 'And you feel as though you've done a million push-ups, you feel well fit and all muscles.' She pressed herself against me. 'Are you starving or shall we go to bed now?'

How could a chap argue with a question like that.

Much later, as we ate cold roast chicken and salad with crusty white bread and salty butter, I told her all about it. What a week it had been, sunshine and showers, slog and hard graft. 'The guys were brilliant Clare, they worked their socks off and we had some good laughs. It was worth it just for the experience.'

'Well, I hope you told them exactly that.'

She'd made a chocolate roulade at her mum's house and followed that with home made truffles to accompany the coffee. They were an odd shape and she looked at them ruefully.

'Lucy gave me the idea so I made almond praline and then mixed it with the chocolate and rum. They taste okay though.'

I tried one. The alcohol content would have pleased Sir Hugh. 'Not bad for something which looks as though it was squeezed out by a rather worried goat.' I told her. The ensuing mock battle ended up with her in my arms again. She really was the most gorgeous kisser.

There was no time for rest. Clare, being the well organised and level headed girl that she is had put all my decent clothes together and ready for packing that night. I was supposed to be going up to Flinton Hall with Sam and Lucy, but both mum and Clare had wangled some time off from work so they were coming up for the first half of the show. I decided to travel up with them to Jeff's place so that I could at least make the introductions before getting Jeff to take me over to Flinton Hall. Mum was quite relieved.

'I won't need the satnav then.' She said. 'And I was wondering what to say to this man I've never even met.'

I put my bags in the Jag, handy that it was kept parked underneath the Coach House, and let Sam know the change of plan.

'See you later then, after I've got the girls settled at Jeff's place.'

Sam and I were both tense, we knew that the garden assessors were examining our work before reporting back to the judges. I'd already had a short interview with them to discuss my client's brief. By the time we got to the showground the decisions would have been made and the awards would have been placed. I was trying not to think about it.

Mum was driving us all in her Toyota and there was a bit of a party atmosphere in the car. We'd never done anything like this before, the only down-side was that Clare and I wouldn't be together.

'Don't worry Simon, your mum and I will take a good look around the show, we won't be under your feet. You're going to be very busy answering questions and being interviewed.'

Clare seemed to have a clearer picture of what the show entailed than I had. She giggled when we turned into Hornyold Road. 'You weren't joking, it really is called horny old road. Is Jeff a bit pervy then?'

I'd texted Jeff when we were about ten minutes away and he'd replied saying he'd put the kettle on. I felt strangely proud, these were my family, but I was bringing them to a new territory, only familiar to me. Mum parked in the space behind Jeff's smart pickup.

'Oh, he drives a Toyota as well.' She said, as we all got out and I heaved their bags from the boot.

'Hello the Sherwell gang. You made it then.'

I turned round and stopped dead in my tracks, Jeff greeted us from the doorway wearing spotlessly clean dark jeans with a black, grey and white checked shirt which had a tiny yellow line running through it. He'd had his thick grey hair cut and was looking smart and very presentable. His dark eyes twinkled with amusement at the look on my face and then rested on my mum, who was just behind me. I thought I caught a moment of pleased surprise on his face then he stepped forwards and shook hands, first with Clare and then with mum.

'You're very kind Mr Hartley, letting us stay when we don't even know you.' Clare said.

'I know, I'm an absolute star aren't I?' Jeff said. 'And my name is Jeff. Come on in, let's get you all settled. Sherwell knows the way.'

'Sherwell can't carry all the bloody bags so give us a hand please mate.' I said, but I was talking to an empty space. By the time I got everything indoors they were all on first name terms and nattering nineteen to the dozen in the kitchen.

A couple of hours later Jeff dropped me off at Flinton Hall. He was picking up fish and chips to take back home with him. They'd voted on it, with Clare insisting on having mushy peas as well. I was feeling quite left out.

'Now then, you enjoy your fine dining tonight, I gather Angela's doing duck. Don't worry about us slumming it over fish and chips.' Jeff said, thoroughly enjoying himself. 'I'll see you sharp and early at the show then. Make sure you get some sleep, don't get pissed and don't be late.'

Lucy waved to me from the garden room so I went up the side steps. Lady Flinton was in the room with her, resplendent in a greenish gold dress with a gold pashmina draped around her shoulders.

'You look amazing.' I greeted her. I'd got the hang of the way this set treated one another, but I wasn't joking. This woman knew how to dress.

'Simon, how charming. I understand you've had a good week. Sam has been telling us what fun you've all had.' She made it sound like a schoolboys' camping trip in times gone by. I had the mad urge to say how jolly ripping it all was. I'd not read Gramps old storybooks on wet summer holiday afternoons for nothing.

'It was hard work, but we got there.' I said. 'Jeff was brilliant, Ian was brilliant, Sam ...'

'Was also brilliant.' Sam was standing at the doorway. 'And you were ...'

'Worried sick most of the time.' I said, accepting a soft drink from Lucy.

Lucy smiled at me, we'd made a private arrangement, no-way was Sir Hugh going to get me pissed since it was such an important week.

'Sir Hugh's just shown me over the job you've been doing here.' Sam said. 'It's looking really good. There's definitely a "Sherwell style". I recognise your way of seeing things.'

I shrugged, a bit embarrassed. 'I dunno Sam, I'm probably just a one hit wonder. Some of the things the other designers were doing were amazing.'

'Are we having first night nerves?' Sir Hugh said, coming into the room. 'One remedy for that, something decent in a glass. Oh, I see you've got something.'

Lucy had given me a glass of tonic water with ice and a slice of lemon. You couldn't tell what was in it. Sir Hugh, being the smart old fox that he was, sniffed.

'I can't smell gin.'

'That's because we're all having a large vodka tonic.' Lucy said smoothly. 'It's odourless.'

Angela's duck was sublime. Afterwards, fortified by a couple of glasses of wine which Lucy had permitted, Lady Flinton took me to one side.

'I want to talk to you about your interviews tomorrow darling.'

'Interviews?' I said faintly.

'Of course, there will be the press, the papers and television. Moulton Show is a special occasion. So I need to discuss your presentation skills with you. I want you to be prepared.'

'Oh cripes. Okay. I'm listening.'

The following morning we were out so early that I thought Sam and I would be the first in the exhibitors' car park. I was wrong. There were plenty of nervous tense faces about and I felt nauseous. My mobile pinged in my pocket with the special tone reserved for Clare.

"Hardly slept, thought about you all night. Good Luck. I love you. Clare XX"

For once I was too nervous to answer. I decided to wait until I had something to say.

'Come on,' I muttered to Sam. 'Let's do this thing as they say in the movies.'

Everyone walked down through the showground without speaking. Today all was perfect, with no signs of the incredible activity that had gone on over the past week. There wasn't a blade of grass in the wrong place, even the sky was the correct shade of English blue. I was barely conscious of the act of walking. I could hear my own breath and the sound of my heart beating. We rounded the corner and walked towards the plot, that little space we'd worked so hard on. I could see that all the plots now had small signage boards erected by them. I knew that mine would have the design name and a brief description of the garden on it together with suppliers' details. I heard Sam say something.

'What? What did you say?'

'I said I can see a card.'

My throat went dry as we got closer and my eyes focussed. There was a card. And it was an Award Card.

'Shit.' I think we said the same word simultaneously.

I was conscious of Sam thumping my back. 'Bloody hell Simon.'

I didn't know whether to laugh or cry so I did a bit of both. Then we thumped each other a bit more and did a sort of a war dance. After that I don't remember much, except for texting Clare with one word.

"*Gold.*"

Jeff and Ian arrived shortly afterwards, grinning broadly. Jeff had got the news from Clare as they were driving.

'Damn near went into the ditch when she told us. Your mum started crying. I had to give her my hanky. We left them at the ladies sorting out their make-up.'

There was a blur of activity. Someone was coming round checking who'd got what and identifying the designer for each plot. A woman in a trouser suit approached Sam and he pointed to me. 'That's your man, that's Simon Sherwell, the designer.'

The woman came over to me. I registered that she was wearing an awful lot of lipstick and eyeliner. It turned out she was organising the timings for people to be interviewed and recording things on a clipboard. 'Old technology I know, but it doesn't crash and the batteries don't run out.' She said, efficiently making notes. 'We'll do a short congratulations interview live to camera, and later on there'll be some recorded footage done so that you can talk about the garden concept and a little bit about yourself. We'll see how it goes. But you have to be here, we have an awful lot to get round.'

Time seemed altered somehow. There were faces, lots of faces and lots of noise. I shook hands endlessly, received congratulations, stood for photographs with my team and with other people. I was wearing the blueish jacket and dark trousers with a pale lilac coloured shirt which Clare had put together for me. She'd folded a purple silk handkerchief into the top pocket and my fingers found a note in the jacket pocket. "With all my love, from the girl wearing your gold ring with the green stone."

At last the news was sinking in and I started to relax a bit. I was beginning to feel as though I'd won the lottery. The four of us managed to get a few moments for a reality check and then over Jeff's shoulder I saw mum and Clare standing watching us. Mum was holding herself together with difficulty but Clare was glowing, she looked radiant in the teal coloured fitted jacket she'd worn to Sam and Lucy's wedding, but this time she was wearing a light summer dress in pale material, with gold drop earrings and a plain gold necklace. She made my heart melt and I walked towards her with my hand held out.

'Clare. Mum.' I held my other hand out to mum.

'You did it Simon. You bloody did it. I'm so proud of you. I'm going to cry again.'

'Please don't Gwenna,' said Jeff from somewhere behind me. 'I've only got the one hanky.'

I smiled down at Clare. 'Come and look at what you inspired me to do. I'll explain it to you.'

A little while later the Flinton's arrived with Lucy, accompanied by Lady Flinton's entourage of media types and actressy friends. Loads more photographs were taken, several for Facebook entries. I got lipstick on my cheek and a couple of people asked me if I had a business card or a website.

'It's early days yet, I'm not really very organised.' I found myself apologising.

'Oh I have some of your business cards Simon,' Clare smiled professionally. 'Let me give them out.'

'Is that your secretary?' A woman asked. 'Cracking looking girl.'

Sam gave me a nudge. 'I can see a camera and a man carrying the sound equipment stuff, you know, the thing that looks like a dead badger on a stick. And there's a rather famous gardening celebrity heading our way.'

The woman I'd met earlier came towards me. She seemed to be wearing even more lipstick. 'Simon Sherwell isn't it. You're on in about five minutes. We're doing well, only forty minutes behind schedule. This part will be brief.'

I was told where to stand, on the curved path between the shallow pond and the golden Osmanthus with the rustic plank bench behind me, which Sam was now referring to as his patented invention. The sound man called for quiet and the television celebrity stepped forwards and shook my hand, a warm dry handshake. He winked at me and turned to camera. I smiled as I was introduced, congratulated on being a Gold Award winning new entrant and the camera moved slowly round while I said something about the fantastic achievement of my team.

'Ah, I recognise a fellow designer, it's one thing to have the idea but another entirely to make it happen. And for that you need a reliable team.'

The reliable team grinned obligingly at the camera, which then moved across to focus more lingeringly on some of the garden features.

'Simon, you've called this garden "The Space Beyond", why is that?'

'It's taken from a poetic description of a Japanese garden, written by a very talented Englishman and garden designer. I believe that by grouping the use of rocks and planting you allow spaces for the imagination, you provide a space beyond the everyday world in which to dream, relax and find peace.' I said, mentally thanking Lady Flinton for rehearsing me last night.

'That's quite lovely, we all lead such busy lives that finding space to dream and relax is vitally important. We shall be returning to Simon Sherwell's garden to learn more ..."

It was over in seconds.

'Well done Simon, that was a good start.' Lady Flinton was assessing me with her cool grey eyes. Remember what I told you last night and the next session will be a piece of cake. By the way, I gather it's Clare's birthday this week.'

I nodded.

'In that case I'd be delighted if she could join us for dinner this evening, I think she should be included in the first night celebrations, don't you?'

By now I was parched and conscious that I'd only managed half a bowl of cereal for breakfast. We weren't allowed to eat and drink at our plots but I reckoned I'd be allowed a quick comfort break and something to eat. After a rapid consultation with the guys Jeff and I dashed to the exhibitors facilities for fifteen minutes before going back and letting Sam and Ian take a break. Later on Ian went off for a stroll round and Sam stood talking to Lucy and mum. Clare was taking pictures on her phone after calling her parents with the good news. I told Jeff that Clare was invited to Flinton Hall for dinner that evening.

'So your mum will be flying solo then?'

'Looks like it. Do you mind?'

'No problem Sherwell, there's a really nice little country pub I know. I'll look after her. After all, I'm a gardener and she's a gardener's mother, we must have something in common to talk about.'

TWENTY ONE

There were more photographs with the bigwigs and I shook hands again with Cecily Reid-Ross. This time she was wearing a patterned dress in violent shades of pink and plum with the traditional fussy ruffles round her neck and yet another maroon jacket. She looked hot and started fanning herself with a programme. Lady Flinton on the other hand was the essence of cool chic, tranquil in cream linen with touches of pale orange and light green and holding a parasol to shade her face. As Cecily stomped away gamely for her next official photograph Lady Flinton smiled sympathetically but turned to me and Clare with a wicked look on her face. 'Poor thing, she looks upholstered rather than dressed don't you think?'

'Time for your slot Mr Sherwell.' The clipboard lady was back again, looking knackered.

'You're doing a fantastic job,' I told her. 'I just wish I could offer you some refreshment or somewhere to sit for a moment.'

'It's okay thanks, I've got a bottle of water in my bag.' But I was rewarded with a grateful smile. 'Problem is that he,' she nodded over her shoulder in the direction of the celebrity garden presenter, 'gets stopped all the time by fans. And he's such a darling that he's never rude. But it holds us up.'

I nodded understandingly, remembering Lady Flinton's instructions. The girl looked at me properly. 'You have a nice suntan, you'll look good on camera, but just blot your face with this tissue. Take any glow off.'

The gardening presenter stepped up to do his job. 'This part is pre-recorded to show later in the week, so any gaffs or stumbles can be edited out. They'll be mine of course, not yours.' He said kindly. 'I'm just going to ask you about your garden design and the reasons behind it, and perhaps a bit about you. Nothing unusual, no trick questions.' He looked at the cameraman. 'I think we'll sit on this handy bench, my feet are aching but we'll look relaxed and informal. Okay with you Simon?'

I sat down as indicated. Clare had already mentioned that the colour of the flower heads on Jeff's Verbena bonariensis toned nicely with my shirt and silk handkerchief. She was a clever girl and so very supportive.

And so it began.

'And here we are in Simon Sherwell's award winning garden, called "The Space Beyond" a first Gold for you I believe Simon?'

I was sitting giving my full attention to the presenter, just as Lady Flinton had shown me, the correct attentive posture, the slight turn of the body and the face towards him. The camera had me in profile and then three-quarters on. I didn't twitch or fiddle about, hands placed casually on my thighs, one leg stretched out further than the other.

'Yes, a fantastic result for me and the team.' I said, not hiding the pleasure I was feeling.

'I particularly like the varied surface and winding shape of the oriental inspired path, leading from and returning to the small terrace. And you can either sit here or on the terrace opposite, giving you views from different angles.'

'Yes,' I responded, 'and of course depending on the time of day you may be sitting in sun or shade or even moonlight. You can sense the movement of the hours in a subtle way.'

'You've included a small pond, always essential in a garden I think, with its benefits for wildlife. But why have you placed it in the centre of the design, and what's the purpose of the rustic steel bowl holding the still water? I particularly like the way it's set to one side on rocks slightly above the pond.'

I breathed in through my nose, looked into the camera, and thought about the woman I loved. Then I smiled into the lens with all that love in my eyes and talked about the five elements incorporated into my design; water, air, stone, fire and iron. I talked about the ritual of purifying your hands in the bowl of water and letting the cares and stresses of the day slip away. We discussed the idea of air movement suggested by the tall waving

Verbena and the Stipa and he complimented me on the choice of gold and purple.

'So you have four of the elements represented Simon, but what about the fifth? I can't see any signs of fire.' Silently I applauded his generosity, he knew perfectly well where the fire was.

'My idea is that's reserved for an intimate drink by candlelight at the table on the terrace.' The camera obligingly moved and focussed on a group of assorted candles attractively placed in a shallow rustic ceramic dish of water on the table. Clare had originally bought them for the Coach House, in various shades of creamy white and lilac. They suited the little lilac painted metal table and two chairs I'd picked up from a shop in Liskeard. Clare had added a matching cushions and Jeff had provided a bottle of red wine and two plain wine glasses.

'Or of course you could have the fire element represented by a barbecue here since there's room for two to eat outside. This is an ideal arrangement for a small town garden. Now Simon, tell me about the planting and your colour choices.'

I was honest and truthful. 'I got engaged at Christmas and the colours you see here are inspired by the dress my fiancee wore that night. I thought the subtle combinations she wore of gold, purple, black and red were stunning so I've translated them into the planting.'

The presenter was looking about appreciatively. 'I particularly like the accent of the clump of red Canna lilies to the side of the pond. They look marvellous against the gold of the giant oats and contrasting with the underplanting of black grass, the Ophiopogon. The bronze Heuchera add some lovely texture too. And of course this red grass here will seed and spread so there will always be a natural element to the design. It looks natural amongst the river cobbles you've placed coming up from the water.'

I was nodding in agreement. That bloody grass would seed all over the place and we both knew it.

'So this garden is all about love,' he smiled and continued. 'But you've got shades of green in your Hakonechloa and Hostas, where does that fit in with your fiancee?' he laughed, 'if that's not a trick question Simon?'

'Emerald is her birth stone, so I bought her an emerald engagement ring.' I smiled lovingly into the camera again.

'And tell me, how long have you been a gardener?'

'I started just before I was ten years old, helping my grandad and then helping some of the old boys in my village in Cornwall. They taught me such a lot. They still do. Then I did a short placement at a local agricultural college, concentrating mainly on design. My family have always had their hands in the soil, my passion goes back generations, it's in my blood.'

The presenter seemed genuinely absorbed, it really felt as though it was just me and him, chatting on an early summer afternoon.

'So this garden has everything, not only the five elements, but love, beauty and poetry. What more can a garden offer? I congratulate you on a beautiful space, imaginatively designed and with wonderful attention to detail. It's talented people like you, Simon, who are the future of gardening in this country.' Said the celebrity presenter, wrapping the piece up.

There was a burst of applause from the people watching, not just my personal supporters, and I couldn't resist it, I gave them all a grin and a small bow of acknowledgement. It was my day and I was on such a high.

The sound engineer gave a dry laugh and looked at me with interest. 'You'll go far son, that was a very nice piece of work.'

As they moved on Clare handed me a bottle of water and smiled at me with bright eyes. 'Simon you were wonderful. That's the best birthday present ever.'

'It's not your birthday yet you lovely woman. And I won't be there when it is, but I'll make it up to you, I promise.'

Lady Flinton waited until I'd had a drink of water and then touched my arm. 'Good work Simon, you're a very quick learner and an excellent pupil. We're going now, we'll see you both at dinner this evening. No need to change, you both look delightful as you are.'

'So how did you do it Simon?' Clare asked. 'I would have been absolutely terrified. Did you have some coaching from milady then?' She indicated Lady Flinton's elegantly retreating back.

'Lady Flinton gave me some tips, she told me to "think of someone you love, look straight into the camera, and let the smile reach your eyes." I think it worked.'

There was a hand on my shoulder and voice in my ear. 'Bloody hell, I can barely believe what I just saw. What a performance! Is that really you, young Simon Sherwell?'

I turned and looked straight into the face of one of my holiday cottage clients from the village. I'd been looking after the garden at his place for several years. It was the owner of Pondside Cottage, the cottage I'd asked if there was a chance of renting when Clare and I were having such trouble finding a place to live.

'Mr Renwick, I haven't seen you for ages.' I shook his hand. 'This is Clare Palfrey, my fiancee.' I would never get tired of saying that.

'Delighted. So you're the very pretty girl who inspired this then?' There were the usual polite remarks. 'My wife is somewhere around here. I stopped to watch the business just now, you know, can't help being critical or interested since it's my profession. And then I realised it was you! Blow me down! Are you still in Cornwall or are you moving on to new and greater things now?'

'I'm still in Cornwall. It's my home.'

'Well, look, you're going to be here for the week aren't you? We're staying with friends. I think you and I need a catch up. Would you be free one evening, both of you of course. I'd rather like a little chat.'

We exchanged business cards, Clare producing another of the cards she'd had made for me as a surprise, amazing girl that she is. He glanced at mine.

'Name and phone number only. Haven't you got a website? Anyway, we'll meet up maybe Wednesday or Thursday evening if that's good for you, I'll check with Amanda, if I can find her, and I'll be in touch pronto.'

Clare watched him go, a balding man in striped blazer but one who projected energy with every bounding step. 'Who was that?'

'Richard Renwick. He owns Pondside Cottage in the village.'

'The one you asked if we could rent? Who said no. Should I hate him?'

'The very same. He's okay, and his wife was very sorry in her email. They've owned the cottage quite a few years now. Rob Williams made the gate, you know, the arty metal one. It looks like water reeds.'

Clare nodded. 'Yes, you pointed it out once. But Simon, I've got to go back on Wednesday, I'm at work on Thursday, and so is your mum. You'll have to go and meet him on your own.'

All Lady Flinton's friends had gone so it was just the six of us for dinner. Sam was in great form. 'I'm as pleased as a dog with two tails, what a brilliant day. It couldn't have gone any better.'

'My face aches from smiling and my hand hurts from shaking hands.' I said. 'But wow, what a fantastic day.'

'I knew you were worth investing in Simon. I can always spot a good thing.' Sir Hugh had handed round after dinner liqueurs and I was nursing a noble and well-aged brandy. I was getting to like this sort of life.

Clare had the giggles, she'd had everything, champagne, wine, a Monbazillac dessert wine and now a small glass of Cointreau. 'I'm turning into a tosspot,' she announced breezily. 'And a groupie. I'm your number one admirer Simon. I'm not embarrassing you am I?' She squinted at me with a dopey look on her face.

'Now there's a girl who will sleep well tonight.' Lucy murmured. 'Coffee anyone? Before I take Clare away to her bed.' Lucy was hardly drinking and had elected to drive Clare over to Jeff's place.

'My lonely bed.' Clare declared. 'Because you're not in it Simon.' She added, as if any further emphasis was necessary. I had the feeling that Clare would prefer to wake up with a hangover at Jeff's rather than at Flinton Hall and anyway, I had another early start in the morning.

'Clare, come into the music room with me, I want to show you a portrait in there.' Lucy said suddenly. 'Bring your coffee and then we'll make a move.'

I saw a glance between Sir Hugh and Lady Felicity which I couldn't interpret. For a moment I wondered if they were anxious that Clare might throw up, although she seemed to be holding her alcohol reasonably well, since she'd only got to the affectionate stage of inebriation. They started speaking to Sam and I excused myself. 'Need the bathroom.' I mumbled. I wasn't lying. On my way back I could hear the girls talking and went and stood in the doorway, they were just out of sight. The music room was a large L-shaped room all done out in Chinese yellow upholstery but the wallpaper was a yellow regency stripe and there was a pea green coloured carpet overlaid with some foreign looking colourful rugs. The colour combinations made me feel bilious.

'I've always thought we had something in common Lucy.' I could hear Clare talking, she was giggly and I realised she was having trouble speaking clearly. 'After all you were a nurse and I'm a veterinary nurse. We know a bit about germs and bad stuff.'

Goodness, she was really squiffy I realised.

'But look at the portrait,' Lucy was saying. 'It's of Sir Hugh's mother, my own mother's grandmother, which I think makes me Sir Hugh's second cousin. Do you think I look like her?'

'I dunno, s'pose you do a bit. Why do you ask?'

'Some people think you and I look a bit alike. I thought you'd be interested.' Lucy said.

'We can't be alike though, we're not related. I know who my mum and dad are, and I've got an older brother. I love them all to bits and I was born in Cornwall. Where were you born Lucy?'

'London. But it doesn't really matter. I'm just interested in family connections. Like the other day when Sally Evans was talking about Simon's possible connection to the Trelerric lands.'

'Oh.' It was all Clare managed to say and I heard Lucy saying she'd better take her back to Jeff's place as it was getting late.

I turned to go back to the others and jumped. Sir Hugh was standing right behind me.

'Everything alright Simon?'

'Yes, fine, I just wanted to check that Clare was still standing. I'll help Lucy take her to Jeff's.'

'Of course. We're turning in as well, shortly. Goodnight.'

Clare and Lucy came out just as Lady Flinton appeared to say goodnight.

'Night then Lady Flick.' Clare beamed at her. 'I'm just off. Smashing dinner. Absolutely smashing house. Thank you so much. G'night.'

Lady Flinton smiled her most dazzling smile. 'Sleep well Clare, it was lovely having you to dinner my darling.' I got the impression she meant it and wasn't at all bothered by Clare's inebriated state.

I helped Clare out to the Jag and got into the back with her. She leaned against me purring like a kitten and with her eyes closed.

'Thanks Lucy.' I said. It was only a short drive and I decanted Clare into mum's arms.

'Did you have a good night?' I asked mum.

'Yes I did, did you? Clare obviously has. She seems a little intoxicated.'

'I'm impoxytated. And the room's going round. I don't like it.' Clare muttered with her eyes shut, a troubled little frown creasing her brow.

I kissed both of them on the cheek. 'Sweet dreams, see you tomorrow, hangovers permitting.'

Mum took Clare inside. 'What a day.' I said.

'One you'll never forget Simon.' Lucy agreed.

We didn't say much on the drive back and Lucy went straight upstairs. I paused and turned into the music room, feeling round the wall for a light switch. I'd never seen this portrait and wanted to take a look. It was a life-sized head and shoulders portrait of a young woman looking over her bare shoulder and straight into my eyes with a defiant expression. I stared, fascinated, then leaned forward and read the name plate. Beatrice Clare Wingfield Flinton.

'Bugger me.'

'You can see it can't you Simon.'

Sir Hugh had come silently into the room, still cradling his brandy. I'd had a busy day, a fair bit of alcohol and I was knackered.

'Sorry?'

'You can see the resemblance to Lucy.'

'Yes. It's remarkable.'

'My mother was quite a beauty in her day, pity she developed into such an unpleasant old bitch.'

'Right.'

'Well, I'll bid you goodnight. It's been a great day. We're all very proud of you.'

'Oh, thank you. Goodnight Sir Hugh.'

He left me staring at the portrait.

'Bugger me.' I said for the second time that evening.

TWENTY TWO

Richard Renwick called me the following morning and I agreed to meet him on Wednesday evening. He texted the details of a pub in Malvern and I checked with Jeff, the fount of all local knowledge.

'They do modern swanky gastro food, you know, scallops with bacon and asparagus, that sort of thing. Too much plate showing. I hope he's paying. It's a bit of a gay boys hang out. Is he that way inclined then?'

'Not that I know of, anyway he's married.' I laughed at Jeff.

'That doesn't mean anything, he might swing both ways. But I honestly don't care how many arms or legs a fella has, what his religion is or what colour he is.'

'Is that tolerance or indifference Jeff?'

'Dunno, I don't really have an opinion to tell the truth. Folks have to deal with their own stuff.' He said obscurely.

I looked at him, today he was wearing dark blue jeans with a dark blue, red and white short sleeved shirt. He was wearing a belt as well and looking pretty decent. 'I like the new get up Jeff. Very smart.'

'What this old thing? I just threw it on, had it for ages.' He laughed. 'I asked your mum if these things went together. She's very understanding. She said she'd rehang all my clothes so that things worked.'

The thought of my mum going through his clothes startled me for a moment, then I smiled. 'She'll chuck out anything she doesn't like. Can you cope with that? I had to put up with it for twenty-five years.'

'Dunno,' he said again. 'Be nice for someone to take an interest in me for once.'

There was something in his eyes, a wistful, soft sort of expression. I thought I understood, Clare was very interested in my appearance. Today I had a pale blue shirt on with the ubiquitous jacket and a dark blue silk handkerchief in the top pocket.

'Did you both have an okay time out last night?' I asked.

'Yeah. She's a laugh, we talked a lot. She's easy to get on with, your mum. Great taste in music. But changing the subject slightly, she's not here this morning because a certain young lady is having a tea towel filled with ice held against her head.'

'Oh dear. Did she throw up last night?'

'Not seen any evidence although your mum did have my washing machine on at dick o'clock this morning.'

I'd not had a text from Clare, although I'd sent her one. Thinking about Clare reminded me I'd still not got anything for her birthday. 'Jeff, is there a nice jewellers in Malvern?'

For a moment he looked alarmed. 'Blimey, for a moment there I wondered if you thought I'd got intentions. Er, but it's your Clare's birthday isn't it, end of the week. I gathered that over fish and chips the other day.'

I asked Sam if he could hold the fort for a couple of hours while Jeff took me into Malvern. I had to get her something.

Later, back on duty, I found it more interesting than I'd expected to talk to the public. There were waves of the beige jackets and bunions brigade brimming with good humour and pleasantries. Some people assumed that I was an expert on garden pests, others wanted to talk about soil pH and problems with struggling plants. Sam was in his element, he was a natural teacher and happy to talk endlessly about gardening. One earnest looking elderly lady all dressed in pearly moth-grey apparel approached me and asked if she could talk to me about my tool.

'Pardon me?'

'You know, the Japanese have a special tool don't they? For cloud pruning.'

'I just use secateurs and shears madam. Best to use what you're familiar with.'

She went away happy but Sam was snorting with laughter. 'Simon Sherwell, the man with the amazing tool.' He found it all hilarious.

It was good meeting interested people, in my experience many people spend a lot of time looking about but don't really see anything. It's not like that with gardeners, they notice things. It was early afternoon before Clare and mum showed up. Clare was wearing a huge pair of dark sunglasses.

'How's the head?' I asked, kissing her gently on the cheek.

'Improving, just. But the stomach is a bit queasy. I might have had a very small puke on the pillowcase. What on earth did I drink last night?'

'Just Sir Hugh's industrial measures of alcohol. He's a very generous man. Lucy warned me about him when I first visited, he nearly had me on my face before dinner. His "preprandials" as he calls them, are lethal.'

'Well I'm not having any more of his prenuptials. I'm not ashamed you know. I had a fantastic evening, I think.'

I just smiled. 'We could go to the exhibitors' tent for a cup of tea if you like.'

Sam was still happy to man the stand. Of Jeff and mum there was no sign, they'd both vanished the moment she showed up.

I settled Clare at a wonky table on grass in the shade. 'It's okay, it's the table which is on a slope, the tent's not spinning round.' I teased her. 'Plain builders' tea and a glass of water. Anything to eat?'

Clare shook her head, slowly. 'Plain water as well, nothing peculiar in it please.'

I drank my tea and ate a huge sticky Belgian bun, enjoying the combination of hot tea and sweet pastry. Clare sipped her drinks and sat quietly. A guy who'd been building a garden just along from mine came by and gave me a high five.

'Heard you got a Gold Award. Awesome. I got a Silver but I'm more than happy. I'll get a Gold next time, we've learned a lot.

We're based in South Devon, if ever you're down that way, or if you need a hand, give me a bell.'

We exchanged business cards and I thanked him but mentally I shuddered, although it was an amazing experience I didn't think I wanted to go through all this again. It was a mental way of proving yourself. After he'd gone I turned to Clare.

'The man from Pondside Cottage phoned this morning. He wants to take me to a gay bar on Wednesday night.'

Clare spluttered into her tea. 'What?' A ghost of a smile lit her face.

'Jeff says it's a bit posh and inhabited by the aspirational and upcoming. Well, he didn't quite put it like that, but you get the drift.'

'He's a nice guy, Jeff. He and your mum are getting on like the proverbial house on fire. I thought I was hallucinating last night, you know, I was feeling a bit ill and could hear voices. But it was them, talking and laughing downstairs. And playing music. And I'm not sure but I think they might have been dancing.'

'Dancing? I've never seen my mum dance.'

'So what does the gay guy want to talk to you about?' Clare asked.

'Richard Renwick, and he's not gay. His business card says he's the CEO of a production company. I've always known he was something in television.'

'Uh.' Clare grunted. 'My head hurts, I can't take all this in. Let me see his card.'

I fished in my wallet and read it out to her. She couldn't see anything in those dark glasses and anyway I doubted she was even capable of focussing. 'Richard Renwick, Pondside Productions. Oh, he's called his business after his holiday cottage then.'

Clare managed a giggle. 'Pondlife Productions? I love it. That should be an interesting evening. Hope he doesn't try to poke you with something slippery under the table. Pity I can't be there.' And she reached out a hand across the table to me. 'Have I told you I love you lately, Simon Sherwell? I love you even when I'm feeling awful.'

'Not lately. But it's nice to hear it.' And we just sat there, holding hands and smiling.

Back at the garden I handed her over to Lucy. 'Madam isn't bleeding from the eyeballs now and she'll survive. She's managed to keep a cup of tea down.'

Clare grimaced. 'Takes more than a few glasses of plonk to sink a Cornishwoman. But I do fancy a dry biscuit now. And a packet of plain crisps would be nice. I need salt and sugar.'

'I don't think Sir Hugh buys plonk. Come on Clare,' Lucy said. 'Let nursey help you.'

'Nice nursey.' Clare giggled and they went off arm in arm, two dark haired girls, like sisters to the casual observer.

My phone started ringing, it was Gramps. 'We saw you on television just now Simon. The beeb are putting an hour on every day about the show. Your Gran shrieked hard enough to deafen half the village. God knows what the neighbours thought I was doing to her. Honestly, I thought she'd had a seizure, I came running in from my onions and there you were on the television. You were brilliant. I'm taking your Gran up to The Wheal tonight, we'll make sure everyone knows about your win. You're going to be famous Simon, we're so proud of you.'

I assured them I was having a brilliant time and rang off. Sam was grinning at me.

'News travels eh?'

'Apparently. I think I might be having my fifteen minutes of fame, or is it notoriety?'

'I'm looking for Simon Sherwell, would that be either of you two gentlemen?' A skinny young woman in jeans with a red t-shirt and a short sleeved denim jacket was approaching us. She had a bag loaded with equipment over one shoulder. 'Bloody long way from the carpark with this stuff.'

Sam and I went into gentleman-mode and introduced ourselves, we were getting quite a patter rehearsed by now and there was definitely a competition to see who could be the most charming.

'I'm Kimberley Scott from the Cornish Echo & Gazette, you're the local celeb of the South West at the moment Mr Sherwell. I'm here to do an interview, or pick up your press pack if you have one. But I could do with a few photographs as well. And Mr Latchley, you're the Trelerric Sam Latchley aren't you? I came to Trelerric Vintage last summer. You're really putting your part of Cornwall on the map these days.'

She prattled on in this fashion and took photographs of us together and several of me on my own, from various angles, holding the Gold Award card and trying not to grin foolishly. We had to explain our working relationship and Sam managed to get a few plugs in for the gardens at Trelerric. I could see that Kimberley was quite taken with him, she flirted and smirked. Then she and I sat on the bench together while she asked me questions and recorded the answers. Once again I talked about my childhood gardening experiences and the influence Gramps and the old boys had had on me. I found myself being drawn out about the Cornish moorland, the landscape and my feelings for the natural rock formations and what they had taught me. She was a skilled interviewer and Cornish herself so I wasn't embarrassed to talk about folklore and landscape spirits, as interpreted by spriggans, the old spirits of the place.

'But this is an oriental-inspired garden isn't it Simon?' We were on first name terms now. 'How does that connect with Cornish folklore.'

'Well, the Japanese have an innate understanding of the spiritual connection of rocks and plants within landscape and the Cornish feeling for landscape is, to me anyway, similar. We celebrate the same ideas.'

'Interesting.' I could feel her attention slipping and her eyes were on Sam who was entertaining a group of onlookers. 'Very nice talking to you Simon. This day wasn't a complete waste of make-up after all.' She smiled at me briefly and asked for my number in case there was anything to verify or add before the article was printed. Fortunately I had one of the business cards Clare had organised.

'This will definitely be in the paper then?'

'Certainly. It's a decent feel good story, people are tired of reading about sex scandals and health cuts and the effects of austerity. And I'm pretty sure your story will be syndicated to the local magazines. Holidaymakers like to read about how happy and creative the Cornish are.' She was being just a little bit cynical. 'Better prepare yourself for a lot of interest, not to mention garden design work coming your way I would expect. You've got a website? Now, where can a girl get a decent cup of tea and a sandwich in this place? Do you think Sam Latchley might show me?'

TWENTY THREE

That evening the gang, as I now thought of us, all went out for a Chinese meal. A few of the other garden exhibitors were also in there and I got a couple of high fives while we all indulged in congratulatory banter. I noticed that Jeff looked after mum and that she allowed him to guide her to a chair, put her jacket over the back of it, sort out what she might like to drink. He wasn't fussing exactly, but they were definitely behaving like a couple and somehow it added to the already happy mood. Earlier I'd asked Clare what she thought.

'At their age if they find someone they hit it off with what's the point in hanging about? And now that you've left home your mum can have a life. Be pleased for them Simon.'

I agreed with her. Meanwhile Angela was glad to be having a night off as the Flinton's had arranged to dine with friends. Sam had some news.

'Seems like things are looking up Simon. Our local agricultural college has contacted me to ask if I would accept some horticulture students on a placement during term time. It means we get free help and they get experience and something different to write up for their student portfolios.'

'Oh good,' I said. 'Someone else to clean pots and do the boring stuff.'

'What's most boring then Sherwell?' Jeff quizzed.

'Pricking out.' I answered without hesitation.

For some reason the females of the party all sniggered and fell about laughing.

Talk turned inevitably to the show. None of us had quite anticipated the effects of being famous for five seconds. Even Ian Marriott had seen his name in a local newspaper article although he was ambivalent about the whole thing.

'It's just advertising for the show really. Gets the local punters in.'

The local news had also broadcast a few minutes about Sir Hugh being the sponsor of a winning garden. We got air time since he was from a long established local family and part of the neighbourhood. Somehow they'd managed to insert some footage of the gardens at Flinton Hall.

'Cheeky sods, looks like they stood on the terrace behind the garden room and shot my garden from there.' Jeff said, his dark eyes glittering.

'They did,' Angela said. 'I saw it all from upstairs, but Sir Hugh was with them so it wasn't as though they were poking about in your potting shed amongst your prize begonias and your secret cache of garden gnomes and porn magazines.' She was dubiously prodding some duck with hoisin sauce. 'Out of a can I shouldn't wonder.' She said to Ian.

'I don't have any begonias, tawdry plastic looking things. I don't like them and neither does Lady Felicity.' Jeff smouldered.

'Ah, but what about the gnomes reading porn magazines Jeff? I'd like to see her face if you put one of those down by the pond.' Sam laughed. 'And then I could borrow it for Trelerric, you know, one of those travelling gnomes, the sort that send postcards to their owners.'

'Having someone posh behind your first prize winning design will help no end Simon.' Ian told me as he speared a spring roll with his fork. 'Prospective employers and clients always like to think they're getting something of value. If you're going to start your own garden design business now you couldn't wish for a better beginning.'

I stared at him, and then at mum, remembering how I'd once asked mum if I was thick because I never seemed to have a plan. I just took opportunities as they arose and worked at them until something else came along. For a moment, amongst the general bonhomie, I felt a frisson of fear and doubt. Who the hell was I? Just a lad from Cornwall who did odd jobs was how Chloe Baxter had once described me, to my face. I felt Clare squeeze my thigh under the table, she'd recovered from the previous night's excesses and was ready to eat, but she was only drinking sparkling water. This was our last evening together, she and mum had to go back home tomorrow which was a pain, I really wanted to sit down with them both and talk about where this might be taking me. The thought of someone waving a wad of cash in my face and saying "your mission, should you chose to accept it, is to design a garden and then go and build it miles away from home" felt scary and just a tiny bit uncomfortable. And no prospective client would be as welcoming and as helpful as Sir Hugh Flinton.

After the meal we all went back to Jeff's place where we soberly drank coffee. Jeff put a Gerry Rafferty CD on and mum hummed along to Baker Street while they smiled at each other. There was definitely something going on there. Clare and I took refuge in her bedroom for half an hour, most of her things were already packed since they were leaving after breakfast. I was sorry about missing her birthday but she told me not to make a fuss.

'This has been amazing Simon. What other girl's fiancé has broadcast on national television that he was inspired to create a Gold Award winning garden simply by the dress she wore the night they got engaged? I can never forget a thing as romantic as that. I'll spend my birthday with mum and dad and we'll do something on our own together when you get home. It's only another few days.'

'Incredible girl.' I kissed her. 'Supportive and lovely, even when you're sozzled. I've got you a present, do you want it now or at the weekend?'

'Oh, when you come home. We can celebrate with a proper snuggle. You do realise I only want you for your body.'

I managed to slip a birthday card into her overnight bags while she wasn't looking.

The next day Sam got a call from his mother with instructions to take a look at the Cornish Echo & Gazette on-line. Apparently there was a photograph of the two of us on the front page.

'Bloody hell Simon, take a look at this!'

"Riding the Cornish Wave" stormed the headline, and the sub-heading had more to say. "Simon Sherwell takes Cornish-Shinto to the Moulton Show and wins Gold Award".

We both stared at it in amazement. I was one of several people who'd won gold, but naturally Cornwall was only interested in one of its own sons.

'Simon Sherwell of "Simon Sherwell Designs" based at Trelerric House has catapulted this obscure corner of South East Cornwall into the headlights with his sensitive garden design abilities inspired by Japanese Shinto.' Sam read out loud. "Readers may recall the outstanding success of Trelerric Vintage covered by this newspaper last summer. It seems that Trelerric House has more than one star in its firmament ..."

'Pass me the sick-bag.' I muttered.

'No, it's great. I love it. Although I'm not so sure about Trelerric being obscure. I wonder what Aunt Flick will make of it tonight.' Sam was enjoying all the silliness.

'You'll have to let me know.' I said. 'I'm being dined at a gastro pub by one of my garden clients. Richard Renwick from Pondside Cottage, he's in television and wants to talk to me about something.'

My phone beeped, it was a text from Gran. She was starting a scrap book about her famous grandson.

Sam finished reading the article and looked at me. 'Well, old son. I think this is your year. Take it by the horns, nuts, short and curlies and make the most of it. Opportunities like this don't come along that often.'

My phone beeped again. This time it was Andy Hauxwell. *"Greetings from darkest Cornwall where the sun don't shine! U got hidden talents. Well done mate. Andy. PS tell Sam the drinks r on him."*

Later I got texts from Steve Bradley, the carpenter and Rob Williams, the blacksmith saying *"Keep the end up for Cornwall!"* and *"Brill news, knock em dead!"*. And finally there was one from Daniel Pencraddoc. *"At last another local celeb, the limelight is all yours. Fiona sends love, so pleased."* Who says blokes can't be sensitive and caring.

That evening Lucy dropped me off in the Jag. It impressed the hell out of Richard Renwick when he saw me getting out of it.

'That's a good looking set of wheels and the chauffeur is something else.'

There was lots of handshaking and bullish back slapping. He seemed inordinately pleased to see me and the front of house manager ushered us to a discrete table for two. 'You won't be disturbed here gentlemen.' He murmured, with a faint but understanding smile.

'Simon, glad you could make it. Funny thing, I've sort of known you for years, but I hardly know you at all. You're quite the unknown outsider aren't you, working with your friend Sam Latchley at Trelerric House and then staying at Flinton Hall. But you're on a winning streak. I gather Sir Hugh Flinton is both a client of yours and your sponsor? Hobnobbing with the nobs. How did you manage that?'

How indeed, I wondered. I couldn't think of an answer and didn't want to tell Richard Renwick something I didn't quite understand myself so I just shrugged, saying something along the lines of knowing the right people and being in the right place at the right time.

'Clearly. And talented with it I think. I'm not so daft as to think you've got this far just by knowing the right people. What shall we medicate ourselves with? We're eating so we shouldn't be over the limit if we pace ourselves with some sparkling water as well. Expect the local filth are shit hot this week with all the show celebrations going on.'

I asked for a virgin Mary, on the rocks with a good dash of celery salt, tabasco and Worcestershire sauce. 'And a dash of lemon juice please.' I asked the waiter. I was getting to like this odd concoction.

'When in Worcestershire drink Worcestershire sauce.' I commented, pulling a face. To my surprise Richard cracked up laughing. He seemed delighted with everything I said or did.

'Cheers.' He was having a tonic water with orange juice. 'So, Simon. I suppose the first thing I should ask is can I afford you now that you've shot to fame? You are still looking after Pondside Cottage I take it?'

I confirmed that I was. I didn't want to let my regulars down, there was a feeling of trust built up over many years. And mum always said, "Never let the bread and butter jobs go Simon, they see you through hard times."

Another waiter appeared, all sir this, and sir that as he handed us the menus, flexing his wrists and standing with his feet placed precisely at ten to two on the clock. Jeff was right, I thought, glancing through the menu. Everything was all hand-cut and pan-fried with jus of varying descriptions and served with micro-herbs lovingly picked by wholesome maidens at dawn. I would probably need to get some chips to stave off night starvation afterwards. Stifling a smile because they really did have scallops with crispy bacon and buttered and steamed asparagus as a starter, I had to order it, it seemed like a good omen. The waiter suggested a glass of chilled pinot noir and I was happy to accept. Richard ordered a game terrine for starters and we both opted for the lobster main course, which came with a Chilean Chardonnay. It was superb. I was making mental notes in order to tell Sir Hugh. He loved all this stuff and I realised I'd be able to tell him that the food was fabulous, where the lobster was caught and where the grapes were grown.

'Well, Simon, you really have come on from the fresh faced young village lad I engaged six or seven years ago. You've not let the grass grow under your feet, if you'll forgive me an unintended joke. So how did you get into garden design?'

I told him that Daniel Pencraddoc's lady had encouraged me after seeing some of my sketches at a class she ran one summer.

'They were both very kind, Daniel gave me help with the IT side of things and Fiona is an artist, she gave me several tips on technique. They're lovely people.'

'Oh, so you're pals with the Pencraddoc's as well. Why not? A dot com millionaire and a couple of landed gentry. You really are a surprising young man. So what are your intentions now? I see from your business card that you're running your own business. Does that leave you with any free time?'

Running my own business. Business card. Hobnobbing with the nobs. These phrases resounded through my head like cymbals and trumpets. Who was playing the tune and was I following it or leading it?

'Well, I'm my own boss for half the week and I work with Sam Latchley the other half. It's flexible.' I said, wondering where this was going.

'Okay, that's good.' Richard Renwick was nodding. 'So you could fit some other stuff in. To make things succinct I watched the interview you did with whatshisname, that garden celeb fella, and I thought you were a natural in front of the camera. I've recently started my own production company over here, just a humble affair but I've had enough of London, and Amanda, my wife, has business interests of her own in the South West. One of the things I'm concentrating on is a soft focus approach to local events and issues, I'm calling it "Events South West" at the moment. The sort of thing you can watch with the kids without being horribly startled. Anything from the local shows, beach cleaning groups to someone getting involved in rescuing a dolphin. That sort of worthy shit. I want a front man who isn't afraid to roll up his sleeves and try throwing a pot, rounding up moorland ponies, blacksmithing, dry stone walling, freezing his balls off star gazing on a frosty night in February on Dartmoor. Get the picture? All the trendy stuff which people like to watch or think they can do, but without getting off the sofa. But I want to delve a little bit deeper, not just showcasing the talent out there but finding out how the talent came about, or the history behind something.' He was in full swing with his ideas and his hand gestures were becoming elaborate. 'I've got a good little team, producers, researchers, cameramen and sound recordists. And I've signed up a girl who rides horses and works as a shepherdess near Exmoor. She's also a wild food forager. One of my researchers found her via her blog. She's older than you so you'll be her bit of fresh, her sofa pet. It will be an interesting combination.'

'So what do you want me for?'

'I want you to be her co-presenter.'

'On television?'

'On the telly,' Richard nodded. 'On the magic box of lights. I think you've got the right face for it, the right look. You're the guy next door. I'd trust you with my granny and my mum, although on reflection maybe not with my daughter.' He laughed but without real humour. 'You can talk to anyone of any age, you've an old head on young shoulders Simon and you're engaging and respectful. And I've got friends in useful places, as a man like you will appreciate. I know an awful lot but I also know some very helpful people. I've not made enemies in my career. The way ahead is to design and run my own thing and to show and sell it to other networks. There's a future in this believe me. And I think that having you involved would benefit both of us enormously.'

I couldn't wait to tell Clare and I phoned her in her lunch break. 'What? On television, working for the Pondlife man? Oh my god!'

'Yeah, as one of the faces, there's a co-presenter already signed up. A girl, I don't know who she is. I've got to do some camera takes or tests or whatever they call them. It's a whole new language to learn. It's only a couple of days work a month at the moment. But Richard reckons it will grow and evolve.'

'Meanwhile you carry on doing your other jobs. It could work I suppose.'

I told her that Sam would be taking on some horticulture students. 'So if I have to be away, filming, he'll still have help.' I felt responsible for my place at Trelerric and conscious of my friendship with Sam. 'And for the hours I'm not working at Trelerric I get paid by the production company.'

'Filming.' Clare echoed. 'Wow.'

'I know, it's mad isn't it. I feel weird anyway. But I've got to go now, Clare, I love you. See you at the weekend.'

Sam was waving to me from the garden plot. Actually he was gesturing quite urgently so I hurried over. Cecily Reid-Ross was with him, resplendent in red, white and blue stripes with the ever present ruffles and pleats.

'Well Simon,' Cecily began in her gushing manner. 'This is definitely your week. I've come to tell you that the people, the visitors that is, have voted you "Best Show Garden". So we need to do another short congratulatory interview and a little award ceremony in an hour. I'll be back shortly, I just need to powder my nose.'

She wobbled off importantly.

'What's she channelling today?' Sam mused. 'Is it tea towel, deckchair or Union Jack?'

I couldn't think of a reply. I was speechless.

TWENTY FOUR

I learned that people had voted for me partly because they loved the romantic slant they'd learned from my earlier television interview but also because they were were tired of what they called garden gimmicks. People were getting fed up with stupidly expensive sculptural pieces in plastic and steel, and responded to my use of what they described as honest materials. One person had written that it was so lovely to see a hedgehog-friendly pond rather than a mens' urinal water feature. The interviewer told me she was going to quote some of the comments in a magazine feature for the RHS.

'Interesting angle I think, a bold challenge is being posed, are the public wanting to return to age old tried and trusted garden features? Are they going back to basics or being reminded of kinder, childhood times? Your use of natural and traditional materials is restful I must say. I might check on sales of garden furniture, purchasing trends and so on, do people want plastic or do they prefer wood? Plastic anything is bad news these days don't you think?' She was thinking aloud and jotting down a list of her ideas.

I didn't really have an opinion, so I said I just knew what worked for me and that I preferred materials which lasted and weathered and would eventually return to the ground. She liked the way I saw things as an eternally revolving cycle so all that got written down as well.

'You're intelligent, decent looking and successful Mr Sherwell. You're a winner in all respects. This is going to be a good article. It will be interesting following your career.' She said. I thought she was just being kind.

After the fuss had died down I stood looking at my Gold Award Card and the surprisingly small Best Show Garden trophy with something like tired disbelief. A trickle of enquiries had already come in asking about my availability for doing some private work. It all felt unreal. For a moment I wondered if everything was happening too quickly. There were all these scenarios, suggestions, invitations and offers, but I had the uncomfortable feeling that my feet weren't quite touching the floor. I wanted to talk to my family and to Clare. I wanted to get back to normal, but normal didn't seem to want to get back to me.

Jeff, Ian and Sam opted to spend half a day each with me for the remainder of the show to enable me to get a break and something to eat. The public continued to come in unabated numbers and the last couple of days went by fast. On the final morning of the show the representative of an insurance company approached me and asked if they could buy the garden. They had an open central courtyard to fill in their new office building up in Birmingham and the Chairman of the Board thought my garden might be relaxing for staff to look out onto. They offered silly money, a ridiculously large amount, and said that as they already had a team of garden contractors currently landscaping the car parking area, they could take this over if I would simply provide an overview or something. Apparently I just had to make a site visit and say if everything was in the right place. I accepted, understanding that this was what garden designers hoped for. And it saved me from having to do something with all the materials.

It made the breakdown a lot easier because we just loaded everything onto the contractor's vehicles. Finally we were done, the organisers signed off our ex-plot and we all felt a weary sense of achievement. Over a last cup of tea in the refreshment tent I thanked the guys for being so helpful and such fun to work with. Later I talked to Sam over a quiet beer.

'Usually men get together to forget their problems, it's only women who get together to discuss them, but I think I know how your dad felt when he said that you all wouldn't do the Trelerric Vintage experience again. It's been the most exciting, exhausting and unreal experience of my life.'

'But it's given you the confidence you need to strike out. You're capable of going places Simon, I can see it and so can other people.'

'That's the nicest thing anyone's ever said. But Sam, I've got this niggle at the back of my mind. Am I genuinely talented or am I just a one shot wonder with a wealthy backer? Sir Hugh has been behind me all the way. And Lady Felicity has been helpful as well.'

'Look at it as though he was your stabilising wheels when you were learning to ride a bike. He's just given you a push. It was you who came up with the goods and won the award, not him. It's up to you now brother.'

'I know. But I'm still wondering what I'm going to do when I grow up. Somehow I can never quite see a plan, or the bigger picture.'

Back at Trelerric it was a relief just to be with Clare. She'd welcomed me home with ecstatic hugs and kisses to a delicious meal, amazing considering the tiny amount of space she had for food prep. I told her she was a miracle worker and we celebrated the events of the past fortnight in a low key gentle manner. Then I gave her the birthday present I'd bought at the jewellers, a pair of emerald earrings with a tiny diamond above the drop. She loved them.

'You'll always be my special girl who deserves green stones.' I told her.

In the failing light of a summer evening we strolled round the grounds and over to the Cherryfields Cottage site. The place was unrecognisable. It had walls, windows, a roof, and had been redesigned to include a covered space for parking vehicles, a wood store and a garden room with an extra bedroom above off the extended kitchen so that Sam could see his beloved new orchard. Not that it was planted yet and I still thought he'd need to put pigs in for six months to clear the ground.

'It's going to be lovely isn't it Simon, they're so lucky.' Clare said wistfully. 'They'll be in by August.'

I put my arm round her shoulders. 'Yes they are, but I think we might start looking around to buy our own place soon. You do the finances, you know what we've got saved between us. And there's a tidy sum on its way from that insurance company up in Birmingham who've just bought the show garden. All I have to do is go up for a couple of days, strut about importantly and tell them if they've put it in right, and charge them another fee for the privilege.'

The way Clare smiled at me made me feel as though I'd hung the stars in the sky just for her.

'And I'm getting some clients lined up. There are two definitely wanting something done, one's in Devon, the other is on the Welsh borders. The problem is I need to get a decent second hand working vehicle, something like Jeff's Toyota. My jalopy isn't going to last much longer and I can't carry gardening kit in it.'

Clare was pondering the idea of somewhere of our own though. I could see she had what she called her "nesting head" on. We both wanted to stay as close to home as possible, we had roots. As Gramps had once said, there's something about Cornwall that suits a Sherwell.

The following Friday night mum invited us all round to eat with her. She was endlessly interested in the recent events and Gran brought her scrap book. I was taken aback to see just how much there was to collect about my recent rise to fame. Mum sat watching all this with a contented expression on her face. Something smelled good in the kitchen and she was, I noticed, looking pretty happy.

'You can Google yourself Simon,' Gran said, the inveterate silver surfer that she was. 'All sorts of things about you, and photographs too. You've made a name for yourself. I'm sure it's because you have a good aspect to Jupiter in your birth chart.'

'What does that mean?' Clare asked.

'Simon's got Jupiter in Libra, and Jupiter is the bringer of gifts and joy ....'

'When are we eating mum?' I interrupted. Once Gran got started she'd never stop. 'I'm starving.'

'Just one more guest to arrive then we'll start.'

'What? Who?' Clare said, looking round.

I heard an engine and a muted beep. Clare looked out of the window.

'It's Jeff!'

Mum smiled, a secret little smile full of expectation. Then she pulled herself together and tried on a graceful hostess expression. It didn't work, I could see that she was thrilled to see him. No one else noticed because they were all looking after Clare who had gone to the door.

Jeff came in smiling, looking pleased with himself and not a bit daunted by a sea of faces. He offloaded a bottle of wine and a bunch of flowers, which at least gave mum something to do for a moment while she collected herself. 'Hope I've remembered my manners, not often I get an invitation to dinner with the family. Hello everyone, I'm Jeff.'

He shook my hand before kissing Clare on the cheek. 'Your mum wanted me to give her some more dancing lessons,' he said to me. 'So I had to come down. Found it okay, no problem with your directions Gwenna.' He casually took her hand and kissed her on the cheek as well and I thought I could feel the crackle in the atmosphere between them.

'Dancing? You're dancing again Gwen, after all these years?' Gran was looking at Jeff wonderingly.

Mum made the introductions all over again and Jeff was accepted immediately, as the man who'd helped me and the man who'd got my mum dancing. Apparently mum had once loved dancing and I'd never known it.

'Is this get up okay Gwenna?' Jeff was wearing a plum coloured striped shirt with grey jeans and a dark blue zipped top, what the assistant in the Truro men's outfitters would call "weekend wear".

'Fine, you look just fine Jeff.' Mum replied, ducking into the kitchen. 'Food's nearly ready everyone.' She called out.

'Staying over for the weekend are you Jeff?' I asked him quietly while I was getting him a glass of cider.

'Might be. Early days yet. Would it trouble you if I was?'

I shook my head. 'I've never seen my mum smiling like that. Just be kind to each other.'

'Gotcha.' Jeff replied, and we rejoined the others.

The good mood intensified as Gran and Gramps got the measure of Jeff and asked him all the same questions they'd asked me when I got back a week ago. They enjoyed the way he called me Sherwell and teased me about the way we had worked together. He also teased Clare about her hangover that night, complimented mum on her cooking and made friends with Ginger. Jeff could do no wrong and I was more than happy.

I'd hardly got my life back into gear when a person with a gravelly voice telephoned me, announced it was Richard Renwick's PA Mickey calling, and called me darling. I was instructed to go up to the studio at the crack of dawn for a few days to sort out the preliminaries, whatever they were, meet the team and spend a day at a sheepdog trials on Exmoor. Mickey had got us all booked into a sizeable B&B close to where the shepherdess co-presenter lived with her husband, a sheep farmer predictably enough. This was her territory and her first piece to camera. We met for the first time in Richard's office. His studio was at a newly converted farm near Bridgewater, just off the M5. It was one of those old nineteenth century Barton Farm models with buildings around a huge central courtyard and renovated with no expense spared. He and his wife lived in some style in the massive old farmhouse.

'Welcome to my humble place of work.' Richard greeted me, bouncing on his toes as usual. This is Miranda, your co-presenter assuming all goes well and you don't hate each other on sight.'

'Hi, Simon Sherwell.' I put my hand out to a diminutive creamy skinned redhead with eyes like searchlights.

She was almost engulfed by the high backed swivel chair she was sitting in and had a fit of the giggles before shaking my hand with a surprisingly powerful grip for a tiny woman. Well, I suppose she was used to throwing sheep around.

'Miranda Linden. So you're the posh award winning gardener bloke. Are you as terrified as I am? I've been trotting to the loo all morning and we're not even filming today.'

Miranda had a refreshingly blunt honesty which made me grin. Richard left us to talk for a few minutes. 'I'm not posh,' I hastened to tell her. 'I'm a real jobbing gardener who just sort of got noticed. I've worked for Richard for years, I look after his holiday cottage in my village, but I don't really know him. He saw my performance at the Moulton Show and invited me to take a look at this idea.'

'Well I'm not really a shepherdess, I just used that name for my blog. I think Richard is a bit of a talent spotter, and probably quite ruthless under the trendy floral shirt and Spanish leather aftershave. But get that guy, the PA, Mickey. What do you think of him?' Miranda said as Mickey walked past the glass door dressed in flat lace up boots, skinny strawberry coloured trousers, a loose pink and yellow top and with a multicoloured fringed scarf wound round his neck.

I wasn't sure what to say, Mickey looked about twelve, wore eyeliner and had amazing eyelashes. His glossy brown hair was cut into a deep fringe but very short at the back. One ear was pierced in three places and he wore a silver metal bracelet with his name engraved on it.

'He's great. We swap make-up tips and give each other neck massages.' I said, deadpan.

Miranda squealed with laughter.

Richard looked in at us with an approving face and called us through to meet the team. There were more introductions, nods and handshakes depending on how people felt. They seemed to be a very relaxed bunch but I noticed the sharp-eyed awareness of people who were professional observers. Then he handed Miranda and me into their care; we were to learn about their world, their way of doing things, their insight into setting the scene and taking the shot. It was both fascinating and exhausting. A producer called Molly got us practising a few ideas in a paddock outside, observed by a couple of laid back donkeys and some curious chickens, and I was surprised to find how the time sped by. It was such a focussed and intense business it left me bone tired from concentrating. One of the sound guys patted me on the shoulder. I'd learned he was freelance and not tied to Richard's outfit, but he did a lot of work for him.

'Well done mate, you're willing to learn. Keep that nice fresh smile you've got, stay off the sauce and don't let your blood sugar crash. Oh, and read the research, rehearse your lines and always turn up on time. It helps and we'll get along fine if we can all go home at a reasonable hour with the job signed off. The most important thing is to keep Richard happy, he's got one hell of a temper if people dick around. But he's okay, he really knows his stuff and wants us all to be successful.'

Mickey told me I was being paid my travelling expenses but nothing else for those few days, since Pondside Productions was covering my accommodation and food. I was immediately anxious about the earnings I was loosing. 'Don't worry my darling,' he said, twiddling his ear studs. 'The readies will start coming in once we've got the schedule up and running and that has to be like super fast, we can't sit around on our arses or nobody gets paid. It's not a fucking charity as Richard keeps telling us.'

Filming was taking place the next day at a small local event being held on Miranda's family farm. She was jittery and

Richard took her to one side to give her a pep talk. I saw her jumping up and down and then swinging her arms, Richard seemed to be a great believer in breathing exercises and I could hear him saying something about expanding the chest area. I watched, with growing respect, as Miranda talked to camera about managing sheep, the particular merits of the breed, a little bit of breed history and so on. She was wearing a peachy coloured t-shirt under green overalls, the old fashioned type with a frontal bib. Her wellies were dark green with a pattern of little fluffy white sheep and she looked cute enough to sit on a toadstool wearing gauzy wings. I looked down at my clothes, I was wearing the brown moleskin trousers with my working boots, a short sleeved check shirt in blue, brown and white, and my cap. I thought the outfit had "country boy" written all over it. Miranda then had to show her prowess with her sheepdog, a six year old boy with a glossy patched black, brown and white coat called Tip. He also had one blue and one brown eye. They were pure poetry as she directed him over the field and brought a small flock into a fold. She was definitely more than a pretty face and her energy was amazing.

The camera guy called it a wrap and Miranda let the slightly bewildered sheep out when something, I think it was a hare, leapt from behind a tussock and started heading our way, followed by a spooked flock of startled sheep and a deeply interested Tip. Realising that one of the crew had left the top field gate open I rushed forwards with my arms outstretched to head them off, yelling at the top of my voice and managing to turn all except one, a big hairy brute with evil eyes that just kept on coming. Acting on instinct I threw myself forward almost in a rugby tackle whilst shouting to anyone paying attention to shut the bloody gate. The sheep and I slithered along the grass together in a close embrace until the sheer force of the animal knocked me down and the beast passed over me. I lay on the grass for a minute, completely winded, before sitting up, minus my cap.

There was a round of applause from the few local eventers and a smattering of laughter. 'The damn thing sat on me.' I said, in surprise as much as anything. Then I realised that the camera was trained on me and that the sound recordist was grinning broadly.

'Welcome to the team Simon, we've got the whole episode. The day Simon Sherwell had a sheep sit on his face.'

'Will they show that sequence?' Sam asked after I told him about it and he'd stopped laughing. 'And are they calling you "sheep shagger Sherwell" then?' He started laughing again.

'I hope not. It's supposed to be a family show although the sound guy said they could replace the risqué dialogue with something he calls "atmos", like just the sound of the wind whistling over the field, sheep bleating and a buzzard mewing and so on. I think it was a rite of passage for me though.'

It was good just doing normal stuff at Trelerric and seeing Clare at home after work. She'd started looking on-line at properties and groaning with disbelief at the prices. Despite the very healthy additions to our savings over the past six months we were still only at the bottom rung of the buying ladder. It almost caused an argument. I'd suggested we should perhaps lower our sights and look at flats but Clare was desperate for a garden. She wanted to grow some veg, keep a couple of chickens and a small dog and did not want to live sandwiched between people.

'They might hear us and we might hear them Simon. I'd hate it. I'd rather stay here at the Coach House despite the lack of a proper kitchen or a washing machine.' She said firmly but with a slight wobble to her chin.

I cuddled her and stroked her silky hair. 'Okay. It was silly of me to suggest it. You're right, I'd hate it as well. We've just got to keep looking and keep working and saving. And we're not having that bad a time are we?'

Clare agreed that we weren't, and said that everybody in our circumstances struggled at first. My reaction was to get on with the requests from the couple of clients I'd landed from the Moulton Show. Jeff was happy for me to lodge at his place while I did the job for the people who lived on the Welsh border and mum took some holiday leave and came up with me, ostensibly to cook and help take care of us. Not that they made me feel like a gooseberry or anything. Jeff helped with the build over a weekend and that made all the difference. The other job was for a retired couple who lived in Devon and were within easy distance of home. Their plot was tiny but had a superb view of the sea. They wanted what they called maintenance free seaside simplicity so I used large river cobbles, gravel and driftwood to some good effect. Any planting was confined to pots. In my spare time I carried on with my usual work until it occurred to me that I didn't have any spare time, I actually worked all the time, harder and more efficiently. Then Richard phoned.

'Okay sunshine, you're on. I put that impromptu clip around of you and Miranda with the sheep, together with Pondside's proposals and we've got a bite.' He went on to outline a schedule, which included several days work a month at a variety of venues, including a dog show, a County show, a rare breeds farm and so on. Richard was using another team following other ideas, and putting a programme out which blended the stories together.

'Kids these days have the attention span of a gnat, so it's lots of stuff in a visual magazine format. You get to do the interesting outdoor things, the others are studio based and deal with people coming in to be filmed.' Richard explained. 'Mickey is grouping everything together as far as possible for you and Miranda, saves me having to send people all over the place, wasting money travelling and so on. I've got other fish to fry and other projects to pursue, so you'll be a small tight-knit team. Call me or Mickey at once if there are problems. I've got to stress this is a trial. You've got four months guaranteed work unless you cock things up. Good luck.'

I felt as though I was diving straight in at the deep end but it was great going over the schedule, and talking about the various animals, with Clare. 'You're my top veterinary nurse advisor thingy, you know all sorts of stuff. I shall be quoting you and sounding like an expert.' I told her.

Clare was handling all my financial business, she was proving to be a whizz at invoices and cash flow. I wondered where she got her good financial brain from and said so one day when Sam and I cadged a sandwich off Maggie in the kitchen at Trelerric House.

'Clare's a natural at business. She's a great manager and absolutely spot on with the finances. I just give her all my receipts and she tells my clients what they owe me. It's amazing. Who does she take after in your family Maggie?'

Maggie had stood rooted to the spot and wiping the same bit of worktop repeatedly. 'I'm not sure I can give you an answer Simon. She's a very capable girl, she was good at maths at school. I thought she might go into accountancy but she went for veterinary nursing instead. Sometimes I wonder if she's wasted at the vets.'

While we were there Gran phoned me. 'I've seen you on telly again Simon, on "Five o'clock Fun", that newsy kids' programme. You were chasing sheep and one knocked you down. It was very funny, like "You've Been Framed". Were you horribly bruised afterwards?'

I told her I was fine apart from being covered in grass stains and that I was going to be filming at a rare breeds farm next. 'Miranda's meeting the fluffy animals and apparently I'm receiving a lesson on how to round up moorland grazing animals, on horseback. I'm really looking forward to it.'

Maggie was impressed. Sam snorted. 'Get you cowboy.'

Actually I was terrified, I'd asked if we could do it the other way round, with me meeting the fluffy animals. 'Miranda can ride, she'd be a natural at this.' I moaned.

'Yeah but you might fall off. That makes it funny.' Richard had said.

Over the next couple of months I found myself expounding knowledgeably about all sorts of things I'd barely heard of until the researcher gave me my homework and I was talked through the presentation. On one occasion I had to stand up to my knees in seawater holding an armful of stinking seaweed whilst talking to camera about fertilisers used in past times. The researcher insisted I called it "olden times", which made me cringe inside, but at least I was in my comfort zone with the information. I explained the uses of seaweed, once called "oarweed", mixed with lime and dung to improve the ground on the banks of the Tamar where the market gardens used to be. The continuity shot took me to some derelict old lime kilns on the banks of the river and I was able to continue the educational slant by explaining the use of lime, which helped neutralise the acid in Cornish soils. And of course we had great fun explaining where the dung came from, all those horses and people in Plymouth. Well, it all had to go somewhere and Cornwall got a lot of it. I greatly enjoyed telling Sam that his beloved Trelerric lands were covered with centuries of human "night soil" and horse poo.

Another time I was supposed to be filmed making a decoction out of boiled foxglove leaves with a mad-haired woman in Devon who used it to control sawfly in her fruit cages. The slant there was supposed to be that plants magically grew together in a way which could be used harmoniously and as a natural pesticide. I wasn't happy with it and personally I was concerned that children might think foxgloves were, therefore, edible. I didn't think the mad-haired woman was even a remotely responsible adult and I made my views known to Molly, that day's producer, which resulted in a call to Richard and she handed the phone over to me.

'I can't do this one Richard, the research isn't right. Foxgloves have another name, Dead Men's Bells. Drying or boiling the leaves doesn't reduce their toxicity, it's best left to the pharmaceutical industry to handle this. If I can I'll convince the lady to make a wild garlic decoction, it grows in her garden, it's just as effective, wonderfully stinky and nothing like as lethal. I'll ask her if she'll change to that.'

I handed the phone back to Molly and heard Richard back me up.

'We're trying to educate and amuse, not poison the little bastards. If Simon says there's a problem then pay attention Molly, he's the garden plants expert, not you.'

To give Molly credit she didn't have a hissy fit. 'You know your plants then. That's giving me ideas, we could do a wild pharmacy slot. It would fit in nicely with Miranda's foraging knowledge.'

I shuddered. 'I'm not keen on the idea Molly. You'd need to find a qualified expert. All I know is enough to treat plants with a great deal of respect. The problems of plant sap and skin reactions and potency and all that.' I finished obscurely, trying to remember something I'd read years ago which had fascinated me.

The style of the show was to engage persons of all ages with things that were cute, furry, smelly, oozy or plain weird. Miranda did the cute fluffy stuff, I got most of the smelly stuff and we both did the weird stuff. Social media started coming into play and Miranda and I discovered that our ratings were climbing. We had a good on-screen relationship and enjoyed what we were doing. So when the four months were up we were both shocked when Richard called us in and told he was going to be dropping the show.

'Why, what did we do wrong?' Miranda was white faced.

'Nothing. I think we've got the angle wrong that's all and it was only a pilot. I've been asked if we could use you for similar stuff but with a less quirky wide-eyed take on things. Viewers like your approach and your obvious interest in the subjects. There's the usual speculation about whether you're having it off with each other but you don't need to pay any attention to that. So we're changing to a weekly hour long slot of four fifteen minute topics. Local network only at the moment, but time will tell. You do two slots each, get to sit on a sofa in the studio with a potted palm and some ugly stuffed toys behind you and do voice-overs and linked presentations. Oh, and I want another body on the sofa.'

'Who?' I asked.

'That bloody dog of Miranda's. Tip is starting to get his own followers.'

'Oh wow,' Clare said when I told her the news. 'I'd love a dog like Tip. He's so intelligent.'

I thought she had a broody look. This girl had a lot of love to give.

I wanted to talk to Clare about my working hours, they were impossible. Sam hadn't objected to me taking time off while I'd done the small rock garden on the Welsh borders. He'd got two horticultural students on day release now so they were covering some of my work but I just didn't feel right going all that way on my own to do a job. I'd covered my costs and made a little bit extra but it hadn't made me happy. I was confused about my reasons for wanting to become a garden designer since becoming seduced by the challenge and fun of the television work, which was looking promising and certainly more lucrative. Clare had an opinion.

'I think it's because you're working with people Simon. You loved the Moulton experience because there were four of you working for a common aim and having fun while you were doing it. I think it's the same with the telly stuff, you're building a working relationship with people you like and respect and you're meeting lots of new people. Whereas with the garden design business you don't have a garden building team and you're working solo apart from that bit of help Jeff provided on the Welsh garden. And it's a lot of hard work, pressure and responsibility. It might work if you team up with those other guys you met at the show, the ones who live in Devon, but it's a lot to think about, and you wouldn't be in control.'

I looked at her, sitting on our little sofa with her feet in my lap. She made it seem so bloody simple and obvious.

'You don't think I'm chickening out of the garden design thing then?' I asked, feeling a sense of relief creeping over me.

'No, it's still something to fall back on and you can do the occasional one if you like the brief, but it's a bit like turning a hobby into a way of earning a living. It can kill the love of the hobby. You'll always be able to turn a garden round because you can see what's needed and how to make things beautiful. But the telly stuff is a different thing, a challenge that's interesting and stimulating. And you're lucky to have been offered the work. I know it's early days yet, but maybe working with Sam and for Pondlife is enough for the time being.'

'Phew.' I felt my shoulders relaxing and my stomach unknotting. She was right, and it was typical of my way of working, I never had a plan, never had a job interview, I just worked hard at whatever came along. 'And what about the holiday cottages?' I'd already had to drop the casual work in the village.

'That's for you to decide. But I'd like to see a bit more of you when I'm not on the weekend shift sometimes.'

'You can see of much of me as you want, starting now.' I lifted her feet up and swung her round so that she was lying against my chest. 'Prepare to be monstered, you gorgeous woman.'

Thinking about keeping Richard Renwick happy I decided to spend Saturday morning tidying up the garden at Pondside Cottage. I'd just parked outside when I saw Chloe Baxter walking down the village road on the other side with her hands thrust into the pockets of a misshapen pink hoodie. She was wearing grey leggings and had her head down, I watched her for a moment and didn't think she was trying to avoid me.

'Chloe!' I called her name and she put her head up like a startled animal. Seeing me she crossed the road. It's a quiet village with about ten cars an hour but she didn't even bother to check.

'Hi Simon.' She said without enthusiasm.

'Chloe. Are you okay?' There were shadows under her eyes and a large spot on her chin. This used to be a pretty girl but she suddenly looked older than her age and a bit defeated. The hood fell back and I noticed her hair needed washing.

'Rough. I look it as well, I know, don't tell me. I've been having a tough time lately.'

She went on to tell me a litany of woes and troubles. Her job in Exeter had been a disaster, her line manager was a bully and had pinched her ideas, the girl she'd shared a flat with had been a nasty bitch and pinched her clothes, her last boyfriend had been a bastard. In fact all her boyfriends had been bastards. I felt as though I was suffocating, she was sucking the oxygen out of the atmosphere. What on earth had happened to her? She'd been out of my reach and now, let's face it, I wouldn't have looked at her twice if I hadn't known her.

'I'm so sorry Chloe. Maybe you just got in with the wrong sort of people. You need a break and a change. You were so full of ideas about going places, you had plans.'

'Yes I did. And I remember saying that you were just a stick-in-the-mud without prospects. Now look at you.'

'You actually told me all I amounted to was an odd-job man, which in a way is still true.' I smiled at her. 'I'm still just doing what the fates throw my way, and I'm still looking after a couple of holiday cottages.'

'Yeah, but your odd jobs are stellar. You won an award for something and now you're turning up on bloody television. And I see you've got decent wheels now. You're quite a surprise Simon. You're the one that got away. Another bloody mistake I made.'

She looked both sad and defiant, a crazy mixed up kid. I remembered my mum once saying that her mother was a neurotic cow or something. I looked at her with some compassion, I had liked her, no, I'd been infatuated at one point, but it seemed so long ago. Now she stood there gazing wistfully at me, wearing washed out faded clothes. Everything about her had seen better days.

'I think you dumped me Chloe.' I wanted her to feel that she'd been in control, the one making decisions and to remember that at least I hadn't treated her badly. Unfortunately she took it the wrong way.

'Yeah, thanks. Remind me that every decision I make is crap. Well, I'll be off, got to get something from the shop. My useless sodding mother can't even remember to buy food these days.'

She turned and left me, hood back up, head down again, fists balled angrily into her pockets. Poor kid, there was nothing I could do for her.

I let myself through the pretty iron gate and got on with the task of tidying up leaves and snipping a few wayward plants. There didn't seem to have been any visitors staying lately and the cottage had a pensive, waiting look about it. I'd always liked this one the best even though it was only a small place, but the garden was pretty and got a lot of sun. It also wasn't overlooked. There was a low granite wall at the front with enough room to park two vehicles in a sort of bay off the village road. As I worked I thought about what Sam had asked Andy Hauxwell to do at Cherryfields Cottage. The garden room extension to the kitchen was a good idea and I could see it working here, making a lovely family area and providing a secluded terrace between it and the sitting room at the back of the house. You'd just have to replace the small windows with French windows and it would be somewhere for a toddler to play safely. I had that peculiar flying, falling sensation that I usually got when visualising something that would really work, when my design-head kicked in. Clare's special flying dream.

Smiling wryly at my imagination I went and peered in through the windows. Cozy, would be how an estate agent would describe it. But it had a kitchen, a sitting room with a small woodstove, a front room currently set up as a dining room and I knew it was advertised as having two double bedrooms and a bathroom. The ground floor could be reconfigured and made much more spacious, useful and interesting. I was lost in my thoughts when a man's voice called.

'Ahoy Simon, is that you back there?'

I called back. 'It's me, who's that?'

It was Rob Williams, the blacksmith. He had something strapped to his chest and a large grin on his face.

'What on earth?' I began. 'Is that a baby or are you wearing a hideous surgical appliance?'

'Thought you might like to meet Joshua Robert Williams, my son and heir.'

'Blimey mate, congratulations.'

The baby was tiny and new. Rob was glowing with pride and love.

'When? And how's Su?' I asked, vaguely remembering Daniel Pencraddoc saying something about IVF months ago, on the day of Sally's historical revelations.

'He was born two weeks ago. Su's at the farm shop, first time out together as a family and I've taken her to buy groceries. How romantic is that? But I'm showing Josh his new home. I'd have thought he'd be a bit more impressed though after being cooped up inside mum for nine months.'

'Wow. Hello Josh. I've never met a Joshua before.'

'Family name, Su's dad is called Joshua. He's a doctor, lives in Perth, Australia. They're all coming over for the christening.'

I asked him how work was going, knowing that like me he was self-employed.

'Okay. I can't concentrate of course, all I want to do is sit and stare at this little chap. We can't believe it.'

'You made the gate here didn't you Rob?' I said, changing the subject.

Rob glanced round at the side gate, all arty wavy reeds and grasses. 'I did, seems like ages ago now. The summer Su and I finally got together. The owner works in television I think, he and his wife wanted something horrible made from horseshoes but I talked them out of it. They had absolutely no taste whatsoever. I remember this place before they bought it, when it was empty, with a rotting sofa up the side and a rusting Ford Cortina at the front. Looks as though it could do with a bit of love and attention now.' He was peering at some rot on a window frame.

I smiled. 'I'm working for the owner, Richard Renwick. He's got a television production company called Pondside Productions, Clare calls it Pondlife Productions.'

Rob laughed. 'Of course, I forgot, you're something on the telly now aren't you. You were the talk of The Wheal. But not too posh to carry on with your gardening jobs then. Anyway, nice to see you Simon, I'd better get back to Su, she doesn't like being too far away from this little guy.'

Later, as I was about to leave, the lady who cleaned the cottage for Mrs Renwick saw me and waved. Mum always described her as a gossipy old tart, but she was harmless enough.

'Still looking after this place then Simon? I've seen you on television, you probably won't be doing this job much longer will you? I doubt the Renwick's are going to keep it anyway, but you see more of them than I do so I expect you know.'

'Sorry, I'm not with you.'

'Well, after the last holiday people left it in such a mess Mrs Renwick said she was fed up with the place and unlikely to take any more bookings. They've moved up Somerset way haven't they, they don't need a bolt hole like when they lived in London.'

'Yes, no, you're right. I suppose they don't.'

'No sign of an agent's board yet though.' The woman was clearly hoping for information but I couldn't supply any.

I took pity on her desperate desire to talk. 'What did the holiday people do?'

'Upset a bottle of red wine on the sofa judging by the stain. Smoked in the bedroom and left a burn mark on the bedside table. Broke a cup and a plate and left the grill filthy. Oh, and put something down the toilet, we had to call a plumber out.'

'Ye gods. The way some people behave. I hope they lost their holiday deposit. But I don't know anything about the Renwick's intentions I'm afraid.'

'Oh well, I suppose it will get snapped up by some other incomers. Good luck with the telly. Nice to see you Simon.'

I decided not to say anything to Clare. There was no point in telling her because we just couldn't afford to buy in my village. Thinking about her, with her lively pretty face and glossy hair and most of all her lovely positive nature made me sigh with relief. She wasn't a moaner like Chloe, she didn't have a bad bone in her body. Suddenly I wanted to hold her very close and tell her these things, tell her just how special she was. My phone buzzed, it was mum.

'Hi mum, okay?'

'Simon, where are you?'

'In the village, just finished doing Pondside. I was about to get some shopping and go home. Clare finishes at two today so I'm picking her up.'

'Simon, can you come here, now I mean. Something's happened.'

'Are you okay?' I said again.

'Yes. But I must see you.'

'Okay, five minutes max.'

Mum was standing at the open door, waiting for me. She spoke without greeting me or even going inside. 'I've had a letter.'

I realised she was clutching an envelope in one hand and I could see that it had been torn open.

'What it is? Is something wrong mum?'

She looked shocked and her eyes had a curiously blind look about them. 'It's your dad. He's dead. I never even knew.'

'Come on, inside with you. Sit down and tell me what's going on.' I took her by the shoulders and turned her round. 'In you go.' I said kindly.

Mum lead the way into the kitchen and in that time honoured tradition I switched the kettle on. Making tea in times of crisis is in the British DNA. Ginger bumped around my legs mewing pitifully, there was definitely something wrong, mum never let him go hungry.

'Can I read it, or do you want to tell me what the letter says.' I asked, glancing at the kitchen clock. I'd wanted to surprise Clare with the shopping done and take her home, but this was clearly important.

'Your father's dead.' Mum said again, her voice sounding as though she was a long way away. 'He died about ten years ago and I never knew. I never even felt anything.'

'So why are you being told now? What's going on?' I put a cup of tea in front of her and sat down opposite, wondering if there was anything else I could do.

'I've been out all morning. It was waiting for me, on the doormat.'

'Mum, you're a postie, it's how letters arrive for us ordinary folk.' Teasing her had no effect. After watching her for what seemed like a few minutes I made a decision. I called Gran and Gramps and briefly outlined the news.

'So can you get round here quick? I've got to go and pick Clare up but I'll bring her straight back with me and help you sort things out. Clare's good in a crisis.'

It was one of those times when you're glad your family doesn't live hundreds of miles away.

TWENTY SEVEN

Clare, to my surprise, was slightly grumpy. She'd got stomach cramps and just wanted to be quiet at home. And there was a hysterical whining dog recovering in the back room of the surgery that had put everyone's nerves on edge and given her a headache.

'Please Clare, mum's in shock. I've never seen her like this. She didn't even know that my father had died. Gran and Gramps came round but I have to be there to see if there's anything I can do.'

Clare nodded. 'Okay then. Let's at least see, but maybe they won't need us for very long. I'm sorry Simon, but I do feel a bit rough.'

Back at mum's house I noticed immediately that the atmosphere had changed. Mum had been crying but they didn't seem to be tragic tears, yes there was some sorrow for things gone and lost, but she'd cried all those tears years ago when I was a toddler. Gran put the kettle on again and kissed us both.

'You look a little bit peaky Clare, not sickening for something are you? Poor little love, go and join the others in the sitting room. Simon will help me bring the tea and cake in.'

Typical Gran, she'd brought one of her cakes with her. It wasn't the end of the world then. I could smell it, date and walnut. I carried the tray and we all sat grouped together around the coffee table, with that moment of family strength and support tangible in the room.

'Now then.' Gramps spoke up. 'Everybody is sitting down.'

'Bill, you're stating the obvious.' Gran admonished him.

'Funny business this.' He had mum's letter in his hand, I could see it ran to a couple of thick, crackly pages. 'Unexpected and right out of the blue.'

'Bill!' Gran was getting annoyed, unlike her. 'Get to the point.'

'It concerns you Simon,' he began. 'And your mother obviously.'

I could see steam beginning to issue from Gran's ears and I pulled a face at Clare. She smiled faintly. I helped myself to a piece of cake.

'It's from the Buckland's solicitor down in Plymouth. Your grandad Derek Buckland has passed away and you're to be his main beneficiary. You and your mum are asked to make an appointment to go down and see about the Will.'

'What? I thought it was about my dad dying ten years ago?' The cake paused halfway to my mouth.

'Yes, apparently Dominic Andrew Buckland passed on ten years ago at an address in Las Vegas.'

'Oh, right. In America? Okay. And his father, my grandfather, died recently then. Still in England I presume?'

'Yes, seems he went about six weeks ago. The cremation has already been carried out. The solicitor had to trace you and your mum, I suppose they do it via the electoral register and electricity bills these days.'

'Bill, this isn't a family history meeting.' Gran said sharply. It wasn't like her to be so prickly, something was going on.

'So what's going on?' I asked. 'There's a Will, so we need to go to Plymouth, mum and I.' Then it dawned on me, Gramps had said the word "beneficiary". 'Oh,' I said. 'Does that mean an inheritance of some sort?'

The appointment was made for mid-morning the following Wednesday. It was a bit tight for me because I was due to be filming on Thursday and needed to check all the details beforehand. Fortunately we were filming in Cornwall so I didn't have to travel too far. We sat in the waiting room for about ten minutes before being invited through into a slightly gloomy office. There were a couple of regency style padded dining chairs opposite the huge desk and I could see at once that they were reproduction, they were stained to look like mahogany but had none of the authenticity of the chairs at Flinton Hall. Files were stacked on the floor along one side of the room and on a long table on the other side.

'Ah, Mrs Buckland and Mr Simon Buckland. I'm acting for the late Derek Buckland, your father-in-law and your grandfather.'

'Er ...' I said.

'That's right.' Mum interrupted, giving me a look.

'I'm Charles Harrison, sorry, I should have introduced myself first shouldn't I.' He gave a thin smile but his handshake was firm and warm.

We already knew his name, it was on the letter he'd sent to my mother. I was wondering why I was being called Mr Buckland. Mum had dropped that name when dad had left us over two decades ago.

'Sad family matters here, Mr Dominic Buckland passed on in, ah, Las Vegas, I understand in straitened circumstances. He died owing some monies and I understand that his father eventually covered his debts, which weren't too great. No problems there. I understand from our telephone conversation the other day that you knew nothing of this Mrs Buckland? He left you and your son here to pursue his own, ah, interests in the er, entertainments industry.'

Mum confirmed this with a curt nod of her head. 'Correct.'

'And you never heard from him again or, for that matter, from your father-in-law either?'

Again mum confirmed that to be correct.

Mr Harrison sat back in his chair and rubbed the bridge of his nose with a forefinger. 'Hmm, no contact then. So sad, what families can do to one another. But no matter. And I understand Mrs Buckland, as we spoke the other day, that you never divorced your husband?'

'No, that's correct, I did not.' Mum said.

It had never even occurred to me. I'd grown up blithely ignorant as Simon Sherwell. Yes, I knew that my birth certificate recorded my name as Simon William Buckland, but I'd been registered at school and subsequently everywhere else as Simon Sherwell. This was confusing.

'And I understand that your, ah, husband as it were never remarried either. Which is fortunate because he would have been committing bigamy if he had done so.'

Mr Harrison wasn't carrying on a discussion with us or even making a wry jest, he was just confirming facts aloud as he consulted papers on his desk, so we said nothing.

'Good.' Mr Harrison picked up his papers and deftly tapped them into order against the desk, as though he was dealing with a pack of cards. I wondered what sort of hand he was about to deal. 'Mr Derek Buckland appears to have decided that the, er, lack of support for his daughter-in-law and his grandson should be redressed. Set right as it were. He was a widower and I understand he had no other dependents or relatives. Following confirmation of a terminal medical condition last year he set all his affairs in order, property sale and so forth, and bequeathed a sum being a percentage of his estate to his daughter-in-law Mrs Gwenna Buckland and the remainder in entirety to his grandson Mr Simon William Buckland. Pending the usual deductions for any taxes, fees and payments of outstanding debts if any, funerary expenses and so on. And of course there is a fee due to us here at Johnstone, Harrison & Parvin.'

We sat quietly, unsure of what was coming next.

My ears were full of noise.

Apparently mum was getting around thirty thousand pounds sterling and I was in line for approximately one hundred and seventy grand. Mum would be compensated for all those years coping on her own at just over one thousand pounds per year. It felt vaguely distasteful and almost insulting, but all I could see was a shadowy figure of an old man trying to reach out to us over all those lost years. Of my late and unlamented father, I could see nothing. Mum was quiet for a long time as we drove back across the bridge at Saltash and into Cornwall. I don't think she'd ever been so surprised in her life. Finally she turned to me. 'Simon, there's only one thing I want to spend that money on right now.'

'What's that? A cruise or something? House improvements?'

'Don't be daft. I'm going to change my name by deed poll. When my time comes I'm not dying as Mrs Bloody Buckland. Do you want to do the same?'

I agreed that I did.

'And then she said that if we wanted to get married she'd use the money for a beautiful wedding for us both, and a honeymoon.' I told Clare. We were walking round the deserted gardens at Trelerric. For once I wasn't seeing jobs which needed doing, all my attention was on the effect this incredible news was having on Clare.

Clare pulled me over to a bench in the evening sun. 'I've got to sit down,' she said. 'I feel all wobbly. It's almost too much to take in. It means our joint savings are putting us into a whole new ballgame. We'll be able to afford somewhere to live Simon, if that's what you want to do with the money I mean, it's really yours to spend as you want. Oh, it's all so unexpected.'

'Of course that's what I want to do. Having a place of our own is essential. But I want us safe and settled before we get married. I don't know why, is that daft?' I cuddled her to my side and kissed the top of her head, huge plans for a home of our own already taking flight in my mind.

Clare didn't have an answer but she got a bit emotional and had to wipe her eyes. 'You're an amazing man Simon Sherwell, an amazing, clever, lucky man. I can't wait to tell mum.'

TWENTY EIGHT

Miranda and I were filming the following day. She was at a trendy bakery being taught about making bread Tudor style by a cookery historian and had to sieve coarse flour through a mesh to make a soft wheat manchet loaf for the gentry's table. She was also cooking and tasting maslin, a more rustic loaf made from wheat and rye which the lower classes ate. There was lots of information about nutrition and why coarse seeded so-called artisan breads had become popular again, especially in Cornwall. It was a nice plug for the bakery. I, meanwhile, was traipsing about on a headland nearby looking for the Logan Stone, a peculiar rocking stone said to have mystical properties. The cameraman called it all a load of old legend crap.

The weather was foul and Miranda definitely had the better day indoors. We wrapped up the day by filming me dripping pathetically, smiling gratefully and taking a big bite of buttered manchet with cheese and raw onion in the snug dry kitchen. It was surprisingly nice and I was famished. As soon as we'd finished the owner shooed us out, complaining that we'd contaminate her clean surfaces.

It was fortunate that the new pattern of our work meant that I had to be up at the studios the next day to complete the job and tie up all the loose ends. I'd found I was very good at being relaxed on the sofa, and Tip was an absolute star, dutifully taking his place between Miranda and me and gazing at his mistress adoringly. He had a habit of placing a paw on my thigh which made me joke about being kept in my place. Honestly, you could talk to that dog and he'd respond, no wonder the public loved him. I could understand why Clare wanted to get a dog.

Richard was pleased with the work we were doing and even more pleased with the ratings. The researchers were unearthing loads of stuff for us to investigate and the work was mounting up. Mickey gave me a wave as we finished the job and announced, gravelly voiced, that Richard wanted me.

'Boss needs you now darling, like pronto.'

I knocked on his open door and he beckoned me in.

'Come in, shut the door.' Richard got up and bounced up and down the floor on his toes. 'Going well, lots to do, going places aren't we Simon, ker-ching moments for us all I think, oh yes.'

He was wearing a dark red and white striped shirt which stretched a little bit on his tummy and he reminded me of an excitable beach ball. By now I was used to Richard's way of collecting his thoughts so I sat patiently with one leg crossed over my thigh and waited.

'Everything okay with you Simon, job-wise?'

'Great. The variety is, er, stimulating. I wanted to see you anyway Richard because there's something I want to ask you.'

'Fine. Good.' Richard bounced back to his seat, completely ignoring me. 'Got a project for you Simon.' He fiddled with his keyboard. 'There's a popular and rather attractive lady art historian wants someone different to co-present an hour on "Art and History in the English Garden". She's doing the history-arty bit and she wants you for the garden history part. She saw you at Moulton and liked your looks apparently. There'll be a horticultural researcher involved obviously but you've got to do your homework, it's the eighteenth century. I hope you know something about that period because I bloody don't.'

'Gainsborough and Lancelot Capability Brown is my guess.' I said casually, remembering one of what I privately called Sam's tutorials in a potting shed conversation on a wet winter afternoon. It's incredible just what high-brow stuff gardeners talk about between themselves when nobody else is listening. Gardeners are not just good in flower bed you know.

'Brilliant. Knew I could rely on you Simon. I think I've heard of those names. Mickey's got all the details, usual contract to sign etcetera. Mickey will fit you in round your other stuff. It's all going okay between you and Miranda?'

I confirmed it was.

'Like a marriage but without the er, complications if you get my drift.' Richard almost smirked.

'She's very professional. We get along well.' I said neutrally. 'But I wanted to see you about something else Richard.'

'Pay is it? I think we might do something about that, ratings and so on.'

'Thank you, that would be nice, but actually it's something else. It's about Pondside Cottage.'

'Oh, that place. Bloody nuisance and a bit less than idyllic. We haven't used it for a couple of years. Amanda has been letting it to holidaymakers until recently. She set her heart on it when we lived in Primrose Hill, but now we've left London and moved here I can't see us needing a holiday cottage. I actually need a London flat. I expect you haven't got time to do the garden anyway now, since I keep you busy enough elsewhere.'

I waited until he'd finished, definitely not feeling as cool as I hoped I was looking. Fortunately performing to camera had taught me something about looking calm and collected when inside my nerves were exploding.

'So you might be selling it then?'

Richard paid attention to something on his screen and tapped rapidly at the keyboard for several seconds.

'Sorry, what was that? Are we done?'

I gritted my teeth. 'Will you be selling Pondside Cottage? Only my fiancee and I might be interested.'

'Bloody hell.' He swivelled round in his chair and peered at me. 'I'm paying you more than I thought.'

The person to speak to was Amanda, his wife. She had her office in the farmhouse and was nothing to do with Pondside Productions. Apparently she ran an accessories business, importing cute girly costume jewellery and other shiny sparkly things appealing to the acquisition hungry teens. Judging by her clothes and the way she'd furnished the farmhouse, it was lucrative.

Amanda was a seductively curvy woman with almond shaped black eyes, her personality as expansive as her figure. She filled the room with positive warmth and a particularly delicious scent. Like her husband she was as sharp as a tack, but unlike him she was calm. I didn't have to say anything more than once and she made fast, logical conclusions.

'Okay Simon, so you've come into an inheritance, have sizeable savings, and want to live in the village you grew up in. Fair enough. Oh, and you're engaged to a local girl, from the next village. A charming picture.'

'It's difficult to find a place locally Mrs Renwick, prices and so on.' I said levelly, looking her in the eye. 'And they get snapped up by rich outsiders on the estate agents' books. Sorry if that seems rude.' I said, thinking for God's sake don't bollox this up Simon, smile at the nice lady.

'So you're interested in buying Pondside Cottage. I've some idea of what I want for it. And in a way it's rather nice that you have an interest, you've looked after the garden for years now and virtually made it your own. Tell you what, I'll find a price and you do what you need to verify and confirm your financial situation, mortgage and so on. Then we'll see if there's some common ground between us.'

I felt desperate, as though something I wanted badly was just beyond my stretching fingertips and it must have shown on my face.

'Courage Simon, what I'm suggesting is the normal thing to do. And before I go anywhere near an agent I shall give you first refusal, if that's an acceptably honest way of doing it.'

It was the best I could hope for. Back in Cornwall I called a family meeting. First I'd had to spring the idea to Clare, which I did by taking us to eat at The Wheal and then strolling along the village street afterwards and stopping outside the cottage.

'Nice little place, I've been doing the garden there for the Renwick's for about six years.'

Clare had a view about second homes and holiday cottages. And her views about estate agents who jacked the prices up were unprintable. 'It's lovely, even though it's quite small it's still got twice the space we've got in the Coach House. More since there are two bedrooms.'

'Mrs Renwick is thinking of selling it.' I spoke softly.

'Shit.' Clare looked at me and I knew what she was thinking. 'Can we ...?'

'Afford it.' I completed her question. 'I've already asked Mrs Renwick.'

Clare's face fell. 'Oh, I suppose we can't then.' She looked so sad I felt awful, I wasn't trying to tease her, this was far too important.

'Mrs Renwick is thinking about it, she wants to know what our deposit is, whether we can get a mortgage and so on. I've called a council of war tomorrow evening with the family.'

'We need more than that Simon, we need to get a solicitor and get talking to the building society. And we'll need a survey doing. Fast. And I think I'm going to either throw up or faint now.'

When in doubt I don't follow the old maxim of doing nowt, I work my nuts off. We needed every extra penny and I threw myself enthusiastically into work, hungrily watching Clare's financial spreadsheet growing. Meanwhile Clare went into overdrive and arranged everything, including a survey which helpfully advised that there was rot in the west facing window frames, damp in the kitchen and insufficient insulation in the loft. Andy Hauxwell took a look over the place and pronounced it a peach of a job.

'Just the sort of thing I want to do over winter, nice indoor renovation and alterations without the rain sluicing down my neck. Use the defects in the report to get the owner to drop the asking price. It's not going to cost all that much to put things right but it's only fair.'

Gran and Gramps said they had some savings and could loan us money, and mum said she'd cover any fees. Clare's parents made similar offers. It almost made me weep.

A couple of days later Richard came along to watch a job we were filming on Dartmoor somewhere near the prison at Princetown. I'd been filmed discussing the history of French prisoners of war and their building skills with an expert from the prison, and was now receiving a lesson in rebuilding a tumbled section of drystone wall in a field. It was an idyllic vista with a little herd of wild ponies in the background. Meanwhile Miranda was being introduced to the minuscule flora and fauna of the local environment and educating our viewers about the essential role of tiny things in the food chain which in turn supported the successful predators. She sounded convincing and passionate.

'Everything lives upon almost everything else, the carnivore upon the herbivore, nature raw in tooth and claw, the wonders of the carbon-cycle.' She was saying to camera. And off-camera she complained, "Who writes this tosh? I'll be banging on about baby calves and baby lambs next."

'Honestly Miranda, you look as though butter would melt in your mouth but you're quite an opinionated little minx.' Our patient cameraman smiled.

'Nice work Simon,' Richard bounded over when we'd done and complimented me. 'I like the way you put your back into everything. The thing with the art history diva starts next month, she's at Castle Drogo here in Devon on another job next week so her people have suggested you meet up for a couple of hours. Mickey's got the details and is keeping you up to date I trust? Big job this one, national television. Can't afford to cock-up so charm the socks off the darling diva won't you? If it goes well I think I'll be looking at getting you involved in some gardening slots, short pieces to slip in to the national programmes. The gardens at Trelerric House would do very nicely for starters. Aim high is my motto. Any problems, call me and only me.' He turned to leave. 'Oh, and before I go, I gather you've charmed Amanda too. She's decided she wants you to have the cottage, says your big blue eyes persuaded her. Good luck with it. At least I won't have to fork out for you to do the garden any more. But I expect I can find a way of compensating you via Pondside Productions.' And he strolled off leaving me speechless. Fruitlessly I tried calling Clare but didn't have a signal, so I decided to stop in Tavistock and get her some flowers to accompany the good news but my phone pinged with a recorded message before I got there. She'd already had a call from the solicitor and I smiled as I listened to her excited voice saying we'd got it, a home of our own. That wasn't a message I would be deleting. I barely noticed the drive back because my imagination was filled with ideas for the cottage and with things I wanted to do with the garden. For the first time in my life I had a plan forming and could see the way ahead.

At the end of the month we were invited to Cherryfields Cottage, Sam and Lucy had finally moved in and didn't attempt to hide their delight with the place. Sam showed me a new date stone over the door to the garden room extension off the kitchen.

'Quite the thing locally Simon. You should do the same when you make changes at Pondside.'

They had a lot of guests for the housewarming and Lady Felicity was trying to convince Lucy that gold tiles in the currently minimalist ensuite and scarlet in the downstairs cloakroom would look wonderful. Lucy wasn't having any of it.

Clare and I wandered about, Clare exclaiming over attention to detail and finish.

'That's what you get with Andy, he knows about materials and he's got an eye for things. He makes it look pretty.' I told her, already anticipating how Andy would approach the work at Pondside Cottage, and wondering how the hell we'd afford it. Buying the cottage was wiping our savings out and I already knew I'd be working as a labourer again to keep costs down, but the whole idea of making a home with my own hands for the woman I loved was more exciting than I could ever have anticipated.

'Yes, I'm a clever sod aren't I?' Andy said behind me. 'Are those your drawings up on the wall in the dining area Simon?'

I hadn't noticed so I went over to have a look and left him talking to Clare about plastering walls and why slate windowsills looked so appropriate. There's no end to what people can become interested in when they have to. Sam and Lucy had framed my garden design, the one I'd given to them as a wedding present last Christmas. It was waiting to be built, now that Andy had finished. God, so much had happened since then, it had been an extraordinary year.

'Penny for them Simon.' Sir Hugh said over my shoulder. 'Takes you back a bit. I thought I'd got you all set up to become a successful garden designer and then you confounded everyone by becoming a local television celebrity. It's a funny old world but I'm glad you've found your own feet and your own way.' He smiled at me. 'You are, in fact, very much your own man. Something tells me you'll go far Simon. And you won't need my help.'

He raised his glass to me. What was it about this man, this curiously paternalistic interest, I'd always felt it was more than just altruism.

'Sir Hugh,' I said. 'You've been very kind to me. I wouldn't have got the television work if Richard Renwick hadn't seen me performing at the Moulton Show, so in a way you helped me there. And I've a feeling you were instrumental in Sam and Lucy letting Clare and me stay in the Coach House. It's been a real bonus while we've saved.' I stopped talking, unsure of what I was going to say next, if anything.

'Hmm.' Sir Hugh's lips twitched, his eyes twinkling. I'd always though he had dark eyes but now I realised they were a familiar greenish sort of hazel. I couldn't help it, I had to ask him a question.

'That portrait in the music room, the one of your mother as a young woman.'

'Ah yes. My mother. I wondered when we might get to that.' His face was sombre.

'I noticed her name was Beatrice Clare. Is there any significance I should be aware of?'

Sir Hugh gave me a shrewd look and nodded slightly. He took a sip of wine as he chose his words carefully. 'Nicely put Simon and I'm impressed by your conclusions. But I'm advised by my dear wife, who is immensely wonderful and wise in these matters, that I should say nothing. Causing distress to the innocent is unforgivable.'

'The innocent in this case being ...'

'Clare.' Sir Hugh said. 'How pretty you look this evening, those emerald earrings bring out the green in your eyes. And I've heard the happy news that you and Simon are buying your own house too. I'm so pleased for you both.'

Clare's obvious happiness made her glow with a dignified kind of beauty and Sir Hugh gazed down at her with obvious pleasure and, I think, a little bit of pride. As she tucked her hand into my arm I mentioned what a gifted financial planner Clare was and Sir Hugh engaged her in talk about being smart with finances, which after all, was his speciality. She was quick, interested and asked him sensible questions and I watched him with respect and something like fondness as they talked. Then I felt a presence and turned my head, Lady Felicity was smiling her dazzling smile at me.

'Simon my darling,' she made a gesture to Clare and Sir Hugh and drew me to one side. 'I've watched your performances and I'm very proud of you. You have a lovely on screen presence. I think you've got a splendid future ahead and before long you're going to have a perfectly lovely wife. I'm already thinking about a wedding present for you both. After all, you're practically family.'

I realised I no longer felt awkward or in awe of this clever, beautiful and very kind woman. To her surprise I leaned forward and kissed her on the cheek. 'Thank you Lady Flick,' I said. 'Thank you for everything. It's been an extraordinary year.'

There was one other person I wanted to speak to and I sought out Rob Williams. 'Can I ask you to make something for me Rob, as a surprise for Clare.'

'Sure, ask away.'

'For the cottage, for when we move in, a present. It has to be a secret and I need something special and ...'

'Unique?' Su his wife offered with a smile. It seemed like a private joke between them.

'Exactly.' I could see an image in my mind, connected with that ethereal sense of time passing and lives repeating themselves. 'I've got an idea, I fancy a clock, a one-off special design, I can draw it for you if you like. I'd like you to make us a dandelion clock.

22074333R00146

Printed in Poland
by Amazon Fulfillment
Poland Sp. z o.o., Wrocław